To, S hoshi

D0174107

Thank you!

DONKEY HEART
MONKEY MIND

by Djaffar Chetouane

Published by CPC
Oakland, California

Book design, cover design, painting, imaging and title page illustration by Reem Rahim. Map drawing by Rachel Jackson.

Edited by Amanda Whitehead (1st edition) and by Rachel Jackson (revised edition).

ISBN-10: 0-615-31407-4
ISBN-13: 978-0-615-31407-4
LCCN: 2009908268

ACKNOWLEDGMENTS

I will forever be grateful to the following for their advice, encouragement, and support: Reem Rahim, for believing in me and being so inspirational; my first editor, Amanda Whitehead; and Alan Karls, who encouraged me to write one story at a time from the very beginning. I deeply appreciate Rachel Jackson, who had a fresh vision of what this book could be and worked tirelessly to bring this revised edition into being; her editing skills made this book much more compelling, even to me. I would also like to thank Andrea Yankowski, who was my very first girlfriend, taught me English, and supported me during my first hard years in America, as well as Jeff Canavan, who was my savior. I would like to thank Ely Jones-Fernandez (a.k.a., Laka Laka), a little boy who ended my fixation with having a daughter and taught me that it would be just as wonderful to have a son: may you someday fly your own plane. I would also like to thank Ely's mother, Tyler Jones, for unearthing the deep love within me. I thank Erin Dunwell for her help and understanding, and for the faith she had in a total stranger. I have profound appreciation for Charles Friends (a.k.a., Todd), who has helped me through tough times, always believed in me, never asked for anything in return, and who continues to feed me delicious oysters from his farm. I thank my mother, who gave me life, and my grandmother, whose wisdom is immeasurable. I am also forever grateful to my maternal uncle, Kader, and my aunt, Ouardia, for helping to teach me kindness and compassion while I was growing up; may you both rest in peace. I would like to express my deepest gratitude for all the people who helped me during both my journey to America and while I have lived here for the last 22 years, including those whose names I do not remember (and those whose names I never knew). I also offer my most heartfelt apologies to those I stole from while running for my life: without your innocence I never would have made it. I am sorry for any harm I may have caused, I hope someday you'll read these words, and I hope to have the honor of being able to thank you in person someday. Last but not least, I do not know how to thank the Angels who obviously always look after me; I can only try to emulate them at every opportunity.

DEDICATION

This book is dedicated to

All the donkeys who helped build Berber villages and
were never appreciated: I appreciate you,

All the people who suffered and/or died during North
African conflicts, past and present, most notably,
Mohamed Bouazizi: May you rest in peace,

Simon Lev Fitch-Jenett and the children
surviving against all odds:
May you live a beautiful life

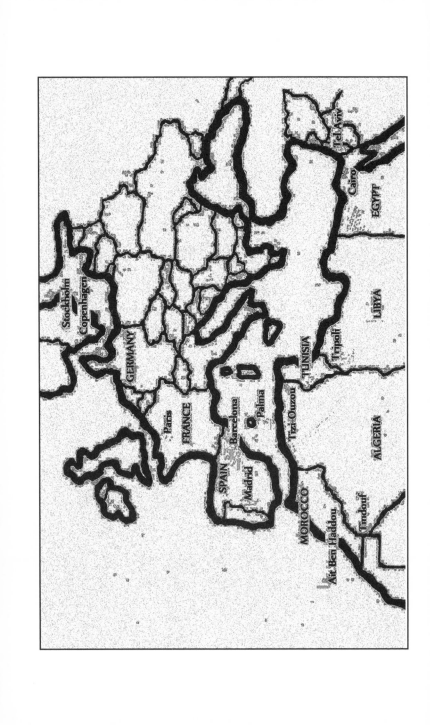

PREFACE

As we go to press, events in North Africa have taken a dramatic and historic turn. Every country in North Africa and many in the Middle East have been rocked by popular protests, with the people ousting brutal dictators, while demanding social and political reforms and a more equitable distribution of wealth. In almost every country I "visited" during my escape, the people have broken the grip of centuries of oppression by neocolonial rulers and are demanding a share of the natural resources that have been stolen from them by their own despots.

While western politicians and corporations scramble to protect their assets in the region, I strongly believe that these very forces bear most of the responsibility for the problems today. They have supported tyrants for decades, providing arms, military and political support—without ever even criticizing their blatant human rights violations or the extreme polarization between rich and poor. Only now that the people are making real change—such as the ouster of Hosni Mubarak in just 18 days in Egypt or the civil war raging in Libya—has the United Nations bothered to get involved. Suddenly the west has a newfound concern for the people, and western military forces are positioning themselves to intervene under the cover of "humanitarian aid."

I am very happy and inspired by the protests that have swept the region since Mohamed Bouazizi's tragic self-immolation in Tunisia. I was once one of the street vendors, one of the disenchanted youth, one of the people who took to the streets—so I fully understand their motivation. And while I celebrate the historic victories thus far, I also fear for the people being arrested and detained, because they are undoubtedly being abused and tortured (as I was, and worse), for voicing the simple demands of human rights, self-determination, and basic necessities like jobs, food, and housing. I hope that new technology and heightened global consciousness will help to expose brutal regimes, and that the people of the world will help to support and protect all who are fighting for justice.

The battle ahead is long and will take enormous effort, time, and dedication to bring about lasting change. My heart remains with the people of Algeria, Morocco, Tunisia, Libya, Egypt, and throughout the region; I was one of the few fortunate enough to leave years ago, but no one should have to flee their homeland to find safety and dignity.

I praise and honor the people of North Africa and the Middle East for their determination and for their will to alter their society, for themselves and for future generations. May God be with them all, or as we say in *Tamazight*: *Rabi Adhyili Yidhssen*.

for you, Brahim,
rest in peace

HANGING IN THE CELL

My toes were barely touching the ground. I'd hung there since the morning, my hands tied by a rope to the ceiling, naked, cold, hungry and miserable. My shoulders strained, and my entire body ached from burns and lashings from a whip.

I was here for the same reason that had led me, two days before, to go out and look for tire repair shops that could spare some inner tubes. I had heard of a trick that I wanted to try, because the next day I planned to be at the front of a potentially violent demonstration. After asking several shop owners, I came upon one that had an abundance of inner tubes. I took several home and started cutting them into long strips that soon filled the storage room of our apartment building. The next day I wrapped my arms and legs in the rubber, put my clothes on top, and immediately looked like I had the muscles of a weight lifter. I became Hercules overnight.

The following day was cold and cloudy. When I arrived on the campus of the University of Tizi-Ouzou in northern Algeria, some of my fellow students noticed how chubby I looked, so I told them of what I had done. We were gathering to march on the municipal building where the governor of our province had his office. There were a few hundred of us, and we anticipated being joined by a bigger crowd in the center of the city. I was not the only one who had taken precautions against violence. I and others had hidden knives in our pockets, and I could see that others had also "bulked up," using my same strategy. Berbers don't know how to have peaceful demonstrations, after having been disenfranchised as citizens for many centuries.

We Berber students were protesting against the city government for not allowing us to have a concert on campus. Supporters of our movement had invited singers and speakers to commemorate April 20, 1980, the "Berber Spring," a turning point in the modern fight for our people's rights in Algeria. We held this celebration every year, but this year, 1986, city representatives had warned campus officials not to allow it, for fear of having the city turned upside down. As the crowd started to move, we chanted, *"Anarez walla anaknou!"* "We prefer to be broken than to bow!" a well known Berber proverb.

About a kilometer away from the center of town we saw the police barricades: officers standing shoulder to shoulder, with batons, big plexiglass shields, water tank trucks parked nearby, and most frightening of all: Dogs. These dogs were the reason for the inner tubes. They were German Shepherds, trained to attack and have no mercy on anyone. In Algeria, dogs are rarely kept as pets. They are working animals, like those the mountain peoples raise to guard their fields and livestock. Police dogs, like those we faced that day, are fierce and hungry, used in any demonstration as the most effective way to disperse a crowd, no matter its size.

Donkey Heart Monkey Mind

We continued our march towards the police lines, and soon what we had expected occurred: the police unleashed several dogs that looked fearless and eager to rip us apart. I pulled my knife out of my pocket, and as soon as the first dog jumped on me, I gave him my arm to bite. His jaws were like a vise, but the rubber had done its work. I didn't feel any teeth. I jammed the knife into his belly and the dog fell to the ground. To my dismay, as he fell his eyes were staring straight into mine, and I watched them going blank as he died. I had never killed anything before (or since), and the image of his eyes remains seared into mine to this day. But there was no time to feel sorry for the poor animal. All around me other people were struggling to fight off the dogs. Some were being dragged to the ground, some were screaming for their lives, and still others were fleeing to safety. Another dog jumped on me, and I stabbed him as I had the first. I saw some people trying to help their friends on the ground by sticking their knives into the attacking dogs' bellies. Next, the police started to shoot tear gas grenades and then they turned their water cannons on us. The pressure from the water seemed powerful enough to knock down a concrete wall, never mind people. In a matter of minutes, protesters were running every which way through a chaos of acrid smoke.

I made my way home safely, and only a few hours later I was enjoying the comfort of my mother's *shurba*, a traditional Algerian soup. The hot liquid was more soothing than ever after the morning's events. As I ate, my mother called out that someone was knocking at the door, and my 10-year-old sister, Souad, hurried to open it. She told my mother that it was the police, and my heart started to pound. I had no doubt about the reason they had come. I stood up from my chair and looked around for an escape route. There was no other door, and we lived on the third floor of our building, so it would have been a disaster if I had tried the window. I tried to hide in the bathroom briefly, but that didn't work. The policemen gave my mother a moment to retreat to another room, since it would be indecent for her to be seen by strange men, no matter the circumstances, and then they came straight in and handcuffed me. As they dragged me to the police van just outside our building, I heard my mother quietly instruct Souad to find my brother, Brahim, and send him to tell my father about my arrest.

When I got to the police station, I was herded into a large cell with about two dozen others, some bleeding from dog bites and many still coughing from the tear gas. The cell was foul smelling and filthy, and the walls were covered with the graffiti of those who had passed through before us. Some writings were phrases from the Koran, some were about the pain the writers experienced while they were there, and some writings were Berber proverbs that spoke of patience and tolerance and having faith that all will pass. We all had some idea of what was coming. I was only 18, and I was about to get first-hand experience with how the government had dealt with Berber people for more than two decades in Algeria.

Imazighen (ⴻⵛ·ⵯⴻⵖ÷ⵉ), meaning "Free People," is the correct name for the ethnic group usually known as "Berbers." My people, the Kabyles, are one of eight Berber tribes in Algeria and throughout North Africa. (Most English speakers cannot pronounce the word *Imazighen*, especially the "gh" at the end, as there is no alphabetical equivalent in English for the way these two letters sound in the Afro-Asiatic and Middle Eastern languages. A close approximation might be the guttural German "r," produced at the back of the throat.) Berber is an English word derived from the Latin word *barbarus*, meaning barbarians, uncivilized, or used to describe a cruel, warlike person. Although many books will tell you a different version of Berber history, the Romans dubbed my people this when they wrested control of North Africa from its Berber rulers in 200 B.C.E. *Imazighen* are an ancient people, and they had ruled the region since at least 10,000 B.C.E. However, control of the North African coast is crucial to control over the Mediterranean Sea, and so the coast has been invaded over and over again, not only by Romans, but also by Phoenicians (who founded Carthage), Greeks (mainly in Cyrene, Libya), Vandals and Alans, Byzantines, Arabs, Ottomans, and the French and Spanish. Under the Arabs, the Berbers were heavily taxed, their lands were taken from them, and some were even enslaved. The Berber language and culture were gradually replaced by those of the Arabs, except among certain pockets of the population, such as that in which I grew up.

It was the Arabs that gave the Berber peoples of my particular region the name *Qabîlah*, plural from *Qaba'il*, meaning "Tribes." In French we are known as *"Les Kabyles,"* and in English, the Kabyles. Kabyles are concentrated in the highlands of northern-central Algeria, especially in the province of Tizi-Ouzou, also known as Greater Kabylia. The capital city of the province is also called Tizi-Ouzou, which is the name of a beautiful flower that grows in the mountain pass. The city lies within a valley in the northern Djurdjura Mountains, 35 kilometers south of the Mediterranean Sea. Like many highland peoples, the Kabyles who live here have remained a pocket of resistance to both conquest and assimilation throughout Algeria's history. Neither the Romans nor the Ottoman Turks ever fully succeeded in controlling our region, and our language, *Tamazight* (written in the *Thifina* alphabet), and Kabyle culture survived even the broad Arabization of most of North Africa.

Djaffar Chetouane

Ironically, some of the deepest conflict came to our region after the most recent colonists, the French, were driven out of Algeria in 1962. As a backlash against French language and culture, the young Algerian dictatorship stressed the Arab identity of the country, and there was no room for recognition of its Berber roots. Arabic was made the official language, and the teaching of *Tamazight* in schools was forbidden. The new Algerian government sought to strip local tribes of traditional rights of self-governance and violently crushed any expressions of Berber cultural pride and political autonomy.

On April 20, 1980, when I was 12-years-old, I got my first lesson in repression. In the early morning, just before 6 a.m., as I was walking to get bread for my family from the bakery about half a kilometer away from our apartment, I came across a military convoy coming from the direction of the University of Tizi-Ouzou. The soldiers were returning from raiding the dormitories during the night and savagely beating the students in their beds, arresting many of them. A little over a month before, in March, the government had banned a prominent author from giving a talk on campus on the use of *Tamazight*, and students and professors had occupied the university in response. The violent April 20th arrests were the government's reply. After the city of Tizi-Ouzou awakened and heard about the bloodshed, there was a General Strike and massive protests against the government forces. Many young men and women were arrested, including my older brother Mustapha. Some 30 participants were killed and hundreds injured. Eventually, the whole city was occupied by the military. These events came to be known as *Thafsouyth Imazighen*, or Berber Spring, and April 20th, the date of the original attack on the students, has been commemorated by the entire province of Tizi-Ouzou every year since. Kabyle singers and poets have written many songs and poems about that day.

From that day forward, I was intrigued by my own people and why my language, history, and culture were forbidden by the Algerian government. I was one of a handful of youths courageous enough to secretly learn to write *Tamazight* during my high school years. When I entered the University of Tizi-Ouzou in 1985, I was eager to learn more. I joined the Berber movement, rallying people to support and promote Berber language and culture. We agitated for the teaching of Berber history in schools, the broadcasting of Berber television programs, and other similar measures. I continued to study the writing of the forbidden language through other students and professors. After I was well-versed in *Tamazight*, I started to write articles and promote Berber language and history to other students. I joined in organizing protests on campus and distributing fliers about meetings. I never did anything secretly, because I wanted other students to see my devotion to the cause.

I was arrested several times at protests, but I was always released within a few hours, a day at the most. But April 20, 1986— when I wrapped myself in inner tubes and faced down the police dogs—was different. As usual, the spark was government refusal to permit a Berber cultural event on campus, and the result was predictable: protests, arrests, more bloodshed, and me huddled with my fellow students in a jail cell, hoping that my sister had gotten word to my father that I had been detained.

One by one, the police called people's names and took them away. It was about two hours before my turn came. Two policemen marched me into a small cell, where the first thing I noticed was the rope hanging from the ceiling. The very next thing I noticed was the blood all over the floor. There were no windows, and the cement walls had darkened over the years. The policemen immediately stripped me naked. They tied my hands and hoisted me up by the rope, making sure only my toes were touching the ground. Then they simply left me hanging for a while. Finally a third policeman, a big, mean looking brute with a moustache, came in with a leather whip. The first thing he said to me was that they saw me killing their dogs and that I would pay for it. He also said he had my father's permission to beat the hell out of me.

As soon as he hit me the first time, I saw stars in front of my eyes as I felt the whip. The burning sensation was so painful, I screamed as if my lungs would come out of my mouth. But he kept hitting me. Each lash made me scream even louder. I pulled myself up and tried to kick him with my feet, but I couldn't reach him. I was used to being hit on my legs; my own father had beaten me on them countless times, and I could stand the pain there. But the lashes on my naked back were something new. Worse yet was the way the fiery, snaking leather would curl around my torso and bite into the skin of my chest. I could do nothing but scream, so scream I did, as loud as I could. And the man continued hitting me until he was tired. He was fat and out of shape, and he broke out in a serious sweat as he worked me over. Still, I could see the pleasure on his face as he left the room, leaving me hanging there, crying and yelling, muscles aching and flesh stinging.

After the cuts and welts on my body had cooled down a bit, I could finally breathe. I expected the man to return for more, but he never did. After a long while, I became convinced that they would soon take me back to the cell. But that never happened. I was kept hanging there for the entire day and throughout the night. My shoulders started aching. I tried many times to lift myself up to ease the pull on them, but I was too weak and exhausted to manage it.

Donkey Heart Monkey Mind

The very muscles and ligaments that I needed to lift myself up were being slowly stretched to their limit by the weight of my body. As the night went on, the pain escalated and became excruciating; now the whipping didn't seem so bad at all. Eventually I wished death would come upon me to simply ease the pain.

In a stupor of pain and exhaustion, I wasn't aware of how much time had passed when the same moustached man returned and slapped me on the face, asking how my night was. As soon as I became aware of him, I began begging him to release me from the rope. Though I didn't see the whip in his hands, I said that he could hit me as long as he wanted with anything he wanted, if only he would let me down from the rope. The words slurred heavily from my mouth; even my facial muscles had been clenched in pain since the day before. The man's answer was that I was going to remain hanging there, because I needed to really feel and understand what I had done. If I ever did it again, he said, the next time would be even worse. I continued begging, and he continued to ignore my pleas.

"I'll send someone to shower you," he grunted as he left. In a short while someone came and splashed a bucket of water over me. The water gave me some temporary relief from the continued burning of my skin, but the searing of my shoulder joints did not abate.

I was left hanging for a long while, eventually losing all sense of awareness and time, until I was awakened by my fellow demonstrators in the big cell. Our captors had dragged me back to the cell unconscious. I noticed the new pain in my shoulders the moment I woke up. Despite their being released, I couldn't move them at all. I also noticed that my pants were on; the people in the cell had put them on for me while I was unconscious. I lay down on the cement floor, and there I would remain for two more

Djaffar Chetouane

days before I would find the strength to stand up and take stock of my surroundings. It was then I saw there were others around me, suffering just as I was.

During the two days I spent on the floor the only thing I kept asking myself was why my father hadn't intervened for me. A successful cab driver, he was well known and well respected in the city and knew many government officials. Furthermore, he carried the title of "Hadj," since he had made the pilgrimage to Mecca, which greatly increased his influence. However, he had always supported the very government that had turned the dogs on university students and that still held so many of us wretched and bloodied in this cell. Still, I was his son. Everyone in our village would have a fair idea of what was going on within these prison walls. It was no mystery how the government treated Berber dissidents. Still I wondered: What father would let that happen to his son if he could stop it? What true Muslim would let it happen, for that matter? But my father was a cold, hard man. He cared far more about his place in society than he did about the welfare of anyone in his family, and I knew deep down that I would be here in this cell until the police were good and ready to release me.

It was the next day, thankfully, that I heard my name bellowed from the other side of the door.

"Come out. Your father is waiting for you!"

I knew I was being released. As I walked towards the door, I looked at the other people in the cell and felt tears on my cheeks. I was so sorry for them. Some of them I knew very well. I even thought of not leaving and staying with them in solidarity, but I didn't dare. However confused and sorry for them I felt, I kept walking.

Emerging into the sunlight, I saw my father waiting in the car. His eyes stared at me coldly. I met them with a look of pure hatred and kept walking. Never in my life had I hated anyone as much as I hated my father that day.

"Get in the car!" he barked. I ignored him and pointed myself towards home.

The walk to our house was less than a kilometer, but it felt like a hundred. I was so tired and weak I could barely put one foot in front of the other. But I wasn't going to give in and accept a favor from my father now. He drove away, and I plodded on with determination. When I finally got home, my father was already there and had informed my mother that I was coming. I headed straight to the single mattress in my room that I shared with my two brothers and collapsed. I had my pants and my shirt on, and no one could see the marks on my body. My mother followed me into the room and asked how I was doing.

"Ask El Hadj. He let it happen," I said to her.

"Don't speak too loud. He might hear you," she said. She had been beaten by my father as many times as her children had, and she was wary of his displeasure.

I lifted my shirt and spoke as loudly as I could, to make sure he would hear me. "Would he do any worse than this?" I asked. When my mother saw the marks she screamed so loudly she startled me. I myself had not been aware of how bad I looked.

"What have they done to your son, Hadj?" she asked my father. My two sisters and my brother Brahim came into the room. My father stood in the doorway wearing the traditional white *djellaba* he always wore at home and during prayer. His big, hairy stomach was visible through the fabric, and he looked mean and satisfied. I hurriedly pulled my shirt down, so he couldn't see my wounds.

"Let me see," he insisted from the doorway. My mother tried to force me to lift my shirt; she even tried to lift it herself.

"Look at what they've done!" she said to him, displaying my broken, bloodied skin.

My father simply turned his head and said, "I hope he learned his lesson." Then he walked away.

My mother left too and came back a moment later with a bucket of water. She asked me to sit up so she could wash the blood off my body. I forced myself up, took off my shirt, and saw my mother start crying as she gently cleaned my torso.

"I'm going to live with my grandmother," I said to her. "I'll never share a roof with him again, I hate him so much."

"Quiet, I don't want him to hear you," she urged. I wanted so much to tell her that if he ever tried to hit me again I would jump on him, but it only would have frightened her. Nevertheless, from that day on, I no longer believed I had a father. (And he never did try to strike me again.)

I stayed in my room for three straight days. The only person who kept checking on me was my mother. Either no one else cared, or no one else was willing to risk my father's anger by coming in to speak to me. During those days I kept thinking about what I had experienced. It was a beating that would make anyone forget their name. Of course, the police could have done much worse to me than they did. Over the brief but violent course of Algeria's history since independence, the government has been known to pull out a person's finger or toenails, cut off their nipples, or burn their genitals. At least my shoulders were still in their sockets. So even though my father had done nothing directly, I probably benefited from his connections. Others who participated in the march were held and beaten for more than two weeks.

From then on I saw my life from another perspective. I was a second-class citizen in a third world country, and I saw no future for myself. There were hardly any jobs to be had in Algeria, so what likelihood was there that I would have an actual career, even if I did stay out of prison long enough to finish school? And if, against the odds, I were to become a doctor or a lawyer, I would still be living in a brutal dictatorship where it was forbidden to learn or teach the language of my mother and grandmother. The police had done their job: I was going to keep a low profile in terms of politics from then on. I lay in bed imagining my life elsewhere. I was 18, barely an adult, and all I wanted was to leave my country and my father behind, no matter how I managed it.

And I did. A short three years later I found myself on a new continent with a new life before me, a life that could never have been possible in Algeria. But the way there was not at all what I imagined it would be. I had to learn the skills that my father was most proud of: taking chances, putting myself first, and exploiting other people. I took risks I had never imagined before, and I also suffered more than I ever thought I would. I spent time in and out of jail in Sweden, Tunisia, Libya, Egypt, Israel and, worst of all, in my own Algeria again—but the last time was not a city jail. It was a military base camp in the middle of the Sahara.

What started as the angry wanderlust of an embittered young man became a desperate run for my life.

APRIL 1987

Where I come from people learn to hustle at an early age, and they stick with it as they grow older. To survive, you have to act as if everybody else's needs come after your own. There is always a shortage of commodities such as sugar, milk, coffee, wheat, construction materials, and especially agricultural materials. You name it—Algerians don't have it. Obtaining basic household necessities always means pushing and shoving and a seemingly endless wait in a government-owned grocery store. There are little privately-owned stores, but they never have the shelf space to keep everyone supplied. To even get bread, the 10 baguettes the average household buys each day, you have to get to the bakery at dawn or wait for hours. If you don't brave the lines yourself, you have to pay double or triple the going rate to someone reselling the goods they fought to buy. Construction materials, such as concrete, steel reinforcing bars, and wood, are even harder to obtain. There is no such thing as a Home Depot. You must find the right person to bribe and then wait for weeks and hope he doesn't double-cross you.

This is not because the country lacks resources. On the contrary, the opposite is true. Algeria is rich in natural resources including gas and petroleum, precious metals and other minerals, and numerous agricultural exports. However, it is also a newly independent country and without strict socioeconomic and political controls, Algerians are liable to be fighting each other in civil wars for decades to come. Therefore, the government keeps a tight hold on the population by not providing everything the people need. When a person is hungry, the first thing on that person's mind is food, just like any animal. There is no way for that person to pay attention to anything else, especially politics. Therefore, you see, in Algeria both the government and the people have their own valid reasons for being the way they are.

I don't know of any Arab or developing country that enjoys true democracy. When a president is elected—rather, when he has been chosen by government officials or fights his way into office—he will never leave his post until he is forced to by death, illness, or war. So you can easily understand how young people brought up under this type of corrupt, ruthless rule will develop the mentality to fight, keep what they have, steal, not worry about others, and always put themselves first. The government does it, so why shouldn't they? This is one reason Algerian people grow up and learn to fight for their lives at an early age, by any means necessary. Some Algerians emigrate to other countries—where people are more educated but also more innocent—and use their street smarts to make it through the day. That's exactly what I learned from the heads of my country and the head of my house: I had to put myself first and not care about anyone else.

My father was considered one of the Mujahideen revolutionaries who fought for Algerian independence against the French during the Algerian-French war of 1954-1962. He fought only indirectly, by transporting letters, money, and arms for the Mujahideen in his cab, but he was nevertheless arrested and imprisoned by the French in 1957. According to his brothers and sisters, my father had been a rebel in his youth. But in prison, he became a pious and self-satisfied Muslim and learned how to read and write Arabic from the Koran. He remained in prison until 1961, when he was released because he had developed rheumatism. Later, after the French had enough of war with their colony and left in 1962, he and all the other surviving Mujahideen, as well as the widows of those who had died, were given special treatment by the new Algerian government. For example, in the 1960s, seventies and eighties, there was a five to ten year waiting period to get an apartment in Algeria, if you were lucky. My father, however, got one immediately, even though he had never actually borne arms in the war. He might have even held government office himself because of the connections he made during the war and in prison, with people who came to hold government posts after independence. Instead he preferred to remain a cab driver until the day he died, enjoying the benefits of being a former revolutionary.

Paradoxically, he actually did bear arms for the French during two previous conflicts. When he was 14 years old, in 1942, the French conscripted him and other Algerian teenagers to fight against Nazi German forces in North Africa. Of course, the French overestimated the loyalty of their colonial subjects, and my father always claimed that he and others had deserted and aided the German side. The second time was in 1948, when he became one of many Algerians recruited by the French to fight in the French-Indochina War. It was not that he felt any more loyalty to the French than

Djaffar Chetouane

he had a few years before, but this time military service offered an escape from danger he had brought upon himself at home: he had stolen some olives from one of his father's wives to sell at the market, and his own father turned a gun on him. Although my grandfather shot to kill, he missed and put a bullet in my father's left heel. Fearing for his life, my father ran away and volunteered with the French. He was paid in advance according to his weight, as was the custom for Algerian recruits, and put to work as a military driver. Driving people around, making contacts and making friends suited him, so he became a cab driver when he returned to Algeria in 1952. When the war for Algerian independence began, he found himself in a position to both stick it to the French and establish himself firmly in the favor of the new government. It was probably fear of falling out of favor with his government cronies that kept him from intervening on my behalf in 1986, despite the fact that he probably had a very clear idea of what was being done to me.

The only thing as important to my father as social standing was money. Knowing how to make money was the most valuable lesson for his children to learn, and money, itself, was the main substance of life—or so we were taught. Although my father had six children, he favored my brother, Brahim, because Brahim bought and sold things (mainly clothes), and then gave most of the money to my father. He called Brahim "the merchant." Being called a merchant in Algeria means that, like a cab driver, you have people skills, know how to haggle, make lots of friends and, most of all, you are smart enough to make money.

My father valued money-making but never gave any money to his children, so we learned to hustle for it. By the age of six, I was growing my own cilantro to sell during the month of Ramadan, when people traditionally break their fast each day with *shurba* flavored heavily with this herb. I was also one of the few youngsters in the family willing to put in the labor to gather the windfalls of figs, pomegranates, and other fruits from our family orchards and carry them to market. When I was about seven, my father taught my brother, Brahim, and me to make money by selling cigarettes and candies on the street at night during the month of Ramadan, the Muslim holy month, and throughout the summertime while we were out of school.

Later on, when American movies, especially Westerns, came to town, I would shove, push, and sneak between the legs of the rowdy crowds until I got to the counter, where I would buy five or six tickets and battle my way out to sell them for double or triple the price. For shy people and the not-so-rough kind, I might go back and do it again (but I would always save one ticket for myself). I even earned small commissions from various family members for braving lines and crowds to buy scarce household supplies for them. But the fact that I was a hard-working person was not enough for my father. I only sold things that sold themselves, choosing not to push people to buy. My father preferred to have a son that really knew how to wheel and deal. Brahim-the-merchant would travel to France and bring back items to resell, making a tidy profit and turning a portion of it over to my father. I, on the other hand, never gave my father any of the money I earned. I always gave some of it to my mother and grandmother, and I hid the rest in holes I dug in different spots on our land. So Brahim-the-merchant was the smart one and "the water stops flowing," as the Berbers would say (meaning, "end of story").

Fortunately, I also had other examples around me. The women in my family taught me deep compassion and pride in my roots. My greatest childhood memories are of my grandmother,

Djaffar Chetouane

listening to the stories, legends, and Berber proverbs she used to tell her grandchildren as we went to sleep next to a fire in her house. Fire, to my grandmother, was a symbol of both life and death, a metaphor in dying wood and living light. My grandmother lived most of her life with no electricity, gas, or running water, so you can understand all that a wood fire would represent: warmth, light, cooking food, and a place to gather with her family. I remember she used to ask us, "Why would you need a television when you have a fire you can stare at?" She called fire by many names, including The Star of the Darkness, The Shadow Maker, The Awakening, and The Untouchable, to name a few. She believed that fire itself was a life form that never ceased to exist, and that we would never be alive without the warmth of the fire that exists within us. She used to tell us looking at a fire lets you see your life, past, present and future. She also always said that if you lead a life of a fire, no one can touch you. I remember once asking her, "What if someone throws water at you? What happens then?" Her answer was that you must evaporate the water before it reaches you.

My grandmother raised four children on her own after her husband emigrated to France in 1952, just two years prior to the start of the Algerian war for independence. Her oldest child was 13 at the time, and the youngest, my uncle, was five. They lived in two rooms, plus a kitchen made from bamboo covered with cow manure and hay, and had a barn attached to their living quarters. My grandfather married a new wife in France and never returned, so my grandmother supported herself and her children by growing and selling vegetables, raising chickens, rabbits, and a dairy cow, harvesting fruit, and weaving traditional Berber dresses and robes. She also supported the Mujahideen during the war by feeding them and occasionally acting as a lookout. She always said she did this by being able to smell the smoke of the French soldiers' cigarettes a mile away.

It takes a tremendous amount of determination and fortitude to survive as a husbandless woman in the Arabic world. Islam forbids women from doing many things other than staying home to raise children. From the time they are born, female children are valued far below their male counterparts. I remember vividly being a child and attending the elaborate parties families would throw when a boy was born, with dancing, singing, and sometimes even slaughtering and consuming a whole cow. When I was eight years old and my sister Souad was born, I was surprised that we weren't hosting a party. I asked my mother why and she answered, "Parties are for boys only." I didn't know at the time what to make of my mother's answer, but I understood when my brother Sid-Ali was born the next year and we celebrated with the whole family. I remember telling my mother angrily that I would have nothing to do with the party, and that when I grew up and had a girl I would throw the biggest party ever.

My mother, like most Algerian women, lost many children before they were born or shortly thereafter. Out of 13 pregnancies, six of us survived. Unlike her own mother, she had a husband to support her and her children. Nevertheless, she may have been better off without him, because my father treated her with the same contempt and violence with which he treated most of his children. Somehow my mother maintained not only forbearance, perhaps because she had no real alternative, but the same warmth and unconditional love that her own mother had always shown. It was this same compassion and generosity towards others that she and my grandmother tried to instill in their children, contrary to the influence of my father, our uncles, and most of the world around us.

Djaffar Chetouane

Once when I was young, I witnessed my father's brother mercilessly thrashing his donkey. The animal had done nothing wrong; my uncle was just venting his spleen on the nearest available victim, as my father so often did. As soon as my uncle was gone, I tried to comfort the animal. The problem was, I did this by pulling up several heads of my uncle's own lettuce crop and feeding them to the donkey. When my father found out, he was furious. Not only had I stolen my uncle's lettuce, but the donkey belonged to my uncle, and I had no right to pass judgment on how he wanted to treat it. Also I think my father may have been most irritated by the fact that I had shown some kind of compassion for a simple beast of burden. He thrust the end of a pole into my belly, crushing my innards back towards the wall so hard that I defecated on myself. It was then that he gave me my nickname, "Best Friend of the Donkey." In Algeria, the most common way to insult a person is to call them a donkey, meaning they are stupid, so my nickname had a twofold cruel significance to my father. Every time he called me that, he was not only telling me I was stupid, but he was reminding me of how I had been humiliated for showing pity to my namesake.

Sometimes, when the whole family would be in the car on the way to visit relatives in the Kabylia Mountains, my father would spot a donkey and say, "There's Jafar's best friend!" Everyone would laugh, of course, although everyone had felt what it was like to be insulted by him at one time or another. I knew my choices were to be cold and mean, as most of them would have been in response, or to find a way to calm myself. I decided to take pride in being compared to a donkey, unquestionably the most patient, hard-working, persistent, and tolerant animal I've ever known. Years later, I even had cause to thank my father for calling me a donkey, when I heard famed Berber singer Matoub Lounes name the donkey as his favorite animal in an interview. Matoub, as the public called him, explained that the donkey had helped build Berber civilization and that the Berbers wouldn't survive without the donkey. His least favorite animal, of course, was the camel, because Arabs used camels to cross the vast Sahara desert and conquer North Africa in the seventh century.

You would be surprised by how much of a load a donkey carries. From water and building materials, to wood and groceries, it is loaded up with basically anything a household needs. Most Berbers are farmers, so they use the donkey to transport their vegetables and fruits to either the nearest road or all the way to the market. The animals walk up steep hills, through narrow ravines, and down rocky slopes, all in the heat of North African summers and the chill of the harsh winters. On top of this, they will commonly be poked and hit with a nail protruding from a thick baton. You can see hundreds of flies swarming around the wounds on a donkey's rump in the summertime. But does it ever refuse or fight back? No. It never does, even though it could easily kill a person with a well-placed hoof. I used to wonder to myself if God really existed, and if so, why He did not intervene on behalf of these animals. I wondered if the Koran specifically condemned the donkey to this type of life. Or, if it is not God's will, how is it that we humans can be so cruel and careless toward an animal whose strength, help, and obedience enable us to survive?

So my father was right about me in a sense: I was the family member who made my way by persevering, and I was proud of that. Very early on, I had became the family member depended upon to find scarce things or obtain items that required long hours in the notorious lines. I worked hard and never refused to do someone a favor. When a child became sick, I was the one who would wake up early to wait in line to get a pass to the hospital for a family member who lived farther away. I would help them plant and cultivate their crops, or take care of their civil documents at the city hall. Sometimes I even went as far as Algiers, the capital city, if someone needed something from there. I took on the jobs that took the most labor but also promised the most reliable rewards. I worked hard enough in school to be the first child in my family to get the grades needed to enter the university, and so for a long time I convinced myself that I could survive in my country and I could survive in my family—if I just embraced being the "Best Friend of the Donkey."

My incarceration and beating at the hands of my own government changed my mind, however. I knew that my life and my happiness depended on leaving Algeria somehow. My dreams took on the only form I could think of: escape to France. Huge numbers of Algerians visit France every year, and many more migrate there. As the Algerians often say, the French were in our country for 132 years, so we already know each other, and it is only polite to pay a return visit. My brother Brahim had visited France in July of 1984, and ever since then, I yearned to see the country that so many people I knew spoke of or had visited. For almost every day of the six months following the demonstration, I thought of nothing else.

In the fall of 1986, the beginning of my second year at the university, I finally applied for a passport in Tizi-Ouzou, the town where I was born. In most cases it would take about 90 days to get a passport. A criminal background check was required for all applicants, and though I had never committed a crime and had never been sentenced to prison, I was still worried because of my political involvement and the many times I had been held at the police station. Little did I know, my political activities were not what I should have been worried about, at least not then. The person who was in charge of the background check knew my father, and he told him of my application for a passport. My father asked him not to issue me a passport—for a few years! Since my father was a Hadj, and since he was well known in Tizi-Ouzou, he got his way.

Over six months had passed before I found out what my father had done. I had left early one morning to wait in line, as always, to check the status of my application. A fava bean crop I had planted was ready to harvest and it was time for midterm examinations at the university, so the news that my passport application had gone nowhere was an even greater disappointment than it would have been otherwise. My mother saw how upset I was later that day and eventually told me the truth about what my father had done.

"A certain man who works for the police department told your father about your application," she said, carefully, and she didn't need to tell me the rest of the story. She claimed that my father simply didn't want me to leave because he knew that if I had the chance I would never come back—but we both knew these were her sentiments, not my father's. The truth was, I didn't live up to his money-making ideal of what he thought a son should be. By his way of thinking, this somehow made me undeserving of a passport. I was 18, but he still claimed the right to control me.

After I left the house, bitterly stewing over what my father had done, I went straight to check on my fava beans. While I was walking in the field, looking over the crop, I remembered something that might help me. During the summer of the previous year, as I was harvesting watermelons that my cousin and I had planted on this very part of my grandmother's land, my distant cousin, Achour, passed by. Achour was deputy councilor of the county where my father was born, in the mountains. He was a tall man with broad shoulders and dark straight hair, and he was wearing a dark blue suit with a red tie and white shirt. He was all politician, well-groomed, with a perfectly shaved face. I waved at him to stop and gave him one of the biggest melons I had. He was surprised and delighted to receive the delicious fruit on a hot summer day. If I ever needed anything, he told me, I should not hesitate to come see him. This is how the system works in Algeria. You do a small favor for someone, nurture your family connections, and if you are lucky, you can call those favors in someday. When I learned of what my father had done, I decided now was the time to take Achour up on his offer. I was very proud of myself for thinking of him, as well as pleased with myself for having offered him that watermelon so long ago. Perhaps I would get to see the world after all.

The very next day, my 19th birthday, I found a chance to go see my cousin at his office. I didn't know the exact location of his office, but I knew it was in the town of Tigzirt, 23 kilometers away, so I started walking. It was a rainy day, and I tried to hitchhike, but no one would pick me up. By the time I arrived in Tigzirt and found my cousin's office, I was soaked like a chicken (as the Berbers would say), so I had to wait more than two hours to dry before I felt presentable enough to walk in. After considerable trouble finding my way through the maze of bureaucratic offices, I arrived at Achour's. To my youthful eyes, the room was very impressive. He had a dark brown desk and black leather chairs, and a big, framed picture of the Algerian president hanging on the wall right above his desk. I particularly noticed that his office was spotless, unlike any other office I had seen before.

Achour was surprised to see me and right away asked the reason for my visit. I told him I needed a passport as soon as possible so I could go to France and buy some agricultural products. This was false, of course, but plausible, and my cousin knew how long I had been working the land. I told him I didn't have time to wait three months for a passport. He agreed right away, telling me to prepare the application, hand it right to him and not to worry; he would have the passport in my hand within a few days. We shook hands, and I left. It was the best birthday present anyone could have given me!

There was one more hurdle I'd have to cross before I could turn in my passport application. In order to apply for a passport in Achour's county, you had to have a birth certificate stating you were born there. My father was born there, and most people in the village knew me, but still the paperwork would have to be forged. Luckily, one of the employees at the counter where they issued birth certificates was always broke from playing poker. I, on the other hand, always had some extra money from the crops I always grew. I offered the man some cash, and suddenly the birth certificate was in my hand. I put the application in my cousin's assistant's hand exactly three days later and walked the 23 kilometers back to my village, feeling like I could have walked to the moon.

A week later, I went back to Tigzirt. My heart was in my throat as I knocked at Achour's office door. His assistant welcomed me and directed me to the passport office, with instructions to ask for a man named Karim. The man who greeted me there was skeptical at first. How did I know Karim, and who had sent me there? I mentioned my cousin's name, and that was that. The man fetched Karim, who walked me to yet another office. He produced a file and leaned over to me.

"Please verify that all the spelling is correct and sign here and here."

I was nervous as I read my name and all the other information written on the passport. I had never had a passport before, and now I was actually touching my own! Soon I would be able leave this country! What a beautiful thought. I walked out of the office with my passport in my hand, looking at it and kissing it over and over again. I walked every kilometer that day without feeling a meter of it. Uphill, downhill, along the river that led towards Tizi-Ouzou, without seeing anything around me or even realizing that it was once again raining heavily. In my head, I was no longer in Algeria. I was flying around the world, seeing my imagination, my hopes, my desires and my search for a better life suddenly right ahead of me. "I'm going to France," I kept telling myself. "I'm going to get out of here. I'm going to have a future and prove to my father that I'm capable of making it out there." I knew there was no use hoping my father would ever love me, but I wanted him to be wrong, and I wanted him to feel remorse for having not given me the respect I deserved. All this was spinning around and around in my head. I was walking but I wasn't really walking. I was floating on the planet.

When I arrived home, I immediately showed the passport to my mother. She knew how happy I was, and she promised not to breathe a word to my father or brothers. Of course, she insisted that I was far more likely to tell such a happy secret to someone myself. But this secret mattered too much for me to risk my father finding out. My mother was also very sad to think of me leaving, not to mention worried about whether or not I was making the right choice for my young life. She was concerned because I wasn't planning to complete my university education. I planned to leave the moment my fava bean crop was harvested and sold.

"Mom," I said, "I know there is a school out there for me where I can actually learn and prepare for a career, even if it's just the school of the streets. But there is no career for me here, even if

Donkey Heart Monkey Mind

I finish school. Besides, I'm sick and tired of learning everything in Arabic. Arabic won't get me anywhere."

"I've never heard you speak about school like this before. You're willing to just give it all up to go to France?" she asked.

"Washing dishes in a restaurant in France will be far better than being a doctor or a lawyer in this filthy dictatorship, and you know it."

"I can't stop you from doing anything you want. I can only advise you to think before you act," she said, looking sad.

"I promise I'll be someone one day."

So I set about making my preparations to leave. First I had to deal with my crop. Once fava beans are harvested, they go bad quickly after more than three days. They have to be picked in batches, according to buyer demand. A mere seven days after my conversation with my mother, I had finished selling the beans, cleared the field for the next family member who would use it, and purchased a ticket to Barcelona, Spain. My dreams had expanded beyond France to seeing all of Europe, and I thought I would start with Spain. I didn't think of the language barrier; my assumption was that everyone in Europe spoke French.

On the eve of my departure, I traveled to Algiers with my friend, a distant relative named Mustapha, and we passed the night in a small, squalid hotel room. I was so excited I couldn't sleep, and I talked so much that I didn't let Mustapha sleep either. The next morning, April 29th, I went to the airport very early, as Mustapha headed off to his job as a restaurant cook. I got to the airport about four hours earlier than I needed to, ready to fly for the first time in my life and eager to get onto the plane. To me, that plane was going to take me away from a miserable country and into a bright future with unlimited opportunities and adventures. My life was about to change forever, or so I thought.

I checked my little bag three hours before departure and took a walk around the small airport. It didn't take long to see everything there was to be seen, so I stepped outside for a little air and watched the planes take off and land. Finally, exhausted from the night before and a little bored, I lay down on a bench, still watching the planes. Before I knew it, I fell asleep. The roar of a jet engine woke me. Horrified, I realized that a long time had passed, and I had missed my flight. I jumped off the bench like it was on fire and headed straight to the ticket counter. I asked the agent if there were other flights to Spain that day.

"There is a flight to Palma de Mallorca in about two hours, and there is room on it," the agent said.

"I'll take it, I'll take it," I replied, relieved that I could still leave that day.

"Well, your original ticket is to Barcelona, but you won't get a refund, even though the ticket to Palma is cheaper than to Barcelona," he said.

"No problem at all, it's okay, I'll take it," I replied with excitement and relief. It didn't occur to me to ask where Palma de Mallorca was in relation to my original destination. All that mattered was that I was leaving.

The agent issued me the new ticket and told me that I would eventually have to go to the airport in Barcelona to retrieve my bag. This hardly bothered me since I barely owned anything to pack in that bag anyway, and I wasn't taking any chances with this flight. I proceeded to the gate as soon as I got my new ticket, two hours prior to departure.

When the time came to board the plane, I suddenly found I was very nervous. I had no idea what to expect from this new experience. I was sitting between two gentlemen, one Spaniard and one Algerian. As the plane began to taxi and then pick up speed for takeoff, I started sweating. I clutched the two armrests as if I was trying to rip them off the seat. The two men on either side of me noticed my anxiety and attempted to assure me that it would be fine. I explained that in my 19 years I had never experienced that kind of speed.

"In just a few more seconds you'll feel better. After the plane takes off, you won't feel the speed at all," the Spanish man said to me in heavily accented French.

"After this you will want to fly again and again," the Algerian man told me.

Despite their kind words, I was still nervous, but then I saw the front of the plane rise up. Just like that, I was flying for the first time in my life. The Spanish man put his hand on top of mine and smiled at me. He was right: I didn't feel the speed anymore. After the plane leveled off, I found the experience of flying quite pleasant. I thanked both of my temporary companions.

The flight from Algiers to Palma de Mallorca only takes about an hour. Just a few minutes after the captain said we would be landing soon, I felt my stomach jump into my chest with the steep descent. In a few more minutes, I started to see land. But when we drew close to the runway, the plane started going up again. The captain got on the intercom and announced that we had to turn around and come in one more time, because he had missed the runway.

The Algerian man commented, "Algerian pilots are so dumb." That worried me a little. But when the plane came in for a second try, we landed smoothly.

"We have arrived," said the Spaniard.

I took a deep breath and said, "Yes we have."

"It's not so bad after all, right?" the Algerian man asked.

"It was fun. I wouldn't mind doing it again, like you said."

"I told you you'd like it."

We proceeded to the exit and through customs, and I found myself in Palma. The airport was much brighter and cleaner than the one I had just left behind, plus Palma's was full of stores, restaurants, and lights. My hopes for a better life were boosted by even that first glance at the airport. But I still needed to get to Barcelona. I went to the information bureau and found a woman there who spoke a little French.

"Can you please tell me where I can purchase a train ticket to Barcelona?" I asked her, still very excited to actually be in Europe for the first time in my life.

"You want to go to Barcelona?" she asked, puzzled.

"Yes, I want to go to Barcelona."

"Do you know where you are?" she asked.

"What do you mean 'do I know where I am?'"

"You're in Palma de Mallorca."

"I know that."

"Then you should also know that you are on an island, so there is no train to Barcelona from here. You have to take either a boat or a plane," she said, smiling. She could see the eagerness and confusion on my young face. Needless to say, I felt very stupid. She pulled a map of Spain from her desk and showed me the Iberian mainland and the island where we were.

"We are here, and Barcelona is here," she explained.

"Can I buy this map?" I asked.

"No, you can have it for free."

"Free?"

"Yes, it's yours," she replied, still smiling at me.

Donkey Heart Monkey Mind

I was stunned. I had owned maps of the world, but they were flimsy paper things that fell to pieces when you folded and unfolded them too often. This map was a nice, glossy one, and this woman was giving it to me for free. Just an hour out of Algeria, and things already seemed promising.

I asked the woman how much a ticket to Barcelona would cost me, and she told me I could make the reservation with her. There were many flights between Palma and Barcelona, and they didn't cost much—only about $60 U.S.D. Unfortunately I only had the equivalent of $200 U.S.D. on me. In Algeria in the 1980s, all banks were government owned, and you could only exchange up to $200 U.S.D. per year. Although back then this was a considerable sum of money for a 19-year-old to have in his pocket, a $60 ticket to Barcelona took a big chunk out of it. Still, a boat would take too long. So I bought the ticket.

That very evening, I found myself in mainland Spain. I went straight to pick up my bag, and once again I was struck by the contrast with my own country. The Spanish were supremely helpful and polite to me; everyone who could speak to me in broken French understood that I didn't know anything about their country and their system. After I found my bag, a woman at the airport information desk wrote down the address of a youth hostel and the bus number I should take to get there. She also provided me with a few key words in Spanish to show the bus driver and directed me into the city. Even the youth hostel was impressive to me; it was clean and friendly. It was full of young men and women speaking different languages, dressed differently, and acting differently, playing games, drinking beer, and just talking. I was most certainly in a different world.

The next day I went for a long walk in Barcelona. I only had my small backpack with me, and I was navigating by a small map (another free map!) given to me at the youth hostel. I used it to walk around and out of the city, and I started hitchhiking towards France. When I entered France, I was immediately amazed by how green the countryside was. Why, I asked myself, would the French have been interested in Algeria when they had a country as beautiful as this one? Why would they have been interested in a brown country that was two-thirds desert? Although I hardly went into towns, I could tell as I passed how clean and organized they were, and this, too, dazzled me. The beauty I was seeing distracted me from how hard the journey actually was. What little sleep I got occurred outside, and sometimes I went a whole day without eating at all. I wanted to save what little money I had left for Paris. Some of the people who picked me up offered me food, and that helped me get through the four days it took to get there from Barcelona.

When I finally arrived in the city that had been in my dreams for three years, ever since my brother's visit, it did not disappoint me. Paris was the most beautiful thing I had yet laid eyes on in my life. Still, I was tired and hungry, so I had to save exploration for another day. I went straight to a hotel and restaurant owned by my father's cousins in Aubervilliers, a Paris suburb.

Upon entering the restaurant, I received an incredible and rather unpleasant surprise: the first person I saw there was my own father. I could hardly believe my eyes. He was as shocked as I was, if not more so. I knew that he traveled to Paris periodically, though I hadn't known about this trip. He, on the other hand, hadn't even known that I had obtained a passport, let alone that I had managed to leave Algeria.

"How did you get here?" he asked, astounded.

"I hitchhiked from Barcelona. I just got into Paris," I answered, smiling proudly and trying to sound nonchalant.

Donkey Heart Monkey Mind

"Are you hungry?"

This wasn't the question I had expected. "Aren't you going to ask me how I got a passport?"

"Ah," he said, recalling what he had done. "No, I won't."

I wanted to pursue the conversation and tell him how wrong he was for not allowing me to have a passport, but I was actually too hungry and tired. Still, I didn't want him to know that I was starving. I wanted to show him that I was capable of being in Europe without his help and that I could take care of myself.

"I'm a little hungry," I conceded. "I heard your cousin makes a good couscous. I haven't had it in a while."

My father saw straight past my casual tone. He could see from my face that I hadn't been eating well, and he rolled his eyes to tell me that I was full of shit.

We sat down at a table together. It was the first time I had sat alone at a table with him as an adult. The last time we had sat down to eat together alone had been in 1980, when I was 12 years old. He had taken me to Algiers to buy a battery for his car. That visit, I remembered, had begun with him slapping me several times across the face for buying us the wrong bus tickets. This time we were on a more equal footing, I thought to myself proudly.

It was a Sunday so the restaurant was full of people from my father's village, all convening there on their day off to chat, play dominoes, drink coffee and smoke cigarettes. The restaurant was clouded with tobacco smoke. My father ordered us couscous. It turned out that he was in France to buy a new taxi. My father changed cars every two to three years so that they would look nice and new for his customers and so that he could show them off to his friends. He asked me what I thought of Paris now that I was there.

"I took a plane to Mallorca, then another to Barcelona,

and I've been hitchhiking from there. Yet all you ask me is what I think of Paris? Aren't you going to ask me about my entire trip?" I asked, challenging him. I wanted badly to tell him that I had seen more of Europe in just a few days than he had ever seen in his whole life. My father knew Paris and Marseille, but he had never traveled for leisure in Europe.

He shook his head and said, "I've never been to Spain. Maybe I'll go through there next time when I buy a car. I'll drive it through."

"It's a beautiful country. You should go sometime," I suggested to him.

"How long were you there?" he asked.

"Just a couple of days."

"Two days and you already know it's a beautiful country?"

"From what I can see, all of Europe is beautiful. I still want to see as many countries as I can. It won't hurt to visit them all."

"Do you have any money?" he asked.

"I do for now," I said, again bluffing to a certain degree. "I may look for a job somewhere at some point."

Even though the conversation was a bit uncomfortable, it gave me tremendous pleasure. I finally felt like a man talking to his father, just as I had always wanted. Finally we could have a decent conversation without him ordering me to do something or finding an excuse to slap me around. One brief shared lunch would never replace all that was lacking in the first 19 years of our relationship, but it was enough to establish a new respect between us. We parted on a new footing: he to buy his car and return to Algeria, and I to continue testing my wings across the rest of the continent. (I never had another chance to talk to my father like I did that day.)

I traveled non-stop for the next four months. I had told

my father that my plans were simply to see as much of Europe as I could, and I did. I hitchhiked, slept outside, and met people from many different countries. In Luxemburg, I worked in an Italian restaurant, though I only stayed there for about three weeks. After that, I just kept moving, managing to see some of Belgium, Germany, Switzerland, Italy, Yugoslavia, Austria, Denmark, and Sweden. Sometimes I went hungry for days at a time, but often the people who gave me rides in their cars would share their food with me. Some even gave me a little money. I didn't settle for just seeing a little of France or Spain, as my brother and many other Algerians had. I explored quite a bit of the continent, and I was dazzled.

THREE CONTINENTS

Towards what would turn out to be the end of my European expedition, I was walking aimlessly around Stockholm and stumbled across the American Embassy. The thought occurred to me to apply for a visa to enter the United States. I had nothing to lose from simply applying—or so I thought. Of course I had no way of knowing that there actually was a lot to lose. If you were denied, your passport was tarnished with a stamp that read: "DENIED - Not Allowed to Enter for 10 years." I applied and my passport was given just such a stamp. But I wasn't worried too much. I still had all of Europe open to me, and my exploration was far from finished.

It was early September of 1987, in a grocery store in Stockholm, that I first tried stealing food. As usual, I was very hungry and had very little money. Whenever I went to a grocery store to buy food, I found things were far too expensive for me to afford. I picked up a baguette, some cheese, some ham, and a bottle of Coke. The cheese and the ham were the most expensive items, so I hid them in my pocket and went to pay for the Coke and the bread. As I was leaving the register, a man stopped me and asked for my receipt. He must have been watching me the whole time. I produced the receipt and within moments two security guards were standing next to me. Of course I didn't understand a word they were saying. One of them held me by the arm and pointed to the back of the store. I thought to myself, "It's okay, I will run away the first chance I get, so I should take it easy until then." I wasn't particularly worried at that point, since I was sure that I could outrun the two guards. But we had barely reached the back room when two policemen arrived and put me in handcuffs.

The cops took me to the city jail and, with characteristic Swedish efficiency, fingerprinted me, took my picture, measured my height and weight, and put me in a cell. Stepping inside, I was amused to find that even European jail cells seemed superior to their Algerian counterparts. This one was clean, with a more comfortable bed than those in the youth hostels I had been lucky enough to stay in when I wasn't sleeping outside. I thought, "Wow, this is a real treat!" I told myself that I would sleep comfortably, I would be fed, and in a few days, once they realized I had no criminal history in Sweden, they would release me.

The two nights I spent in that cell were indeed luxurious compared to my prior experiences with jail. I was allowed to cross the hallway to use a real bathroom, and I was very well fed. Then, after the second night, a guard came in and told me to follow him. A woman who spoke French greeted me in a nearby room and said, "Good news. You are about to be released."

I was thrilled. They gave me back my belongings, at which point I expected to just walk out. But then another police officer told me to put my hands behind my back. The woman who spoke French had already left the room, so I couldn't ask what was going on. I was loaded into a police car and driven away through Stockholm. We kept going and going, and when I couldn't stand it any longer, I demanded to be informed of our destination. The policeman didn't speak French, but he guessed what I wanted to know.

His answer was a shock to me: "Airport." I started screaming and yelling, but there was nothing I could have done.

We finally arrived at the airport, and I was put onto a Scandinavian SAS airplane, headed to Rome. Another translator was waiting for me on the plane. This woman told me I was being sent back to Algeria, but that my flight had to connect through Rome. Once in Italy, she said, my passport would be given back to me. She took off and the plane departed. When the plane arrived in Rome, two gentlemen escorted me off the plane. One of them spoke broken French, and he immediately made himself my friend by saying, "There is no need for you to walk out in handcuffs. Besides, there is nowhere for you to go." They released my hands, and we walked up the gangway.

We were in the international zone of the airport, and the two men told me to follow them to their office. When we arrived, one of the men punched a few keys on the computer and told me that the plane to Algeria would leave in about two hours. He told me that if I needed to walk around and stretch my legs, I was more than welcome to do so. To ensure my return, he explained that he would keep my passport until I got onto the plane to Algeria. I agreed, telling him I would very much like to take a stroll through the terminal.

I immediately began evaluating my surroundings and my options. The guards were fools to think I wouldn't try to escape.

Djaffar Chetouane

They had no idea what I would be headed back to if I let them deport me. I had left my country because I knew there was no future for me there, except a narrow, Arabist educational system, no career to be had, and only a lifetime of scraping a living from the dirt to look forward to. If life in Algeria had seemed dismal and cruel before I had seen Europe, it now seemed insufferable compared to the abundance and beauty that I had been introduced to over the last few months. So I embraced my present situation: I had been deported from Sweden, but I was now in Italy. I thought there must be something I could do to keep from being sent home.

Walking around the international zone, I saw a couple of guarded exits and wondered if there might be other ways out. I kept walking, passing different gates marked with various destinations. There were bars and restaurants with beautiful pictures of pasta and other dishes decorating their walls, and many stores selling clothes, perfumes, shoes, purses, and the like. Then, all of sudden, I spotted a gate marked New York. I caught my breath, and my mind started racing.

No one I knew had ever been to New York. Even the idea of traveling the great distance to get there is, for most Algerians, far more daunting than the short hop from North Africa to Europe. What's more, it is an English-speaking country and, most importantly, you have to obtain a visa to travel there. An Algerian like me lacked both the money and the political influence required for an American visa. I had never even met an American, even on my travels through Europe, though I assumed I must have heard English spoken in one youth hostel or another. But since I didn't speak English, I didn't know how to meet Americans. To me, Americans were only something from movies and television. In Algerian movie theaters, we had all loved watching Westerns—you know, white people killing Indians. I didn't have an inkling of the history between white colonists and Native Americans, but the movies portrayed the Native Americans as villains and the whites as heroes; naturally, we Algerians liked the "good guys." So every aspect of America was more or less only fantasy to me.

Back at the airport, for the moment, I just kept walking.

When I circled back around and passed the New York gate again, I found that people were boarding the flight. I stood there for a minute, watching the passengers. There was a lady standing and taking the tickets. (Of course in the 1980s, plane tickets were all paper, with two or three carbon copies.) As the ticket taker tore the top portion off each packet, she would put the carbon copies down on a stool next to her. Without having any kind of clear plan whatsoever, I headed towards her. Somehow I ended up behind her, facing the large window, from which I could see the huge plane. I stared at the plane for a few moments, amazed at its size.

I turned around, and the batch of paper tickets caught my eye. Still without really thinking, I picked one up, just like that. Although I was very sneaky and cunning, it was fast even to me. The lady remained busy tearing tickets. At this point adrenaline must have taken over, holding my thoughts firmly in the present, leaving me unable to plan or really analyze, able only to act. Shaking, I took the ticket and got in line. There were only a few people ahead of me, and suddenly I was standing in front of the lady and handing over the carbon copies. I began babbling to her in French, telling her that I was sorry but I must have dropped the other half. She just looked at it, said something in Italian, and waved me through. I could not believe what was going on. Proceeding past her, I walked down the gangway and actually boarded the plane.

Djaffar Chetouane

The plane seemed about 80 percent full, and there were some seats in back that weren't occupied. Choosing an aisle seat next to an African-American man, I discovered that he spoke a little French. The anxiety I had felt the first time I had flown was nothing compared to what I felt now. My blood pounded through my veins as I thought of what I had just done and what might be coming next. I tried to make conversation with my neighbor, feigning calm, and before I knew it, the plane had taken off.

I never really calmed down during that whole trip. At one point, I went to the bathroom with my little backpack and tore up every piece of paper that had anything to do with Algeria, anything that had Arabic writing on it. I thought over and over of ways I might get out of the airport once we got there. No English. No money. No friends. No family. And, of course, no passport. How the hell would I get past immigration? What would I tell them? The thoughts collided, crashed and tumbled over one another for the duration of the flight.

My seatmate was extremely kind and friendly, and he let me ask him question after question about New York City. His French wasn't very good, but he tried to answer as best he could. And of course he had a few questions of his own. I confided in him about exactly how I had gotten on the plane, and at that, he smiled the biggest smile I'd ever seen. He had a big mouth full of bright white teeth. It was a beautiful smile that I will never forget. Once I had told him most of my story, he reached into his wallet and gave me some money. I cannot remember how much it was but, more importantly, that man was my first American friend. (I still wish I could see him again and repay him for his kindness to such an unusual stranger.)

I was way too nervous to sit still, so when I wasn't quizzing my new friend, I was taking advantage of the size of the plane by walking up and down the aisles. I kept telling myself that I really needed to come up with something good to get myself into New York City. Even though most of the people around us slept, I could not. At one point, I considered stealing money from those who had dozed off, but the thought of my new friend wouldn't let me. Besides, I was too preoccupied with how I would get out of the airport. Just before I thought I would go crazy from speculation, the plane began its descent. I sat down and looked eagerly out the window, trying to see New York City, but I couldn't (since we were landing at Kennedy International).

Once the plane was parked at the gate, I followed everyone else off. I tried to act like I knew where I was going, like the casual, experienced traveler who already knows the drill. I proceeded to the immigration officer, and I told him in French that I had no papers. At nineteen, I was naïve enough to hope he might actually tell me to go on through. What wishful thinking! He said something I didn't understand, repeating it several times. And I, too, repeated myself saying, "I don't have papers." Then I said I had no passport, and he understood that immediately. He picked up a phone and asked me to step aside. In less than five seconds, two more officers appeared and told me to follow them.

They took me into a little office, where one of them stayed with me while the other went back out. In a minute or two, the first two were replaced by two new officers. They started talking to me, but of course, I couldn't understand a word. At the same time, one of them searched my little backpack. We were getting nowhere, so the room eventually fell silent. Within a few minutes, a woman walked in. She wore civilian clothes and she asked me if I spoke French. I thought to myself, "Do men ever speak any languages other than their own mother tongues?" Once again I had a woman translator coming to my rescue.

The translator began asking me questions, and I asked her how she knew I spoke French. She said that they had found an Algerian voting card in my backpack—the one thing I must have forgotten to dispose of.

"How did you get onto the plane from Rome to here without a passport?" she asked. I told her she wouldn't believe me if I told her the truth. She relayed my answer to the other officers.

"Well, tell me," she said. So I did. I told her the whole truth. As she translated for the officers, I saw looks of disbelief spread across their faces.

"So your passport is with the Italian authorities?" the translator asked.

"Yes," I said.

They conferred for a moment, and then she turned to me and said, "This gentleman will make a phone call to Rome, and in the meantime you have to wait until they decide what to do with you."

She asked me if I was hungry. I told her no, but that I could use a drink. She left with the officers, and one of them came back with a can of Coke. As he handed it to me he was smiling. I think they were simply bewildered, unsure of what to make of me. It was about half an hour before the other officer and the translator returned. She told me that my story had checked out and that the Italians had laughed very hard when they found out what had become of me. Then she told me the bad news.

"We have to send you back to Rome, on the same plane you came in on. It is leaving in about three hours."

Up to this point, some part of my brain was still indulging in the fantasy that my fate would take a turn right here—that I would give them the slip, get lost in New York City, and begin my young life anew in this fabled place. I had kept a keen eye on my surroundings the whole time I was marched to the office, just in case I saw an opportunity to escape. But I was too closely guarded, and these officers had guns in their holsters. This time the translator dispelled all my fantasies, and my few months of freedom from my old life were coming to a close.

I became increasingly desperate as the time to get back on the plane drew near. I couldn't believe that I had managed to scramble my way from Algeria to Europe and from there as far as America, only to be shipped right back to the hopeless place from which I had started. As I was finally sent onboard the plane, I was agitated and nervous, starting to sweat. I took a seat in the very back of the almost empty plane. My body settled, but my mind did not. "I have to do something. I have to do something. I have to do something," I said to myself over and over again.

There was only one action left that I could take, or the plane would take off with me on it. It was already starting to taxi back from the gate. Just like that, I stood up from my seat, turned around, and headed for the Emergency Exit. The last thing I saw was the Italian flight attendant screaming at me, and then I simply opened the door and jumped out. If you have never jumped out of a jet plane, you would be surprised at the distance from the emergency door to the tarmac. I hit it hard and felt my left ankle twist badly. Still, I stood up and tried to take off running. I had no idea where I was going, so I hustled and limped my way towards a nearby warehouse. Of course I had barely made it inside before I found myself cut off by two officers in a jeep, with machine guns pointed at me. In any language, the meaning is clear when someone points a gun at you: you get on the ground and put your hands on your head, period. And I did just that. To my surprise, though, the officers handcuffed me very gently. They put me in the jeep, and we headed back towards the terminal.

We were greeted there by the same two officers and their French translator, wearing predictably astonished looks on their faces.

"What were you thinking?" the woman asked, incredulously.

"I didn't want to go back," I told her.

The officers exchanged a few words with her and she turned around to say, "They've never witnessed anything remotely close to what you just did. You could have been killed." They took off the handcuffs, and I sat in a chair while one of them picked up the phone and made a call. Shortly thereafter, a big woman with light brown skin, long curly dark hair, and a kind face came in with ice in a plastic bag. She put the plastic bag around my left ankle and began gently cleaning my face with a white towel.

"Are you feeling better?" she asked through the interpreter, wiping sweat from my face and gently smiling. I could feel through my skin that she was one of the most caring and loving people I had ever met.

"Yes, much better, thank you," I responded gratefully.

They soon took me to another office, where the interpreter started asking me questions again.

"Why don't you want to go back? Are you afraid to go back to Algeria? Did you do anything? Are the authorities looking for you?"

"No, I just don't want to go back. There is nothing there for me."

"You jumped out of a plane! You must have a reason for not wanting to go back. What are you afraid of?"

She kept repeating the same question, and I could tell she

wanted as much as the officers to know why I would risk my life just to stay in America. But her tone eventually changed, and I could see she was getting agitated. Maybe she was tired of dealing with me.

"Are you politically involved in Algeria?" she asked.

"I'm a Berber. Of course I'm involved," I answered.

"What do you mean?" she asked, now with a new look on her face.

"Berbers are always involved with politics," I explained. "We've been oppressed ever since the French left Algeria in 1962. And before that we were oppressed by the French."

"Is the government looking for you because you're involved with the Berber movement? If they are, then you must prove it. Then you can ask for political asylum, and they may let you stay here while they see if your story checks out."

Either because I was just a kid, or because I was in a tremendous amount of pain, clearly I wasn't thinking straight. The Algerian government wasn't looking for me now, but they certainly had been on more than one occasion. I surely could have said something that would have gotten me at least temporary political asylum. But I didn't understand that and let my chance pass.

"The government is not looking for me," I said. "I haven't done anything wrong. I just don't want to go back."

Eventually, finding they were getting no new answers by asking the same questions over and over again, they took me to yet another room. There they fingerprinted me and took my picture.

"We have to do a background check," the translator explained.

"What background? I've never set foot in this country before! I don't have any background for you to check!" I responded, laughing.

"They still have to do a background check," she explained.

Djaffar Chetouane

"It's standard procedure for anyone who tries to sneak into the country, especially a person who jumps out of a moving plane! In the meantime, you'll have to spend the night here."

My heart leaped a little at that. An overnight stay would mean yet another chance to make my temporary stay a permanent one.

"Where will I sleep?" I asked.

"They'll figure something out for you."

In a short while, an African-American officer wearing more gold jewelry than I had ever seen in my life entered the room. The interpreter explained to me, "This officer will take you to a hotel, where you'll stay until they figure out what to do with you tomorrow."

The officer looked like he was in his mid-thirties, with broad shoulders and a shiny, shaved head. In my head, I dubbed him "The Gold Man." He wore gold earrings, a gold watch on one wrist and a gold bracelet on the other, a few gold chains, and several rings, and he even had a couple of gold pens in his pocket. "This man must be worth a fortune," I said to myself. "America must pay their police officers very well."

I followed The Gold Man, and he drove me in a police car to a hotel full of cops, just minutes from the airport. I scrutinized the adornments of all the cops there, and was impressed to find that many of these, too, wore gold jewelry, though none as much as my escort. He gestured to ask if I wanted to eat something, and I responded by eagerly nodding my head. At the hotel restaurant, we got in line with the other police officers, and I happily served myself a big plate of steak and baked potatoes.

As in Stockholm, I was very impressed with how these people treated suspected criminals. When The Gold Man led me up to a sixth floor room after dinner the impression continued, even though the room was plain by American standards. Though simple, it was clean, with a red-patterned carpet, two single beds, each with a blanket and pillow, and of course, a television. Above the beds, in the center of the wall, hung a crucifix, and a Bible sat on the nightstand next to the remote control. The Gold Man gestured for me to take the bed next to the window, and he sat on the one nearer the door, flipping on the TV.

We began watching a man talking to an audience, with everyone laughing, including The Gold Man. He said something to me through his laughter, though the only word I could understand was "English." I continued to stare at the screen for an hour, maybe two, as image after image flickered across it. Then another noise caught my attention. Could it be snoring? I couldn't believe my luck: The Gold Man was asleep. Immediately, all I could think of was getting out of there. I tried making a few little noises, to see if he would wake up easily, but he didn't. I made a few loud noises, but still he didn't stir. Slowly, I stood up and headed for the door.

I opened it nice and slow and closed it quietly behind me. After hurrying down the hallway, I pushed the elevator button. In a few seconds the elevator door opened, and an unfamiliar police officer got out. He stared at me and said something in English, but I tried to ignore him, getting in and pressing the button for the first floor. Just as the elevator doors were about to close, he got back inside and started to talk to me. I didn't answer him, and just as we were about to arrive on the first floor, he grabbed me and handcuffed me.

After he escorted me back to the room, I gathered that he had been sent there to check on us. As soon as we entered, he started yelling at the other officer, waking him up with a start. After they had argued back and forth a little, the second officer took the handcuffs off my right wrist and cuffed me to the leg of the bed. The Gold Man left, and my new guard lay down on the bed to which I was handcuffed.

By that time it was quite late at night. I sat on the floor, my hand attached to the bed, feeling thoroughly sorry for myself. Still, I thought, my hand was only cuffed to the leg of the bed, and if the officer fell asleep, I still might have a shot. I kept thinking back and asking myself, "Why hadn't I taken the stairs?" Maybe I would have had better luck that way, I thought, and continued to debate with myself. I was determined not to give up until I had exhausted every possibility.

To my surprise, luck was with me again. The second officer fell asleep, too! I noticed that the digital clock sitting on the television read 3:45 a.m. I slowly lifted the corner of the bed, being careful not to disturb the sleeping policeman, and slid the handcuffs off the leg. Once again, I made a few noises to check that the officer was deeply asleep. Once again, I crawled carefully to the door and let myself out.

This time I headed towards the stairs at the far end of the hallway. I opened the stairway door, shut it behind me, and then froze. I couldn't decide whether to go up or down. I was sure they wouldn't look for me on the highest floor, but how long would I stay up there before it might be safe to come down? I decided to find out if there were a door to the roof, so I headed up. Before long, I found just the door I was looking for, but I could see that it was rigged to some kind of device and labeled in big red letters. It had to be an alarm. I decided to just lay low for a while and then walk downstairs. In the meantime, I tugged and twisted at the handcuff, trying to work it off my wrist, and I kept an ear open for the sounds of a search. For the moment, I could simply enjoy my freedom.

About half an hour later, I decided to head down. Still limping on my swollen left ankle, I made my way down flight after

Donkey Heart Monkey Mind

flight of stairs. When I reached the bottom, I cracked the door. To my surprise, the door led to the main lobby, which was full of chatting policemen. By now, it was almost dawn, and cops strode in and out of the hotel's entrance continuously. I shut the door and tried to think, but I didn't know if there were any other ways out of the building. Deciding to take a chance, I held my left hand with the handcuffs behind my back and headed out into the open.

I tried to walk quickly yet casually, but the moment I passed the first group of policemen, one of them turned and saw what I was concealing behind my back. He yelled at me, and I tried to hurry, but my ankle wouldn't let me run. In no time at all, I was surrounded by three cops. Not one of them was sure who I was, but all of them were sure I was up to no good. They made a few calls on their radios, and soon their questions were answered. My second guard hurried downstairs and picked me up, returning me to the room for the last time. After berating me for a while, he handcuffed his hand to mine, put us both on the same bed, and fell asleep for a few more hours. He seemed able to sleep comfortably, now that he could be sure I wasn't going anywhere, but I lay wide awake, anxious and frustrated.

In the morning we went downstairs for breakfast. But before we could enter the dining room, I asked if I could go to the bathroom. The policeman accompanied me to the bathroom in the lobby and told me to go ahead, but he didn't want to uncuff himself from me. I gestured to him that I didn't just need to urinate, and then he had to consider his choices. I wasn't lying. I really did need to use the toilet, but of course I was still hoping to make a last-ditch effort at losing my escort. He decided he could let me as far as a stall. He took the handcuffs off and said something that I interpreted as, "I'll be right here in front of the door."

Djaffar Chetouane

I went inside and saw a window above the toilet that the policeman must not have spotted. I did what I had to do in a hurry, then opened the window, and bingo—I was outside! I started limping and hopping away as fast as I could, without a clue about where to head but no less determined to go. Of course I wasn't gone for long before I heard a siren and looked around to find a cop on a motorcycle pulling up behind me. In seconds he had knocked me to the ground with his foot, tackled me, and hand-cuffed me. A car came and took me back to the hotel, and when my guard greeted me, he was laughing. I can't imagine what he thought of this disheveled foreign kid with an ankle swollen like a melon who just wouldn't seem to give up. My luck had finally run out, however, and he knew it. I stayed attached to that same cop by the wrist for the whole rest of the morning.

That afternoon, two Italian detectives came to interview me. One of them spoke a little French.

"Well, we've heard about all that you did," he said.

"What did you hear?" I asked.

"That you jumped out of a moving plane, and that you attempted to escape from the hotel many times."

"I don't want to go back," I said. "There's nothing for me in Algeria."

"How did you think you would stay here while your passport is in Italy?"

"I would do whatever it takes if it lets me start a better life here," I replied, with total conviction.

"Well, we're here to take you back, and if you think of doing anything like that again—" he pulled back his jacket and showed me his gun, "I'll shoot you."

"Don't worry. I won't."

Donkey Heart Monkey Mind

"We will be leaving shortly for the airport."

"Can I just ask for one favor, please?" I asked the officer, crestfallen.

"What is it?" he replied politely.

"I made it all the way to America and didn't even see New York City. Would you please take me through New York? I want to get a glimpse of it just once. I promise I won't do anything at all."

"New York is out of our way," he said.

"Just a quick look. Please," I pleaded.

The two detectives conferred, and I think the one who spoke French felt a little sorry for me.

"Okay, I'll take you to see it from the highway. We won't actually go into the city though. There's too much traffic, and we'd miss the plane."

"It's okay. Just a look," I replied happily.

I was handcuffed to the one who spoke French, and the two officers took me to their car. The translating officer and I got into the back seat, and off we went. As we were pulling away, I noticed ruefully that the Emergency Exit stairs had been on the outside of the hotel building the whole time, and that there was a door on every floor. A Berber expression came to mind: "My name just wasn't on those stairs."

To my amazement, we drove onto a seven lane highway. I had never seen anything like it before, and I couldn't stop turning my head in all directions. There were so many things to see! New York City was visible in the distance, and I could see the World Trade Center towers rising into the sky. How could anyone build such a tall building? Seeing that skyline, I was convinced that America was in fact the most powerful country in the world.

Partway to the airport, the officers changed their minds.

"We'll take you in for a little while," said the one who translated for me. "I think we'll make it."

"I don't know how to thank you!" I said to him.

We drove into the city, and my face was illuminated with joy. Where else but in a city like New York can you see so many things in so little time?

"Would you like something to eat?" the officer asked me.

"Yes, I would like that!" I replied, with a big smile.

"But I won't take the handcuffs off, okay?"

"Okay."

They pulled over to a McDonald's window and started ordering food. I was amazed. I had never seen a restaurant serving food from a window before. The officer handed me a little paper bag. I don't remember what I ate, but I clearly recall that it had french fries with it and that it was all delicious.

We drove on while we ate. When I had finished my meal, the officer asked me if I wanted anything else before we got onto the highway.

"Can you do me one more favor?" I asked, feeling encouraged.

"What is it?" he asked, seemingly gratified by how much fun I was having.

"Can you get me a couple of postcards to send to my friends in Algeria, to impress them?"

"Is that all?" he asked.

"Yes, that's the last thing I'll ask of you, and I'll pay for them myself. I have money in my pocket."

"No, that's okay. I'll pay for them. You should save your money," he said with a smile.

The officer who was driving pulled over next to a small

store, went inside, and came back with five cards and stamps.

"You have to write them quickly. We have to head back," my translator told me.

"I'm only writing a few words. I promise."

I wrote the postcards very quickly, and he jumped out and mailed them for me. I thanked him with all my heart, assuring him that I would never forget his compassion.

When we got to the airport he said, "If you want, I can take off the handcuffs now, but you must not try to do anything. If you do, I promise I'll shoot you."

"I won't," I said, truly meaning it. I had tremendous respect for him for being so nice to me, and I couldn't break a promise to a person like that. We walked through the airport to the plane, one of them close on either side of me the whole time. I was sandwiched between them as we sat and waited for the flight, and I walked between them again right up until I was on the plane.

All the way back to Rome, I thought of the remarkable time I had spent in the United States. I couldn't ask for more: I had been to New York City, I had eaten a McDonald's meal, and I had sent postcards to my friends as proof that I had been there. More importantly, I had met a woman who made me feel very special just through her gentle touch and her compassion to a stranger. I never knew her name, but her face is one of those that remain in my mind. Likewise, two Italian police officers were very kind to me, even though they had no responsibility other than to take me back to Rome. I had made it to New York once in my life. I told myself that I would have to make it there a second time someday.

When we arrived in Rome, the officers who had picked me up from Stockholm greeted me again. They were laughing their heads off. It was quite funny for them to see me strolling off a plane from New York, when they had last seen me heading off just to "stretch my legs" in the terminal. They, too, had heard about my hijinks in the American airport and hotel. One of them joked that they should just let me go, that I deserved to stay in Italy if I was willing to try that hard to not go back to Algeria. I certainly was willing to try all that and more. I had no choice this time, but I knew that I would make my way back out of Algeria again as soon as possible. And now my sights were set far beyond Barcelona or Paris.

Algeria looked more bleak than ever to me in September of 1987. I had spent all of my money in Europe and, since I had been traveling instead of growing crops, I was completely broke. All I could think about was what to do for money so that I could leave again as soon as possible. Four months in Europe and one wild day in the United States had convinced me that I simply had to emigrate. My trip had confirmed for me the reality of places like Paris, where you could sit down for a civilized meal with your father instead of being cursed at and cuffed by him; or Stockholm, where they were rich enough to feed you and gave you a comfortable bed in jail; and finally, there was America, where the policemen dripped with gold jewelry and stayed in hotels where they could have all the steak and potatoes they wanted. How could I go back to scraping pocket money from fava beans and taking classes at a provincial university controlled by a government that had outlawed the teaching of my own mother tongue?

One option for money, at least in the short term, would be for me to get a crop in the ground as soon as possible. But I saw several problems with that. My family's land, including that from both my mother's and father's sides, is extensive, but not all of it is near a road or has direct access to water. Use of land with road and water access requires permission from the family elders in the summer or winter. The right to use these parcels of land rotates among the various immediate families, and it wasn't my family's turn. Using the land that doesn't have road and water access is extremely difficult. The planting is hard, keeping the crops watered is even more strenuous labor, and the worst part is the harvest, toting bushels and bags of produce back and forth across the fields.

I would have done it in a heartbeat if I had arrived home during the spring or summer, but winter labor is grueling. For example, potatoes require tilling the soil around the head of the plant just after the leaves are halfway grown. Carrots require very little care as they grow, but they must be cleaned after you pull them out of the ground. On top of that, winter weather is very unpredictable. You have to work in cold rain, mud, and sometimes snow. Imagine carrying your crop across the fields through sucking mud so you can get to a road. Then, if there is too much rain, the crops drown, and if there is too little, they wither and die. I wasn't willing to risk it this time. I wanted an easier solution.

One appeared one day in the form of a villager nicknamed "Bootooje," who approached me because of my reputation for being able to obtain things that were hard to get. He knew that a few years earlier, my brother Brahim had started raising chickens for money, and Bootooje was interested in obtaining a quantity of young chicks to sell.

The chickens were destined for New Year celebrations that would take place about two months later. The Berber New Year, *Yennayar*, is traditionally celebrated on the 12th of January with a feast that always includes chicken. The holiday celebrates the founding of the 22nd Egyptian Dynasty by the Berber Pharaoh Shoshenq, around 950 B.C.E. It is said that Shoshenq and his followers celebrated their final, decisive victory over their rivals by slaughtering chickens, and so chicken is as much part of *Yennayar* as turkey is a part of American Thanksgiving. All Berber families are ready to pay good prices for chickens for *Yennayar*. Of course, in villages, they don't go to the supermarket and buy a pre-plucked, gutted, plastic-wrapped bird, as they do in cities in some countries. They buy live birds in the fall to slaughter later, preferring the taste of birds that have been raised at home. (Berbers refer to commercially produced birds as "electrical chickens," because they are raised with electricity to speed their growth.) It takes about 60 days to raise a chick to full size, so demand for them is high in mid-November. People even reserve them several months in advance, at excellent prices. I thought to myself that if I could find a few hundred chicks for Bootooje, plus some for two friends of his who were interested, I could make a good commission on the sale.

What I needed to find was a person with an incubator; someone rich and well connected enough to have bought an incubator and be hatching chicks for sale. I knew that finding such a supplier wouldn't be easy. First of all, anyone with that kind of expensive setup was unlikely to be of my class. Secondly, they probably already had all kinds of people better connected than I, begging them to produce and reserve chicks for them, especially at this time of year. Algerians eat so much chicken that the chicks from hatcheries are usually sold out weeks before they hatch, year round, even months before the eggs are in the incubator. This makes for a reliable, profitable business for those who can afford to get into it.

Where I come from, some villages are made up of a single extended family, and big villages like mine are made up of several large, interconnected families. Men and women do not mix, but the men know all the men, and the women know all the women.

Donkey Heart Monkey Mind

People know to whom your cousin is married, who your friends are, what your skills are, and whether you owe someone a favor. Villagers marry each other, fight each other, help and hire each other. Bootooje, for example, lived in the center of the village and had managed to buy a pick up truck, so people knew and hired him as a transporter and delivery service. I was known throughout the village for my determination to get things that were hard to get, so Bootooje had come to me when he had trouble supplying his clients with chicks. Now I just needed to figure out whom to ask so that I could supply Bootooje.

I thought through my network of family and friends. One of my best friends from childhood, Cherif, had a much older brother, Mahmoud. Cherif and Mahmoud's father and mine were long-time friends, and my father spoke of Mahmoud with great respect. I learned that Mahmoud had gotten into the hatching business recently, which made him the first and only person on my list to ask. Of course, it would not be appropriate to approach Mahmoud directly. I asked my friend Cherif to put me in contact with Mahmoud, but even this was not as simple as it sounded. Although the men were brothers, Cherif, the younger, owed Mahmoud, the older, a formal debt of respect, so they would never be close. It would not be appropriate for Cherif to ask his brother to sell me a thousand chicks, Cherif said, since he had never had anything to do with his older brother's business. So for Cherif to put me in contact with his brother was out of the question. I thought briefly about asking my father to approach Mahmoud, who would have acceded to such an important man's request in a heartbeat if it were a matter of me planning to raise the chicks myself. But the chicks weren't really for me, they were for Bootooje and his friends, so I couldn't ask my father to do it.

Djaffar Chetouane

I decided to take a chance and go straight to Mahmoud and ask him myself. At least I would have the advantage of being able to use my father's name. In Berber villages, when you introduce yourself, you use four names: your name, your father's name, your grandfather's name, and your great-grandfather's name. So I, for example, would say, "I'm Jafar, son of Hadj Arezki, son of Hadj Mezian, son of Said."

Mahmoud was a well-educated man by Algerian standards, having obtained a four year electrical engineering degree in Yugoslavia in the 1970s. He was one of many who the Algerian government sent on scholarship to study abroad in the 1960s and 1970s, in an effort to cultivate an Algerian intelligentsia. Not all of these students returned to Algeria, but of those who did, many worked for meager government salaries just long enough to establish good connections and then used their influence to open some kind of more profitable private business. This is exactly what Mahmoud had done with his incubator business.

When I went to his establishment and introduced myself, I was lucky at first. Mahmoud told me he would see what he could do, although he had already sold out all the chicks that would hatch from the machine this round and everything he would produce for the next six months. But still, he assured me, he would come up with the 1,000 chicks that I needed, just because I was the son of Hadj Arezki. But before I left, he asked casually, "Are you going to raise them in Tikobaine with your brother, Brahim?"

"Yes," I said, hesitating, "but I'm not doing it with my brother."

"Did he not make any money the last time he raised them? I was the one who told him where to get the chicks, because I didn't have any at the time," Mahmoud replied, curious.

Donkey Heart Monkey Mind

"I'm sure he did," I said, trying to avoid explaining to him that I was not only not planning to raise the chicks with my brother, but I was not planning to raise them at all.

"Your father spoke highly of Brahim," Mahmoud interrupted. "He said that he is an excellent merchant. I'm surprised he is not doing it again."

"I think he is going back to France to buy some clothes to sell," I said, evading the question. "He is doing well with that sort of commerce. It is cleaner than chickens, more profitable, and has a quicker return."

"Your father told me your family had built a shed big enough to sustain 2,000 chickens. Why are you looking for just a thousand?" Mahmoud continued his questioning. This time I had no problem answering his question.

"That's all I can afford by myself. I can only work within my budget." I thought this would be the end of the conversation, but that wasn't the case.

"Well," he said, "if you want I could advance you the other 1,000 chicks, and you could pay me later, when you sell the chickens. Your father did many favors for my father, and I remember your father picking me up and dropping me off at home when it was raining several times when I was a kid. I don't easily forget that sort of kindness."

When I heard the words "your father," I wasn't sure what to say. I realized that I might have made a mistake in this fledgling attempt to work the system of interfamilial favors. My father had not given me permission to trade on his name and ask his friends for things. If Mahmoud were to run into my father in his cab in Tizi-Ouzou, or if Mahmoud's father were to say hello to mine in the mosque, the whole story would unravel. My father would know that I had gone behind his back, Mahmoud would learn that I had lied to him about what I planned to do with the chicks, and the deal would be off. This needed to stay between the two of us, at least until I delivered the chicks to Bootooje.

"It's not just the price of the chicks that I can't afford, it's the price that comes with them during the next 60 days. Besides, the amount of work would be double. I just want to make sure I raise the thousand comfortably," I said to him.

"Well, give me some time. I'll figure something out for you."

"How much time are we talking about?"

"Well, the next two batches are already sold, and there is nothing I can do. But in a month and a half, I could reserve you the 1,000 you need."

"But I want to raise them to sell in *Yennayar*," I protested.

"There is no way for me to get you the chicks you want any sooner than a month and a half," he insisted.

It seemed all my clever negotiating had been for naught. Either my answers had not been good enough, or there really were no chicks to be had. I tentatively asked Mahmoud if he had ideas about who else I might ask, but he stated simply that at this time of year it would be very hard. I had no choice but to thank him for his time and leave, disappointed.

I considered my options. No matter my skills as a pro-curer, I couldn't make baby chickens appear from nowhere. So I could either come up with a crazy scheme to find a person I had never heard of and persuade them to supply me with chicks during the time of highest demand in the year, or I could go to Bootooje and tell him that I had failed. The first option was a fantasy, and the latter option wouldn't get me out of Algeria. I wasn't thinking about the families who were looking forward to their *Yennayar* dinners or the people who were looking to raise the chicks to make a living. I was only thinking about how I could get enough money to leave for Europe. So a third option presented itself: I could tell them I had lined up the chicks, take payment in advance, and just go. I could always pay them back after I made a pile of money in Europe, as I planned. In the end, that's exactly what I decided to do.

We met a few days later. Bootooje and his poor friends brought me a large amount of cash, the equivalent of six months of a good salary, and I told them I would deliver the goods the next day. I was so excited that I took the money straight to Tizi-Ouzou and bought a plane ticket to Madrid, paying far too much just to be able to leave the next day. I told a couple of my friends where I was spending the night, inviting one of them to the hotel to have coffee with me, just to lay a false trail for when the three men eventually came looking for me and their money. After coffee with my friend, I took a taxi to Algiers, spent the night in a cheap hotel, and was on my flight to Madrid the next day.

When I arrived in Madrid, I called my brother Brahim and told him where I was. Of course he already knew exactly whom I had swindled and that they were looking for me. They had told our father about the whole thing, and if he caught me he would kill me. Brahim warned me not to come back without everyone's money. I assured him that of course I would not.

People in the village never forgot the story of the little chicks. The next time I saw Bootooje was 19 years later, in 2006. Fortunately, by then the sting of our prior transaction had worn off. He recognized me within seconds and smiling, he called me *Petit Poussin*, meaning Little Chick. That's what people had started calling him after I stole his money and took off. Some people would imitate chicken wings with their arms whenever he passed

Djaffar Chetouane

by in his car.

Algerians will persist with a nickname for life, especially if it's a funny one, until they either drive you crazy or you give up and embrace it. To this day, almost 24 years after I took his money, some people of his generation still call Bootooje "Little Chick."

MADRID

Even though I received a considerable amount of Algerian money for the fictional chicks, it wasn't worth much in Spain in November of 1987. It was only a matter of a few days of sight-seeing and exploring in Madrid before my wallet got so light that I knew I had to find a job. One day, as I was walking through the city, I saw an Arabic-looking man selling cigarettes and candies from a small table on the sidewalk and immediately recalled my childhood experience of doing the same thing on the street. Of course, I didn't have any legal papers or a work permit. It was no secret to me that many Arabs worked and made a living in Spain without any papers. As long as they were not involved in any crimes, the police and immigration officers never bothered them. So I figured this fellow could help me. I approached and asked him where I could get a job like his. He told me he worked for an Egyptian man who was always looking for people to be sidewalk vendors.

Djaffar Chetouane

The vendor gave me his boss's phone number, and I called the man and explained that I was interested in working for him. The Egyptian said he was definitely looking for honest people to work for him, and he gave me an address to report to. That same day, I showed up at the address he gave me to find a little warehouse in an industrial zone, full of all kinds of things one might find at a drugstore or convenience store. We talked for a bit and soon settled on the commission he would give me for selling his goods. If I gave him my information and came back the next day, he said, he would have a table ready for me. The idea was to start me out selling just a few items, so I could get the hang of it, and then give me more items when I had proven that I was reliable. I was very excited to have this opportunity and eager to start.

The next day, I went back to the warehouse and was given a small table and a duffle bag containing a few cartons of cigarettes, some candy bars and other such things. The Egyptian came along to train me on the sidewalk near the *Plaza del Sol*, in the heart of the city. After a little while of working with me, he seemed to feel comfortable enough to leave me alone, though I think he was watching me from a distance to see that I wouldn't take off with his stuff. I'm sure it had happened to him before; he only employed Easterners and North Africans, and we are known for pulling just the kind of stunt that I had so recently pulled to get here. I had never done such a thing before then, and I wasn't planning to do it again now, but the Egyptian didn't know that. He only knew what all those from our region know: if you aren't careful, a North African can steal something from between your crossed legs and you won't feel a thing.

At the end of the day I came back to the warehouse and gave my new boss an account of what I had sold, as well as what was left. He was very impressed by my work, because I had kept a written inventory throughout the day. He counted his money and counted the items left over, and the numbers tallied with mine exactly. To my great satisfaction, my commission amounted to about two weeks' worth of work for someone in Algeria. I was very impressed and very happy to have already found such an easy and clean job.

Most of the Egyptians I had known in Algeria were my schoolteachers, and they had not given me a positive impression of Egyptians in general. They, along with many Palestinians and Iraqis, had been hired by the Algerian government after the end of the war for independence. All state education had previously taken place in French, the language of the colonists, and initially there were no Algerian teachers available to teach in Arabic. The Egyptian teachers were particularly unkind to Berber students. They not only insulted us and called us stupid, but they would pull our ears, yank on our hair, hit us, and put pencils between our fingers and squeeze. Altogether, they had made me very suspicious of their countrymen. But now I was outside my country for the second time in my life, and my horizons were already expanding. This new boss had given me a good job and paid me a decent commission, and at the end of my first day he even took me to dinner at his hotel. Everything seemed better outside of Algeria.

For about a week, I sold basically the same merchandise as on the first day. At the end of that week I convinced my boss to give me a bigger table with more items, because people were asking for things that I didn't have. I assured him that I had the hang of it, and that I would do my very best to make as many sales as I could. He agreed, and the next day when I arrived at the warehouse he had a much bigger table and a heavier duffel bag ready for me.

Djaffar Chetouane

We set off for my usual corner in downtown Madrid, and when we arrived he showed me the best way to arrange the items on the table, so that they were most visible for customers. That day I neatly kept my written inventory, as before, and at the end of the day the expanded stock had made a palpable difference in my commission. The Egyptian was as pleased as I was by my sales.

Things went on this way for about two months. I enjoyed my job and impressed the Egyptian with my organizational skills, never misplacing an item or miscounting money. I especially remember working on New Year's Eve, 1988, selling bottle after bottle of champagne from my little table. I even got to sample the champagne myself, and it all made for a New Year's Eve like no other. Altogether, I was very happy. I had my hotel room that I paid for by the week, and I had money in my pocket. So even though I had no papers, living illegally and poor in Madrid was far better than living legally and rich in Algeria. Besides, it was just a matter of time, I thought, before I would become familiar with the Spanish system and would become a legal resident.

A few weeks later, however, things took a dramatic turn for the worse. At the end of every workday, all the vendors would gather at the warehouse to hand over the money we had made, turn in our bags of unsold merchandise, and receive our cut of the profits. One day I was distracted, chatting to a couple of the guys while we waited our turns to settle up, and someone stole my duffel bag. It can only have been someone who had finished up with the Egyptian and was on his way out. When my turn came, I couldn't find the bag anywhere. I had the money in my pocket, but there was no bag and no inventory to return. I was furious, and I tried to convince my boss of what must have happened. But gone was the nice man who had taken me out to dinner on my first day of work.

Donkey Heart Monkey Mind

He told me point blank that the bag was my responsibility, that I must pay for everything in it, and, worst of all, that I couldn't work for him again until I had paid for what was lost. I had lost it, and I must pay for it, end of story.

The cost of everything in the bag was far more than I had, and if I didn't work, how on earth was I going to make up the difference? I came back the next day and tried to reason with him again, but he wouldn't hear of it. I was outraged by how unfair the Egyptian was. For almost three months I had worked for him, never losing a single item, always giving him the correct amount of money at the end of each day, keeping a written record, and never once stealing from him. I was a hard-working person and very honest with him. And now I found myself with no job and no money, all because he couldn't forgive me for someone else's crime. I had made a good faith effort, and he wouldn't even let me make one mistake, leaving me not only with no money but no way to make it up.

Many young North Africans live in Europe and make their living stealing from tourists. I had witnessed theft after theft on the streets of Madrid. For these young people, stealing had often become a matter of survival, for they had no education and no job prospects. I suppose that I, too, had been stealing the chicken money from my fellow villagers but not simply for survival, rather as a matter of desperation and urgency. I needed to leave the country as soon as possible, especially after my experiences in jail. However, I never went to Europe to steal. On the contrary, I had actually gone to Europe to get away from that kind of living. Still, I was not incapable of it. Like most Algerian children, I had stolen from those who cheated me, hurt me, insulted me or had stolen from me. I had been raised to know right from wrong, but I had also been raised to know that you sometimes had to hustle. Now,

Djaffar Chetouane

despite my best efforts to do an honest day's work, I found that I too would have to look out for myself or risk starvation. My Egyptian boss did not care that I had been truthful and hard-working for him, so I decided I couldn't afford to care about anything he might have done for me in the past. What mattered now was the present, and in the present, he didn't care about me at all. I wanted to be compensated somehow for my honesty and hard work, and there was only one way to make that happen: Steal from him.

I thought back to one night when I was in the Egyptian's hotel room. He had picked up a teddy bear and pulled a wallet full of cash out of it to pay a man for some items. The memory was especially vivid because he had paid the man in U.S. $100 bills. The wallet in that teddy bear became my target, and I came up with a plan to go to his hotel room and steal it. I knew a couple of Moroccans, and I asked one of them if he was willing to help me get into the hotel room. There would be a large quantity of cash there, I told him, and he agreed with no hesitation.

We took off for the hotel. The plan was for me to distract the receptionist while my Moroccan friend stole the key to the Egyptian's room. The receptionist and I had chatted a few times before. He was from Chile and had been living in Madrid for only four months. A skinny young man with dark hair, he was not yet familiar with the North African style of deception. I was certain I would succeed. As we approached the reception desk, I spotted the key hanging behind it—we were in luck! I pulled an envelope containing only a blank piece of paper from my jacket and asked the receptionist if I could leave it for the man who lived in room 413. The receptionist knew me since I had been there from time to time to visit my boss, and he was happy to oblige.

When my Moroccan friend and I left the hotel, I asked

him if he had the key, and he said no. He wasn't able to reach behind the desk without being noticed.

"We have to go back. I have another idea," I told him.

We approached the receptionist once again.

"I forgot to add something to the envelope. Also, if you don't mind, could I talk to you for a moment?"

The receptionist picked up the envelope and stepped out from behind the desk to get closer to me. I held him by the shoulder, like an old buddy, and turned and led him a few steps away from the desk.

"It's his birthday and I want to surprise him," I told the receptionist, as I pulled out my wallet and put a couple of bills in the envelope. I took a big risk by letting go of the only money I had, but I was sure I would be rewarded if my Moroccan friend succeeded in getting me the key.

"I would like to bring in a birthday cake, too, if you don't mind putting it in his room," I added.

"That wouldn't be a problem. I think he would be very pleased," the receptionist replied with a smile.

I turned around and looked at my friend, who winked at me. As we walked out of the hotel door, my friend handed me the key. I turned around and went in again immediately.

"I'm sorry, I really need to use the bathroom," I said to the receptionist.

"Of course, no problem," he replied with yet another smile.

I knew the bathroom was on the first floor, and my friend waited for me outside as I climbed the stairs. From the first floor, I hopped onto the elevator to the fourth floor. My heart was about to pound out of my chest, I was so nervous. When I got out of the elevator, I walked straight down the hallway and let myself into room 413. There was the teddy bear on top of an armoire, and there was the brown wallet inside it. As it had been before, it was full of $100 bills. I stowed the wallet under my belt and left in a hurry, my hands shaking as I locked the door behind me. Once inside the elevator, I added another layer of deceit to my scam. I pulled out the wallet, took out two $100 bills and then put them in my pants pocket, and hid the wallet with the rest of the bills in my sock. Getting off at the first floor, I walked back down the stairs to the lobby.

To my great surprise, the first person I saw there was the Egyptian, talking to the receptionist. I thought for a moment that I actually felt my heart come out of my chest this time. Undoubtedly he was asking for his key, because I heard the receptionist telling him it must be with the room cleaners. I had to pass the desk to leave the hotel, so I kept walking.

"Don't say anything to him yet," I said to the receptionist, smiling.

"Don't say anything about what?" The Egyptian guy asked, still looking at the receptionist. Then he turned around and saw me, demanding, "What are you doing here?"

"Don't tell him until I leave," I said to the receptionist, while I headed towards the front door.

The Egyptian kept asking, "What?" turning his head to look alternately at me and the receptionist as I left. The receptionist looked too surprised to know what to do or say. He was paralyzed and confused.

As soon as I shut the front door behind me, my Moroccan friend and I ran like cheetahs. We didn't slow down until we were many blocks away.

Panting, my friend asked, "Did you get anything?"

Donkey Heart Monkey Mind

I pulled out the two $100 bills. "These are all I found!" I exclaimed, swearing and trying my best to look very pissed off at not having found more. "You can have one, though," I told my friend.

As he took it, he made a face that clearly said, "All that for just this?"

I shook his hand, thanking him and apologizing for the small reward for our efforts, and we parted ways. I ran straight to my hotel room, hardly able to wait to count the money. To my amazement, there was $3,000 U.S.D. This was a huge amount of money, especially for an illegal Algerian immigrant kid in March of 1988. I packed my bags in a hurry and headed straight to the train station, where I got on a train to Barcelona. What I did was certainly, terribly satisfying at the time. I saw it as what I needed to do to get money to survive, as well as what I needed to do to repay the Egyptian for not appreciating my hard work. My revenge was not only sweet but very profitable.

I only spent one night in Barcelona before moving on to Bordeaux, France. It is hard to describe how intoxicating it felt to be a 20-year-old from a developing country standing in the middle of Europe with that much cash in my pocket. Not knowing what else to do with it, I started shopping. I began treating myself to nice things I had never been able to afford before. I spent one day and night in Bordeaux, then took another train to Paris, where I continued shopping. Shirts, sweaters, pants, shoes, and underwear—all helped sooth the sting of the injustice I felt I had suffered at the hands of my former boss. I filled up two new suitcases with new outfits, imagining myself looking like some kind of rock star when I went home to Algeria one day. Back there, having nice clothes was the next best thing to having a car. It would make people think I was smart and rich, an important person they needed to know.

Djaffar Chetouane

Even my brother Brahim had never looked quite that good, and at my young age nothing really mattered to me except looking nice in other people's eyes. I had so much money that I almost thought I could never spend all of it.

Of course, predictably, I noticed my stack of cash was shrinking after a few weeks. Again I faced a choice. I could either find a way to get more money or go home. I certainly didn't feel like I was done with Europe, so I had to make some money. But my first experience working as an illegal immigrant in Spain had made an important impression on me. The way it looked to me, hard work got you nowhere, but stealing was easy. I had had a taste of what it was like to have a very fat wallet, and continuing to steal was going to allow me to keep enjoying that feeling.

I began to work my way south through France, heading roughly towards home, but taking my time. In each town in which I stopped, I would stay at a youth hostel, and it was there that I would make my money. I had seen that the people that stayed in youth hostels were from elsewhere, youths from different backgrounds from mine, seemingly with money to spend. They had the chance to be something that I never would, I thought, and I saw no reason not to take a little something from each of them. And so I would blend into the motley crowd at the hostels, and as everyone slept, I would pick their pockets and bags.

I justified my actions to a certain degree by never entirely cleaning somebody out. I would take a few notes from a wallet here, a camera there, maybe even a credit card or a passport. But I never took so much cash that anyone would notice first thing in the morning. The cameras could be sold in camera shops, and the passports were bought by North Africans, who would eventually forge new ones from them. I told myself that losing a passport was

Donkey Heart Monkey Mind

just an inconvenience, and that one could easily be replaced at an embassy. (And while it was true that it was easier to replace a passport then than it is now, I was still deceiving myself.)

In Castres, a small town in southern France, I nearly got caught trying to use a stolen credit card. The merchant became suspicious and asked me for identification, and I fled before he could call the police. That was the first time I tried dying my hair. I bought a box of hair lightener, thinking I could make myself look blonde and European, but of course I was mistaken. Instead, I ended up with a mass of reddish curls sitting above black eyebrows. Still, after brushing and blow-drying my hair and putting on a new pair of sunglasses, I was impressed at how different I looked. I was so pleased with my transformation that I even took a picture of myself in a photo booth. The next thing I did was get to a train station and take a train to Toulouse.

In Toulouse, I continued my stealing rampage. There I bought another box of hair color, but I just ended up a darker redhead than before. After a couple of nights in Toulouse, I headed to Barcelona again. In each place I stopped, I left my heavier bags in a locker at the train station, just taking a few things with me to the hotels and hostels where I continued to stay. This turned out to be a good thing in Barcelona, where I had yet another close call with the law. After a successful trip to a leather store to deck myself out in a couple of pairs of leather boots and a very expensive jacket, which I thought made me look just like an American cowboy, the merchant at the next store I entered got suspicious. It was easy enough to run away again before I got in any real trouble, but I realized my mistake when I got back to the youth hostel. As soon as I entered, the receptionist and I exchanged a look, and he picked up the phone right away. I realized that I had used the same credit card that I just ditched at the store to pay for my room. In a moment I had grabbed my small bags from my room and was hightailing it to the train station. I gathered all my suitcases and took off for Madrid.

Madrid was the last mistake I made on that trip. I booked into the same hotel where I had been staying when I had worked for the Egyptian, and it was only a matter of time before I found a threatening note from him in my mailbox. Of course I packed my bags and got ready to leave right away, but he was there in the lobby before I could make it out the door. He started in right away, shouting at me and swearing, and I told the receptionist to call the police. In just a few minutes the cops came and, because the Egyptian spoke excellent Spanish, he convinced them to handcuff me and take me to the station. There, they took off the handcuffs and took me into a room to question me, and they searched all the bags I had on me (of course, the bulk of my things were in a train station locker, as usual). Over and over again, they asked me if I had any drugs on me, but all they could find in the bags were clothes and some presents. No matter what the Egyptian must have told them, I had never so much as experimented with any drugs, let alone sold them, and most of the cash I had on me was in French francs, which wasn't particularly suspicious. There was no evidence to support the Egyptian's claims that I had stolen his money, and the police told me I was free to go. I took a deep breath and gave quiet thanks in my head that I hadn't had any stolen passports and credit cards on me. Then, when the police let me go, I went out and paid cash for a hotel room far from the places where North Africans tended to congregate.

I knew I was done in Europe. In preparation for making a clean getaway home, I went out to a real hair salon and had my hair professionally bleached, eyebrows and all. The next day I went to

Donkey Heart Monkey Mind

an area of Madrid where Arabs traded in passports. My passport still carried the stamp denying me entry to the United States for 10 years, so I decided I was done with it, too. I sold it to a Tunisian who gave me very little money for it, since it was "only" Algerian. A European passport would have been worth far more. The way I saw it, it was better not to have a passport than to have one that would keep me out of the U.S. for 10 years.

The next step was to go to the police station and report that I had lost my passport. The Algerian consulate provided me with a temporary permit to enter the country, though not before the receptionist took a long, suspicious look at my blonde hair and asked if I was really Algerian. I stayed out of trouble for four days, and then I finally boarded a plane to go home. Here, too, my hair seemed to capture everyone's attention. Unusual hair styles may have been the norm in Europe in the 1980s, but they were unheard of on an Algerian man. "Crazy or gay," was probably the verdict of the other Algerians on the plane, and of the two options, crazy was definitely preferable. Being considered gay in a Muslim country would mean unbearable shame to my family, and if I were labeled that way, it would only be a matter of time before my father would shoot me dead and not serve a day in jail for it.

When I arrived in Algiers, the immigration officers kept me overnight to verify my identity. I spent the night in a cell near the airport, having a great time laughing with the guards and another person who also claimed to have lost his passport (he had undoubtedly sold his as well). My cellmate and our guards thought it was hysterical that I had chosen to become blond like a Swede. They had never seen such a thing.

I arrived home the next day. It was my mother who answered my knock, and when she opened the door, she didn't recognize me.

Djaffar Chetouane

"Who are you?" she asked.

"You don't recognize me?" I replied, smiling.

My mother knew my smile, of course, and it was only then that she began to recognize her own son.

"Jafar?" she asked, furrowing her brow.

"Yes. It's me!"

Her mouth fell open. "What did you do to your hair?" she asked, covering her mouth in amazement.

"I just colored it, that's all."

"What will your father say?" she asked. What I had done would not be by any means acceptable for the son of a Hadj, in my father's eyes.

"He will kill you," she said, completely seriously. "You had better cut it right now, before he sees it."

"Should I also cut my eyebrows?" I asked, laughing.

Mom opened her eyes even wider, because she hadn't even noticed the eyebrows.

"Oh my God!" she shouted.

But I had found new confidence during my travels in Europe. I had defied my father by getting a passport and by leaving Algeria twice. I had proved that he was wrong to think that I wasn't capable of surviving away from home. And I returned with more money than most Algerians had ever seen.

"No. I won't cut it," I told my mother, "and if he wants to kill me, so be it. I'm no longer a kid, and I won't obey him about stupid things."

But she knew what would really matter to my father, far more than my hair.

"How about the money you took from those people? Do you have it?" she asked.

Donkey Heart Monkey Mind

"Yes, I have it. And a lot more."

She looked relieved. Then she told me about the ordeal I had left in my wake. Apparently, the people I had stolen from had kept coming to our home and harassing my father to reimburse them. My father refused to pay them back at first, on the grounds that they didn't consult with him before giving money to his 19-year-old son. At some point, however, he grew tired of the pressure he was getting from them and considered paying them back just to shut them up. First, however, he went and consulted with the "Sheikh," who was the head of the Mosque and the most respected person in the village. Was it my father's obligation to pay my debt? The Sheikh's answer pleased him (and was a blessing for me). He said that my father should be proud of having a young son who was smart enough to fool older people, and that he should not punish me for being smart. The Sheikh told my father that he would talk to the three people and order them to stop harassing him, because it was their fault and no one else's. No one disobeys the Sheikh, and so my father was left alone. And because everyone listened to the Sheikh of the village for his advice and orders, my father also listened to him. My father finally realized that I was smart and said so to my mother.

When my mother told me this, I knew that my father really and truly believed I was smart. Otherwise he would never have admitted it to my mother. He had never called me that before, and he still never said it to my face. Nevertheless, I was relieved.

When my mother got over the surprise of my arrival, she decided that the best course of action would be to tell my brother Brahim I was home and let him tell our father. She also made sure that Brahim would tell him that I had the money to pay everyone back, because that would ease the sting of my prior deceptions. The word money was the first word out of my father's mouth when I saw him that evening. Before I could even give him the traditional kiss on the forehead with which one greets a Hadj, he was barking at me.

"Do you have the money that you took from those people?" he asked, scowling.

"Yes, I do," I replied.

"Let me see it."

I pulled a stack of French francs out of my leather jacket and saw my father's eyes grow wide at the sight of the money.

"Here, this should cover all of it, plus 20% for their losses," I said to my father. Handing him still more cash, smiling, I added, "and this is for you."

"This is for me? Where did you get all this money?" he asked. My father knew it was very hard for a young man to come back from Europe with that much cash. He was implying that it was stolen.

"Have you ever heard of me stealing from someone before?" I asked, standing firm.

"Yes, you stole money that you were supposed to use to buy chicks for people," he replied with a smile.

He had already softened. He loved getting cash from his kids, and I had seen the same satisfied expression of accomplishment on his face many times before, like when Brahim had handed over a portion of his earnings.

"I didn't steal the money. I only took it because I needed it," I insisted.

"Ah, right. You took it, but you didn't steal it. Is that what you think?"

"Has anyone ever complained to you about me before?

Have I not been a hard worker all my life? It was just a little inconvenience, that's all."

"Why didn't you ask me for money?"

"Have you ever given me money before?"

"You never asked."

My mother interrupted, saying, "No harm is done. Those people would probably have made less from raising those chicks than what you're giving them now. I'm sure they'll be very happy to get their money back, especially since you're adding something for their trouble."

"It's quite a lot of profit you're giving them," my father commented.

When I heard him say that, I was absolutely sure that I was out of trouble. And he hadn't even mentioned my hair yet.

"I handed you the money," I said. "You talk to them and decide what's fair."

That was the master stroke. I was completely forgiven.

By the time my father was done with my creditors, they had admitted their mistake, apologized to him, and they understood that it was I who had returned their money, not my father. They happily accepted 90% of their original money back, conceding 10% to my father for the trouble they had caused him. Of course he never mentioned the extra 20% I had planned to give each of them (and I heard later that they were quite pleased to get most of their money back and forget that the whole thing ever happened).

My father did have something to say about my hair, of course, but it was just that he didn't want to see me with it in the house again. In response, I simply stayed out of the house for the next month. It was the talk of the town for a while, of course, and there was a nickname associated with it: I was christened "Jimmy."

Djaffar Chetouane

Some people did accuse me of being gay, and I got into a few fights over that, but it was mostly in good fun. My father did not find it as funny when his friends made fun of him for having a blonde son, but there was nothing he could do about it. I relished how much it annoyed him, and I relished the fact that he had no control over me anymore. I had made my point, both to him and to myself. I didn't cut off my "crazy, Swedish" hair until the black roots had grown well in.

ACROSS NORTH AFRICA

It was the end of April, 1988, when I made my triumphant rogue's return from Spain, and this time I was ready to stick around for a while. It was perfect timing to plant crops for the coming summer, so I paid a lazy uncle for his turn to use the best land. He was easily convinced by the offer of real French francs, and I used my extra cash to plant 20 acres of watermelon.

Watermelon would have been an ambitious crop to choose, even if I wasn't planting so many acres. It requires constant attention to keep it sufficiently watered, and it has to be guarded every night in case of thieves. But once the fruit matures in the middle of the hot, humid summer, it fetches a price that makes the labor well worth it. At lunchtime in the summer, when the North African sun is high in the sky, the melons are a favorite delicacy to serve cold at the end of a meal. It is said to clean your liver, and it seems to slake your thirst (but I suspected that all the sugar in it probably made people thirstier).

Djaffar Chetouane

I also had a second reason for wanting to plant watermelon: I planned to give a large portion of whatever crop I planted to the poor, to settle my moral account with the innocent people I had stolen from in Europe. I would never see those people again, but I felt the angels might look kindly on the gift of such an expensive and desirable item as watermelon to those who couldn't usually afford it. Still, I probably rationalized my stealing by thinking of it as "only" an inconvenience to those I had stolen from. I hadn't thought about the fact that they were young men like me, who were staying in youth hostels because they were cheaper than hotels, and that they might have worked quite hard to earn the money they were using to travel. Still, I at least understood that I owed something, if not to them then to the universe at large, and I did my best to repay the debt that summer.

One night, while I was guarding my field with a couple of friends, we started talking about Europe and how beautiful it is. I didn't have a chance of going back there anytime soon, because Algerian law states that if you lose your passport, you cannot apply for another one until your previous one expires. This is, of course, to discourage people from selling them, as I and so many others had done. But I was telling my friends about my trips to Europe and the things I had done there when something clicked in my mind: I remembered the first passport that I had applied for but never received because of my father. That application might still be able to be processed, or the passport might even be ready by now. I figured that I had applied for this first passport long before I lost my second one, and that might be a way around the law.

I was so eager when I thought of this possibility that I went to the passport agency the very next day. To my surprise, they told me that my passport had been ready for a while. All I had to do was provide a stamp and I could walk out with it in my hand! I was thrilled. I went straight out and purchased the required stamp and did indeed walk out with a new passport. I couldn't believe it. I would have left that same day if it were possible. As it was, I would just have to wait for my crop to come in, and then I could take off for another adventure with plenty of spending money, this time legitimately earned.

By the end of July, I had sold and given away all my watermelon, cleared the land, and prepared the field for the next planting season. I was in the airline office as soon as I could be, buying another ticket to Madrid. But when I got to the airport, there were two police officers waiting near the gate with a piece of paper in their hands, looking back and forth from the paper to the faces in the crowd. I could tell right away that they were looking for me. I tried to hide my face in the crowd, thinking I could get away with it. But it wasn't to be.

When they spotted me, they came up and asked, "Are you Jafar?"

"Yes," I responded. They asked me to follow them.

When we got to a small office, I was introduced to another officer who asked me, "Did you lose a passport back in April and enter the country without one?"

"Yes, I did," I responded, nervous but trying to look innocent.

"How did you obtain another passport?" he asked.

"Well, I applied for one and I got it," I answered simply.

"Did you know that you cannot have a passport until your previous one expires?" the man said.

"I wasn't aware of that," I answered, attempting to look surprised.

Djaffar Chetouane

"We have to confiscate this passport, and you cannot leave the country again until your lost one expires," he said firmly. "It's the law here. We will also be investigating how you got this passport, because you shouldn't have been able to get it."

They turned me loose, and I left the airport, frustrated and dejected. I had no passport, I had paid good money for a useless plane ticket, and I was now officially stuck in Algeria. I felt fire run through my entire body. What's more, I had given up my right to use the family land for the summer, so now I had no work. I had told everyone that I was leaving for Europe, and I didn't relish strolling back into my village and confessing I had been detained at the gate and my passport confiscated. I took a bus back to Algiers and checked into a small hotel.

The urgency I felt about getting out of the country at the time was not only personal, but also political and social. Kabylia, the Berber homeland, was not the only area in which political tensions had been mounting throughout the decade. Nominally, the Algerian government at that time was socialist. But its most important characteristic to those of us who lived under it was its authoritarianism. For its citizens, there was really no way to understand the Algerian government, except to say that it was corrupt, disorganized, and really did not seem to care about growing and developing the country. Most of the wealth the country possessed (and government officials mostly pocketed) was based on oil sales, and oil prices had plummeted in 1986. This left a government uninterested in providing for its less able citizens and even less willing to do so. After years of repression, people were beginning to call for change. As I sat in the hotel in Algiers, protests were springing up, some led by members of the government itself, some from Muslim fundamentalists, and some from members of the general population, especially the bored, frustrated, undereducated youth.

A huge percentage of the Algerian population was fairly young at the time. When the French left Algeria and there was finally peace in the country, Algerians started getting married and having kids by the dozens. My own mother was a typical Algerian woman, and if she had not lost any of her children to miscarriage or early death, there would be 13 of us today. After independence Algeria had a "baby boom" of its own, to the point where over 50% of the population in the 1980s was under the age of twenty-five. Certainly, more than seventy percent of the unemployed were under this age. Even if the government had not been hopelessly corrupt, it would not have been able to keep up with the needs of the massive young population in terms of schools, health care, or housing. As it was, the government didn't really care about any of these issues, and the politicians' plates were full with other priorities, such as what they could do with the cash they still had left from gas and oil.

I hold the French partly to blame for the problems the general population of Algeria had in the 1980s. They could have done a much better job of advising and guiding the transition to power of the young Algerian government. The French government was supposedly assisting Algeria with its financial needs, in part by buying gas and oil from the former colony. If the French really cared about the Algerians, however, they would have done a much better job of stabilizing the young country they left behind. Certainly the Algerian government was also to blame for its lack of interest in helping its own people and developing its own country. As it was, Algerians were so hungry for the political power and money that were suddenly up for grabs after the French left that they didn't have time to think about future generations.

Djaffar Chetouane

So there I was, a member of one of those future generations, just coming of age, stranded in a hotel room in Algiers. I sensed the political tension around me, and I was unwilling to participate for fear of another experience with the police like the one I'd had in 1986. There was nothing for me to do in Algeria, I thought to myself, so I had to go somewhere.

But where could I go? After a couple of days of thinking, I decided to forget about Europe and head in a new direction. I had never seen the rest of North Africa; why not try Tunisia, our eastern neighbor? A passport was not required to get into that country, only a national identity card, and I still had that. This seemed as good a plan as any. I bought a train ticket to Annaba, one of the larger cities in Algeria, located near the Tunisian border. The next day, I walked across the border and started to hitchhike.

On my first day in Tunisia, I got picked up by a guy who started asking me a suspicious number of questions. He was headed to Tabarka, a little more than one hundred kilometers over the border. When we got there, he said he would drop me off at "a special place," and before I knew it, we had pulled up at a police station. He parked his car, announced to me that he was a cop, and demanded that I get out and follow him inside. It was just to carry out the standard procedure of a background check, he insisted.

"I've never been here before in my life. This is my first time here," I protested. "You won't find any record on me."

"It doesn't matter. I just want to know you check out all right," he responded.

What could I do? I went into the station with him. I was then taken aback when he told the officer at the door that he suspected me of being a drug trafficker.

I looked at him dumbfounded and replied, "I'm not a drug

trafficker! You just said to me you only wanted to do a background check, and now you're saying I may be a drug trafficker?"

The officer at the door thanked the man and told him that he would take it from there. I was there for more than three hours before they released me and drove me back to the border in a police van. I couldn't be in Tunisia, they said, though they couldn't give me a reason why not. Tunisians and Algerians have always treated each other with suspicion—as so many citizens of neighboring countries do—and I am still convinced that the man who picked me up and turned me in to the police did so simply out of prejudice. He certainly did nothing to foster international understanding that day, as I returned to the Algerian border a very bitter young man indeed, swearing that I would avoid Tunisia and Tunisians for the rest of my life.

After another night spent in Annaba, I decided that Libya might be the next place I should explore. Entering Libya was supposed to require a passport, but I knew there were ways around such things. The logical way there was directly east, through Tunisia, but of course that route was closed to me. I would first have to travel south. It took me three days to hitchhike to the southern tip of Tunisia, where the western Libyan border with Algeria begins. From there, I would aim for the closest Libyan city, Ghudamis. It took less than a day hanging around the Algerian side of the border to find people willing to guide me across illegally. They required a fee, of course, and they had to gather enough people to make it worth their while. A few days later, a man I had made contact with came to my hotel and told me to get ready to leave that same night.

Eight of us gathered at a particular street corner, and when our guide gave the word, we started walking. In the end, it really couldn't have been simpler. I had no idea where we were, but we followed our guide all night, and by dawn we had reached Ghudamis. Next we went to our guide's friend's house and laid low until it was day, at which point we went our separate ways.

From Ghudamis, I had planned to head for Tripoli, the capital. I changed all the Algerian money I had on me into Libyan currency, and was dismayed to find that Algerian money was worth less than Libyan. The next two days held nothing but long bus rides across hundreds of kilometers of uninterrupted desert. It was not a promising beginning, I thought, remembering the green beauty of Europe.

Tripoli itself was also terribly boring to me. I decided that Libya was worse off even than Algeria, economically, politically, and socially. Muammar al-Gaddafi held tight control over his people, far more than even the repressive Algerian government. It was more like a vast private property than a country. There was no trace whatsoever of democracy, and no one could do anything without the knowledge of the government. Not even the appearance of the city could excite me. I did notice that Tripoli was far cleaner than Algiers, but I had not traveled all this way to see something clean. I was looking for the elegance and grandeur I had seen in Paris and Madrid.

Adding to the feeling of suppression and unease was the fact that I hardly saw any women on the streets. In Algeria, though men and women did not socialize, women were everywhere. I was told that for every woman in Libya there were seven men, though this was probably an exaggeration. Still, for a Libyan man to get married, he had to have plenty of money.

Whatever disadvantages an Arabic woman may have, in Libya she can at least choose the richest man she can find. He then has to put a monetary guarantee in a bank account in her name, in

Donkey Heart Monkey Mind

case he ever divorces her (because once she is no longer a virgin, it is highly unlikely that she will be able to remarry, and she certainly won't be able to get a job to support herself). In fact, when a man marries a woman in Libya, it is more like he is buying her than marrying her, as far as I could tell.

After a few days there, I found out from other immigrants that the country would issue a working permit in a heartbeat to anyone who wanted to work, because its population was too low to support the demand for labor. I met people there from all over the African continent, but I had no desire to join the workforce there. Though I enjoyed meeting all the new people, especially the black African immigrants, Tripoli depressed me deeply.

After six days there, any vague thoughts that I might have had about migrating to somewhere in the Arabic world were evaporated. I decided that this trip would just be an adventure, and that I would continue eastward, taking it one day at a time. Most of the Libyan coast is desert, unlike the mountainous and fertile coasts of Algeria, so I looked at a map before setting out, thinking that I needed to aim for an interesting destination. I decided to head for Benghazi, the country's second largest city, and I set out hitchhiking again.

It didn't really occur to me that I might be in any real danger traveling around alone like this. Hitchhiking was more common at the time, and I was young and strong. I could run fast and fight if I needed to. My main concerns were finding places to eat and sleep and trying not to come to the attention of the police. About halfway to Benghazi, I found I had failed at both.

I stopped in a town called Surt, where I met a couple of men strolling on the beach. They were very friendly to me and offered me their beach cabin to sleep in. We spent a long, lovely evening chatting about all kinds of subjects, including the politics of both our countries. One of them even brought me food from his house, which was not too far from the beach. Then, after a while, they left me alone in the cabin to sleep.

The next thing I knew, I was waking up with a knife at my throat. As adrenaline surged through my system, a voice said, "I want to have sex with you, and if you resist I'll cut your throat."

I tried to struggle, but the man was behind me forcing me against the wall. I recognized his voice: it was the man who had brought me food, the cabin's owner. He was pressing his body against mine, the knife held firmly against my neck, and I couldn't move too violently without risking the blade cutting in. My assailant's friend came in and tried to hold me down by pressing my legs on the bed. Before long, the friend had gotten my pants off, and the man with the knife started to unzip his pants.

"You'll have to kill me before I'll let you do that!" I yelled.

I continued to struggle as he tried over and over again to aim his penis at its mark, but I wouldn't stay still long enough for him to do it. After a short while, both men had to let me go, though they still pointed the knife at me as they clambered off the bed. I grabbed my chance and stood up. There was a shovel in the corner of the room, and I grabbed it.

"I swear if you get any closer I will cut your heads off with this!" I cried, holding the shovel up high and ready to strike.

"Get out of here," snarled the first man.

"After you," I answered.

They both started backing up, and when they opened the door, I saw that there had been a lookout standing at the door. All three left, leaving me there. I hurriedly put my pants on, grabbed my bag, and came out, the shovel still in my hand. I went straight to a police station that I had noticed while I was on the beach, and from there, two policemen accompanied me back to the cabin on foot.

To my surprise, when we got there, all three men were at the door of the cabin. They shook hands with the cops and said hello as if they knew each other. My accusation was repeated, but the man who had held the knife to my throat said, "I've never done anything to you." Then he pulled a police badge out of his pocket. "I'm a cop, and if you don't get out of here I will arrest you for lying," he barked.

I knew there was nothing else I could say. I immediately left the scene, determined to get out of that town as soon as possible. It was dawn by this time, and I could start hitchhiking eastward towards Benghazi. But not even putting days and miles between me and that beach cabin helped at first. For many days, I traveled much more warily.

When I arrived in Benghazi, I had to leave my identification at the entrance to the town. In my new, mistrustful mindset, I was inclined to be suspicious of such an unusual practice. Fortunately, it turned out to be harmless. The youth hostel there was the most beautiful one I had ever stayed in. It had high ceilings with complex, Byzantine decorations, and there were spacious rooms and clean beds. The floors were made of marble, as were the columns that stretched from floor to ceiling, and there were Berber carpets everywhere. It was like a museum, and its beauty seemed particularly rich after the boredom of desert travel and the ugliness of what I had left behind in Surt.

The next day, I continued east. Following the coast, I entered Cyrene, one of the largest and best-preserved Greek ruins in Africa. From there it took me two days to get to Bardia, a town very near the Egyptian border. Here I was once again deceived by false hospitality, though not nearly as vilely as the last time. I met a family that invited me to stay in their home and fed me a nice dinner. They asked me question after question about Algeria and Algerians, telling me they had never met any before me, and I thoroughly enjoyed our talk. It was late at night before we went to bed.

Again I was awakened by an assailant—this time someone grabbing me and pulling a hood over my head. I could tell that there were two or three others holding me, and through my fear I heard them tell me they were police officers and that I should calm down. That was, of course, no comfort. I struggled and screamed for a while, until I finally realized I wasn't being harmed. The whole group of them then led me away on a short walk to a room in another location. There, they took the hood off of me. Showing me their police badges, they asked for my identity card.

"Why didn't you just wake me up and ask me for it?" I demanded, handing it over.

"We wanted to make sure you're not an Egyptian spy. Are you one?"

I was still shaking from the ordeal as I handed them my identification, explaining as I did so that I was just an Algerian traveling through Libya and nothing more. After a few more questions, I was free to go. But before I left, I asked them why they had come looking for me there. It was the family I was staying with, they said, who had brought me to their attention. "They're just trying to be safe. I'm sure you understand."

"What weird people," I thought to myself. The Tunisians didn't trust the Algerians, the Libyans didn't trust the Egyptians, and in both cases it was a harmless traveler who suffered.

The next day I started following the coast, figuring that I would just cross into Egypt at some point. The land was rocky, with no beaches, and it was miserably hot. I was walking in the coastal desert, absolutely nothing around. As late afternoon approached, I was walking and enjoying the view of the ocean when suddenly a man in military uniform literally popped out of the ground and pointed a rifle at me. Surprise and fear blunted the absurdity of what had just happened, and I obeyed his shouted order to lie down on the ground with my hands on my head. In just a few seconds, two more men had appeared, also seemingly out of nowhere, pointing their guns at me. I really almost urinated in panic. In no time there was a cloth tied around my eyes, and I was hustled away across the rocks.

When the blindfold was removed, I found myself before the three men's commander. They were patting me down and searching through my little bag as the commander demanded to know what I was doing there. I answered as best I could. To my relief, after a while, the commander started laughing. He turned to me and asked, "Did you know where you were walking?"

"What do you mean 'where I was walking?'" I shot back, not really understanding his question.

"Where did you come from?" he asked, still chuckling. I sensed that any imminent danger had passed, but I still didn't quite understand what was funny.

"I walked from Bardia," I responded, smiling tentatively.

"You walked all the way from Bardia?" It just seemed to get funnier and funnier to him.

"Yes, I did."

"Did you know that you were walking through a minefield? You must be the luckiest guy on earth! You could have been blown to pieces!"

"Really?" I exclaimed, aghast. It was immediately clear what was so funny, at least to him.

"What were you thinking?"

"I didn't know. I guess I am lucky."

"Did you also know that Libya and Egypt are not so friendly to each other?"

"I had no idea." It was absolutely true that I knew nothing about the history of hostility between the two countries.

By this time the commander had stopped laughing, and he asked me more seriously, "Tell me about your trip in Libya."

"Well, there is not much to say. I started my journey from Tunisia and really didn't like what I saw, so I decided to continue coming this way. I thought I would explore Egypt, since I had never been here before. Besides, I don't really like the Libyans." I told him about both experiences I had had in the country, including how I had been suspected of being an Egyptian spy the day before.

He believed me, thankfully. Then, having heard all he needed from me, he sent me to a single cell made from dry bamboo and said I would have to wait there until they figured out what to do with me. I was given a big cup of water and a bowl of *ful*, a traditional Egyptian dish made of dried fava beans. I recognized it from the Egyptian television shows the Algerian government bombarded its citizens with after independence, in an effort to broadcast material in Arabic rather than French. I had hated those TV shows, always full of sad stories and tears, but they were said to be very popular among Algerian women, who had no other way of seeing the outside world. And to my great surprise, the *ful* itself turned out to be delicious.

I spent the night in that cell with the guards nearby. In the morning, they transferred me to the police station in a town called Sallum, where I spent another three nights. Finally they had to let me go.

The police chief in Sallum explained, "I have no choice

Donkey Heart Monkey Mind

but to release you. You haven't done anything wrong except immigrating without a passport. If we could, we'd send you to Cairo and make your embassy pay to send you back home. That's how we deal with illegal immigrants. If their embassy won't pay for their plane ticket, they're in jail for quite some time. You, on the other hand, are lucky. We are a small town without the budget to send you to Cairo. We can't just send you back to Libya, and we certainly can't pay to send you home. You're free to go. But if I see you here again because of wrongdoing, you'll be here for a long time. So you'd better not come back."

I was very happy to hear that their limited finances meant I got to go free. However, I had my own budgetary concerns.

"Can you please tell me where I can exchange Libyan dinars into Egyptian pounds?" I asked the police chief.

"That's your problem. In this country we don't use Gaddafi's filth," he answered angrily.

"So, you're telling me this money is worth nothing at all?"

"I'm telling you that the money you have will not get you anything at all in Egypt. Egyptians don't accept Libyan currency. So you might as well throw it away in the next garbage bin you see. Didn't you know that?"

"No, I didn't," I replied. I now had a bigger problem than being in jail, I thought. No money, no friends, and no family. What was I going to do?

The police chief saw this thought cross my face and reached into his pocket. Out came ten Egyptian pounds, which he handed to me.

"I can only give you this. I'm not rich and I have a family to feed. It will only pay for your next meal, that's all, and then you have to try to figure out some way to go back to your country. It will be very hard for you here with no money."

I thanked the man and was out the door.

It was about two o'clock in the afternoon when I walked out of the police station, feeling very happy to be free. But I only had £10 on me, and the sun was at its hottest. Here I was in a city where I didn't know anyone and didn't have any money, any shelter, or any destination. At that moment I wished I had never left Algeria. But I quickly began to think of all the places I could visit in Egypt. We had studied the pyramids in school. How could I resist trying to see them? I asked a few people for directions then walked out of town on the road that led to Alexandria. In the middle of the afternoon heat, I headed on my way.

I must have walked about five kilometers before I was finally picked up by a truck heading to Alexandria. The driver told me that I was crazy to be on the road in the middle of the heat. He quickly offered me water. I spent a day and a half with that truck driver, both of us talking so much that I hardly noticed the miles we covered. I was the first Algerian he had ever met, as well as the first person he'd met who had crossed over from Libya, and he was fascinated by how I had managed it. He declared that I was very courageous, but I didn't think of myself as courageous, of course. I just hadn't known about the political relationship between the two countries, and I certainly hadn't known to expect minefields. I was just lucky. The truck driver was so kind that he bought me food and gave me £100. So far, I had had far more luck with the Egyptians (at least in Egypt, if not in Madrid) than I had with either Tunisians or Libyans.

From Alexandria, I continued hitchhiking towards Cairo. When I got there, after a whole day of being picked up and dropped off, I found it to be a massive city, full of overwhelming numbers of people, cars, camels, bicycles, and motorcycles, all mixed together. I knew right away that it was not a city I would want to live in. It was too dirty, too crowded, and too noisy. Even when I got to the pyramids, the atmosphere was much the same. There were tourists everywhere with their cameras, Egyptians with their camels hassling tourists to climb up for a picture, kids selling all kinds of souvenirs. The whole area was full of chaos. Of course the pyramids themselves were breathtaking. I had never imagined how big they would look. I was astonished by their size and the mystery of how in the world they could have been built. Each step was at least two feet high, and I counted them as I climbed the Great Pyramid (though I have long since forgotten how many I counted).

It just happened to be the end of the day when I climbed the Great Pyramid, and that was how I managed to see the most amazing sunset of my life. I felt as though I were back in the Pharaoh's era, 5,000 years ago. What did Libyan dinars or Egyptian pounds matter to the sun and the vast sands turning red beneath it? What did it matter what country I was in now or how I got there? What was the urgency of my 20-year-old desires and concerns? It was an inexplicable feeling of freedom that I have never felt before or since. I was adrift in time.

But I was not destined to stay in Egypt long. Having seen the country's greatest monuments and having had my fill of Cairo, I began thinking of where I might travel next. I had met my first Israeli in Cairo, and he told me a little bit about his country. It sounded very much like it was the Europe of the Middle East. I also decided it was time I learned something about Jewish people for myself. Like so many people in the Arab world, I had been taught that Jewish people were not to be trusted.

Yahoodi, or "Jewish," was something you called someone

Djaffar Chetouane

who betrayed others, left someone to starve, or did some other such dishonorable thing. I had never understood why a person would be called a name that represented a whole ethnic or religious group. I remembered how in Islam classes and history classes in school we were taught that the Jews betrayed the prophet Mohammed, and how the prophet himself declared war against them. (Of course, there was never a word mentioned in those classes about the Second World War and the kind of loss the whole world suffered during the Holocaust.)

So I began hitchhiking once again, this time towards Israel. I knew I would have a hard time entering the country without a passport, but I wanted to take my chances. After I had traveled with a few different passersby, I got picked up by someone heading to Tel Aviv. When he started asking me quite a few questions, I knew right away that he must be police or military. I decided to tell him my whole story, with one rather key alteration: I told him that I was an Algerian Jew, and that I was running away from my country.

My story was plausible enough since there have been Jewish people in North Africa for as long as there have been Jewish people. Some are indigenous to the area and others migrated there with traders or settlers, while others had been deported there by various regimes (such as the Roman or Spanish) over the millennia. There are even some Jewish Berber tribes. Some of the North African Jews in Algeria left with the French in 1962, some remained behind, some were converted to Islam, and some were killed. And so I said I was an Algerian Jew, on my way across North Africa to try to find refuge among my own people.

The man believed my story and seemed sympathetic to my plight. To my disbelief, when we arrived at the Israeli border, the man showed some kind of an ID to the border agent and we were waved through without a single question.

I said to the man, "You're a military person, right?"

"Yes, I am. Are you afraid?" he responded, speaking to me in Arabic.

"On the contrary, I'm feeling very safe," I responded, with just a trace of concern on my face.

"Don't worry. I'll drop you off in town, and you'll be free to go wherever you want."

"Can I ask you a question?"

"Yes, go ahead," he replied.

"Is it hard to get papers here as a refugee?"

"Well, just tell them what you've told me and you'll be fine," he said casually.

"Fine is something I haven't been in a while."

"Do you have any money?" he asked.

"No, I don't have any at all."

The man reached in his pocket and gave me all the money he had on him.

When we reached Tel Aviv, he dropped me off in the center of town, and we took leave of each other. I thanked the man for his help and started looking for a small and cheap hotel.

Less than two hours later, I was taking a nap when I was startled awake by loud knocking on my door. I opened the door, half awake. Two men with badges were standing there: Police officers.

"Is this your identity card?" one of them asked.

"Yes, it is," I responded, barely able to see the picture on it through my sleepy eyes. But I recognized its light green color; it was the only ID I had on me, and I'd had to leave it at the reception desk.

"Do you have a passport?" the same man asked.

"No, I don't."

"Well, will you come with us to the station so we can ask you a few questions?"

"Do I have a choice?" I asked.

I picked up my little bag and put my shoes on, and off we went in their unmarked vehicle. By this time I had gotten used to police and police stations. Of course, this time they didn't handcuff me or pull a hood or a blindfold over my eyes, which was already an improvement. I thought I would just tell them what I had told the man who picked me up, and then they'd set me free, just like he said.

When we arrived at the station, they took me through a series of questions about how I had entered Israel without a passport. Unlike some of the other people I had faced on this trip, these officers would not believe me no matter how much I persisted. I told them the truth about crossing the border again and again, but they simply could not believe my story. "It is unheard of," one of them said. "You simply can't enter Israel without a passport, no matter who you are."

After I spent the night there, we went through another round of questions the next day. My story never changed. I told them how I had been with the man in the car, how he had shown his ID, and how we had passed through the border.

Finally, one of them said, "Well, if you want to stay in Israel, you have to tell us the truth about how you got in. We always welcome Jewish people who want to live in Israel, no matter where they come from, no exceptions whatsoever, but you have to help us as well, so we can correct the flaw you exploited in order to enter. Then we'll set you free. We just need to know the truth."

"I've told you the truth. Whether you believe me or not is up to you," I answered.

Donkey Heart Monkey Mind

Convinced that I would not change my answer, they said, "Well, we have to check you out and decide what to do with you." By now I had heard "We'll decide what to do with you" so many times since I left Algeria that the phrase seemed commonplace.

"How long will I be here?" I asked the last man who interrogated me.

"I don't know. In the meantime, we have to transfer you to a bigger place, where you'll stay for a few days," he answered.

I was transferred to a prison with a cell that held more than 20 Palestinians. They told me they were all political prisoners, awaiting various transfers, trials, and deportation. All of them were there in transit. As soon as I entered, I noticed that the cell was filled with mattresses, one next to another, with barely any room for the prisoners' personal items. Some had a couple of plates next to their mattresses; some had books (primarily the Koran), letters, or magazines. All of them, without exception, had the rug they used for prayer.

When I got there, I was welcomed warmly by all of them. They had never met an Algerian before. One of them offered me one of his two mattresses, another offered me a pillow, and another gave me a sheet. And the next morning, they woke me up very early.

One of them said, "Aren't you going to get up so we can all pray together?"

At that, of course, I was obliged to act like a devout Muslim.

"Yes, of course I'll get up," I immediately replied. I knew that my "Algerian Jew" routine would not play well here. If I didn't acknowledge that I was a Muslim, they would treat me as an outsider. For once I was thankful for the single-minded Arabist Muslim education that meant I had learned how to pray in school.

I had prayed with those men for more than a week when

Djaffar Chetouane

I decided I had had enough of our cramped quarters. I was quite tired of praying five times a day, plus participating in discussions of the Koran after every prayer. So I decided to play a game and see if I could be transferred to a cell all by myself. I asked to talk to the police officer in charge of the section where I was, and I was granted a meeting with him.

"Listen," I said, "I'm Jewish. That's the reason I came here, not to live with Palestinians and pray five times a day. Please, if you could transfer me to a different cell, anywhere but here, I'd be very grateful." I was transferred right away and given a cell all to myself, just as I had hoped.

Over the next several days, I would tell the guard about the history of Jewish people in Algeria. He was particularly fascinated by the story of the seventh century Berber warrior princess Dihya, called *Kahina* ("The Seer"), by her invading Arab adversaries. She is supposed to have been a member of one of the tribes that converted to Judaism, although some scholars have disputed this. She led a successful resistance to the encroaching Arab Umayyad Dynasty in the 690s, before finally being defeated after five years or so. As I know the story, when the Arabs killed Dihya, they decapitated her and burned her head in the center of town. To this day, Berbers celebrate her life by burning various herbs in the Kabylia mountains. In the spring, you can see smoke rising to the sky from most Kabyle gardens to commemorate the way she died.

After two weeks in the Israeli prison, a man entered my cell at midday and said, "We'll take you back to Egypt today."

"I didn't come here to go back to Egypt! I'm Jewish and I have the right to be here," I said to the man, with all the conviction I could muster.

Donkey Heart Monkey Mind

"I'm sorry, I'm only following orders. They couldn't verify anything about you, and we don't even know your true identity."

"All you have to do is contact the Algerian Embassy, and you'll find out all about me."

"We don't have any relations with your country, so you're a mystery to us. We don't have any choice but to send you back to Egypt."

I was taken in an unmarked vehicle all the way to the Egyptian border. There, they handed me over to the Egyptian authorities.

Back in a city jail in Cairo, I met people of many different nationalities, including a fellow illegal Algerian immigrant. We were all held in the same room, much bigger and cleaner than the one in Tel Aviv, with bunk beds. Over the course of a few days, we were each taken to the immigration office for fingerprinting and so they could put our names permanently on file. The Algerian prisoner escaped from a bathroom window at the immigration office the second day they took us there. For the next couple of days, we saw very small articles in the newspaper about him and all had a laugh about it.

After being there for a week and after being taken, by myself, to the Algerian Embassy, I was transferred to a maximum security prison called *Siggn el Guanatir*, Prison of the Bridges. It was the worst prison in the country, by some accounts. I spent more than two weeks there, with criminals that had all kinds of backgrounds. In that prison, I had to be very smart. I went straight to the Sheikh of the Muslims, Sheikh Said, a Palestinian. I introduced myself as a devout Muslim and told him my story. I also told him that I was afraid, because I was. I was petrified as soon as I entered the place. The prisoners were filthy, with faces that would kill your appetite if you hadn't eaten for a week. They were very scary looking: maimed, disfigured, and scarred from years of living in such a brutal place with other brutal people. And they were all looking at me: young, fresh meat from the outside. Most of them were sentenced, I found out through a couple of Palestinians, to years in prison. If it weren't for the Muslim brotherhood's protection, I would have been sexually abused again and again, without any recourse.

I am still not sure why the authorities took me to that prison. I was told that it would be a temporary stay while my embassy tried to arrange passage home for me on a plane, but I ended up staying there for more than two weeks. While I was there, I prayed the five Muslim prayers each and every day with Imam Sheikh Said, my protector. I also spent most of my time with him, listening to his speeches on the Koran and Islamic stories so I could avoid being noticed by the criminals. Sheikh Said was very effective at turning anyone into a devout Muslim. I myself had never really believed in such religion, but even I was somewhat persuaded. Sheikh Said was absolutely a true Muslim, with all the characteristics of a genuine person with a profound belief in God.

A small part of me was glad I was in the prison. I learned about Egypt and its system, learned about how Palestinians were treated in the Arab world through Sheikh Said, and most of all, I learned never to do anything, no matter how small, that would land me in prison. Prison is the worst place a person can be. I concluded at the time that whoever came up with prison as a means of punishment, back however many years ago, must have really understood the psychological effect of being there. The act of confining a person seems simple, but it makes monumental changes in the way it feels to simply exist in the world. I had felt trapped in Algeria, but I had not truly understood the meaning of the word until I saw that Egyptian prison.

Finally, one day, I was taken back to the city jail, and the next day I was taken to the airport and flown home.

OCTOBER 1988

      I arrived back in Algeria on October 15, 1988. The timing could not have been worse for someone who had once been on the government's long list of political troublemakers. While I was in the Israeli prison, the frustrations of the poverty-stricken, politically disenfranchised Algerian people had come to a head. Labor strikes had turned into massive anti-government demonstrations, and riots eventually broke out all over the country. It started in a Berber village called Michelet, a well-known village high in the mountains. On October 4th, political activists there burned down a police station to protest against government corruption and abuse of power. The next day, October 5th, Algiers followed, and eventually the whole country was swept up. Algeria was in a state of chaos.

      In a period of civil strife that would later become known as "Black October," the president called on his long-time friend, army General Khaled Nazzar, to use the military to take control of the populace. But the general did not limit himself to just calming the situation; in some instances he ordered his troops to open fire on demonstrators. By the time the government had regained control, there had been as many as 500 civilian deaths, more than 2,000 injured, and 3,500 arrested, according to some estimates. But the control the government gained was not destined to last long.

Throughout all this, the Berber people continued to fight for their own rights. The beloved Berber singer and prominent political activist, Matoub Lounes, was shot in the stomach five times by a member of the National Police Force. On October 5th, as chaos was exploding around the nation, Matoub was on his way to distribute fliers asking the Berbers not to participate in the violence that we all knew was about to erupt in Algeria. Berber leaders wanted the conflict to remain within the government itself and between the government and some vocal Muslim fundamentalists. They didn't want Berbers to be caught in the middle, because Berbers always paid a high price for political involvement. Still many Berber activists did participate. And once Matoub was injured in the conflict, the Berbers' own outrage at many years of government oppression exploded. There was no going back; Kabylia became a war zone. Like activists around the country, Berbers protested by burning and breaking into government buildings, schools, police stations, government-owned stores, and gas stations. Tizi-Ouzou was burnt to a shell.

Matoub survived the shooting, but as he was leaving the hospital months later, greeted by a cheering crowd, someone attacked him and stabbed him with a knife. Matoub went right back into the hospital and, in all, ended up spending two years in recovery in hospitals in Algeria and France. With all the surgeries he had, he lost five centimeters of length in his right leg.

In the aftermath of the October 1988 ordeal, the government did institute reforms. The constitution was amended to allow the existence of other political parties besides the ruling National Liberation Front (Front de Libération Nationale, or FLN), apparently in an attempt by those in power to appease their most vehement opponents and draw them into the existing political process. By the time I came back from my travels across North Africa, the situation was seemingly under control. Schools were open and everyone went back to business as usual. Controversy and violence still simmered under the surface, but they would not erupt again for some time.

In the meantime, I, too, decided to go back to school. I had no passport, I had no money, and I was exhausted from all the time I had spent in jail during the course of my travels. I had no choice but to suppress my urge to leave the country and wait for another chance to present itself. My mother was pleased that I was returning to school, and my father had just come back from France with a brand new car that he had driven down through Spain and Morocco. Looking at his Renault 12, a French car, I remembered the conversation I had with him in Paris when he told me he might one day drive through Spain. He had done it, but it was his last visit to Europe. And the lunch we shared in Paris would be the first and last time I sat and talked with him as an adult. (The next closest thing I had to a conversation with him was over his grave. He died on November 2, 1988.)

When my father died, I was the only member of the family who did not shed a single tear. Later, people speculated that I was happy he had died, and you might say that I was. I was mostly happy for my mother—glad that she would never, ever suffer violence at his hands again. As for me, my father was so mean that I never had a chance to love him, only to fear him. The combination of not having a loving father and the misery of living in a country where I would never be free made me unable to stop burning for a better life, away from my father's house and away from Algeria. In the end, it was shortly after my father's death that I would begin the journey that would take me out of Algeria forever. He died two weeks after I came home and exactly two weeks before I was to be arrested for the last time.

The government did not rely on democratic reforms alone as a way to preserve calm; it also started making massive arrests throughout the country. Along with the carrot of change, the government wielded a huge stick. They were arresting everyone who had any ties with any political organization, including the Berber rights movement. Of course these arrests were not widely publicized. They occurred in silence, so as not to incite further unrest. But many thousands were imprisoned, to prevent them from ever disrupting the business as usual of the government again. This was how I was to get another chance to leave Algeria, though it wasn't the chance I had been looking for. Rather, one might say that it was the chance that had been looking for me.

Ironically, I was sitting in political history class on November 16, 1988, when my past activism caught up with me. Two military gendarmes (military police) walked in and bellowed my name. I stood up, shaking.

"Are you Jafar?" one of them shouted in Arabic.

He spoke as if I were a kilometer away. His partner was holding what looked like a picture of me.

"Yes, that's me," I responded, as the whole classroom turned to look at me.

"Get over here," he barked. I walked cautiously up the aisle of the classroom, and as soon as I was within reach, he grabbed me by the back of my neck.

Donkey Heart Monkey Mind

"Son of a dog," he snarled, jerking me out the door.

The other officer slammed it behind us. They immediately handcuffed me, squeezing the cuffs so tight that in just a short while I couldn't feel any blood in my hands. As we exited the building I saw that other students were being dragged to a van parked just outside. None of us, I thought, was resisting our arrest, but they still bullied us like shepherds hurrying reluctant sheep across a river so they can get home before dark. In a moment, there were seven of us crammed inside the van.

We all knew each other from having been active in the Berber movement at the university at one time or another. We were all scared, and no one spoke. I thought to myself that this was just another regular arrest: they'd release us just like they always did, eventually. After they interrogated us and maybe beat us a little, we'd be free. It had happened that way many times before. I thought briefly of my father. If he were still alive, I would have gotten out of this somehow. Even that escape route, however distasteful to me, was no longer an option. Perhaps because of this, and perhaps because of the current political climate, I was quickly changing my mind, sensing that something very different was about to happen.

One of the students was bleeding from his mouth, apparently punched by one of the gendarmes. Two of my friends were particularly scared.

I told one of them, "Don't worry, they'll just interrogate us, maybe we'll get a little beating, and we'll be having dinner at home tonight," though I doubted every word I said.

"I don't think so," he responded firmly.

"Is this the first time this happened to you?" I asked another friend.

I was trying to make light of our plight, raise our morale,

give us some courage and reason for optimism, but of course I didn't even believe my own words.

"It's happened to you, too, and you know it just as well as I do," said another friend, with a look that said, "Please don't try to encourage us while you're in the same hole."

"Well, that's exactly what I'm saying: they'll beat the shit out of us and we'll all go home. I'm telling you, this is no different." I spoke with confidence, even believing myself for just a few seconds.

When we arrived at the *Gendarmerie Nationale* of Tizi-Ouzou, they put all of us straight into a cell. We sat quietly, speculating to ourselves about the outcome of every approaching minute. But there was no word, no beating, and no interrogation—yet. We spent the entire night there with no food, water, or any kind of explanation. The hours went by in silence and conjecture.

Very early the next morning, we were brought out of the cell and loaded into the back of a camouflaged military truck with two armed gendarmes. In just a few minutes we were on the road, without a clue about our destination. It must have been about two hours before we were told to get out of the truck. From the sound of vehicles and traffic, we could tell we were in a big city. Hunger was still not on our minds, although it was very much in our stomachs. As soon as I got out, I knew we were in Blida, a town about an hour away from Algiers. The entire military administration of Algeria is based in Blida, and this meant that we were being turned over to some kind of military tribunal. We were in no position now to hope for justice, civil rights, or a quick release. We all realized that our predicament was much worse than we had thought.

We were marched into a building and immediately separated into individual cells. Each of us was now by himself, with no one to draw even false encouragement from. Alone, I became suddenly much more aware of my physical self. My head, my hands, and my body were all I had for comfort or company. I knew they were all I needed to be alive, and they were all that could give me hope. I blocked every thought from my mind in order to preserve my sanity.

I spent two days in that cell, fed just a piece of bread each day, and no water. On the third day, mid-morning, a military officer in fatigues opened the door and shouted for me to come out.

"It's your turn, son of a dog."

The officer talked to me as though I had killed his mother, that is, if he ever even knew her. Many of those engaged to serve for life in the Algerian army are orphans, the abandoned children of prostitutes and the poor. As officers with some power but few other options in life, they have total disdain for those who serve only their obligatory two years in the military, and they have no mercy for servicemen who commit infractions that land them in military prison. I could only expect this officer to reserve a special contempt for civilians and political activists who found themselves confined there.

When I came out of the cell, he struck me hard across my face with the back of his hand.

"Traitor!" he roared at me in Arabic.

I looked at him and tried to respond. Before I had a chance to speak, he kicked me as hard as he could on my buttocks with his steel-toed boots. I looked at him again and he kicked me once more, like he was trying to launch a soccer ball across a field.

"Walk, you dog!"

We soon got to a room where two more officers sat behind a desk, these two with stars on the shoulders of their uniforms. I could see that I had been brought there to be judged. I was told to sit down, but when I did, I realized how bad the pain was on my backside.

"Sit down," one officer said.

"I was just kicked twice in the ass and it is so painful that I would rather stand than sit," I offered quietly.

I was immediately slapped on the back of my head by the guard that had fetched me from my cell.

"Sit down, don't even breathe, and keep your eyes on the floor when you talk."

As he forced me into the chair he continued, "Just answer what's been asked of you, don't be a smart ass, and make sure you finish your answer with 'sir'."

"Your name is Jafar, correct?" the first officer began, staring me down.

"Yes, sir," I answered.

"You were born on (such and such) date?"

"Yes, sir."

He continued the questions while the other officer looked through some papers. His demeanor was as cold as the room felt.

Finally the second officer asked, "Are you a Berber from Tizi-Ouzou?"

"I was born a Ber—"

Before I had a chance to finish my sentence my guard slapped me on the back of the head and said, "Didn't I tell you not to be a smart ass and to just answer the questions?"

"Yes, sir."

"And your answer is?" he prompted me.

"Yes, I'm a Berber from Tizi-Ouzou, sir."

I saw a quick smile cross the face of the second officer, but he immediately scowled when he realized that I had seen his expression.

The questions kept coming at me for about an hour, with breaks here and there so they could look over their documents—yet the interrogators never spoke to one another. Finally the first officer said, "Well, just wait here while we discuss your case, and then we'll give you our answer."

He never told me his answer, and I never saw his face again.

As soon as they left the room, the officer who had been guarding me grabbed me by the arm and said, "Come with me." He took me back to my cell, and I was held for six more days without a single word of explanation.

Nine days after I was first arrested a new officer came to my cell and announced, "You're in for a long promenade. Today is your lucky day. Get up and let's go."

I stood up eagerly, thinking I was going to be let outside for the first time in many days and that I would get to smell the fresh fall air. Instead, when I was escorted out of the building, I was met by two other officers with a truck. I was thrown in the back, and someone who looked like a nurse climbed in after me.

He said, "This will make your journey quite pleasant."

"What are you doing to me?" I asked, my legs shaking with fear.

"I told you, this will ease your journey."

"I don't need anything to ease my journey," I protested, backing further into the truck. He turned his head and signaled to the other two officers.

They climbed in, irritated, and one of them said, "Sit down, it's for your own good. I wish I were getting there like you."

They held me down by both arms. One of them pulled up my left sleeve and the nurse gave me an injection. After they left

Djaffar Chetouane

and closed the doors of the truck, I felt the truck start to move. I wasn't aware of anything after that, and later I woke up by myself in a new cell, in a totally different place. I didn't know where I was, what day it was, or how long I would be there—let alone what might be in store for me.

AT THE EDGE OF THE WOODEN BED

My cell was very plain. It had a wooden bed with no mattress or pillow, only a blanket. The door of the cell was made of wood and it had a small barred window through which I could see the wall across the hallway. The floor was made of hard rock, and the walls were adobe. These materials and the smell of the desert told me I was somewhere in the Sahara, but I had no idea where.

I spent two days in a state of shock and disbelief before I came to my senses. I then found the courage and the words I needed to ask the guard who passed some food through the window if he could tell me the name of this place.

"This is your home and I'm your mother, but I only have less than a year and then they'll bring you a different mama. Maybe she'll be nicer and more talkative to all of you."

I could see both anger and sorrow on his face as he replied. I didn't get the answer I wanted, but he had told me more than he thought. I now knew that I was in another military compound, because this poor slob was here serving out his two years of obligatory service. He had no insignia on his uniform, so he was of low rank, and he clearly felt sorry for himself for having to fulfill his term here among prisoners. He seemed to be in charge of feeding the entire prison by himself, though I had no idea how many of us there were.

The most important information I gathered from his reply was from his accent: he was not an Arabic person, and he was most likely a Berber from somewhere. Excited thoughts raced around my head. I decided to strike up a conversation with him in *Tamazight* the next time he came by. If he were in fact a Berber, I would actually have a person to talk with, and he might even answer some of my questions. I might only have brief conversations with him, but they would be much better than nothing at all. "I'm about to have a friend," I thought. By the time I left off thinking long enough to taste the noodles in broth he had brought, it was cold. The entire night went by in silent wondering.

The next day, I heard him passing food to the other inmates. As soon as he reached my door, as he passed the food to me, I told him in *Tamazight* that I was a Berber. His eyes flashed to my own as though we'd met before.

He replied, "I'm from Bejaia."

Bejaia is a beautiful city on the Mediterranean coast, 130 kilometers from Tizi-Ouzou. Because of its location on the coast, it contains ruins from many civilizations, from as far back as the Roman Empire. Bejaia is also known as Little Kabylia, because it has the next largest Berber population after my own town.

"I'm from Tizi-Ouzou," I replied quickly, before he could move on to the next cell.

I was so happy. It was almost as though someone had

released me from my cell. To be in a place like this and to find someone who spoke the same language as me—someone with whom I'd be having regular contact—put me in much better spirits. He was even from my region. Perhaps he could do me some favors.

"I can't speak to you right now. Maybe when I come back to pick up the plate and if there isn't anyone else around I'll—" he cut his sentence short as he moved on. I was relieved by his answer. I knew he'd be back and that he would talk to me about something. Anything. I was like a desert that has received the first drops of rain after decades of drought. They were just a few drops, but it was enough to know that rain did in fact exist. His few words were just enough to bring some comfort in this new, unknown place.

The rest of the day went by in silence. I kept obsessing about what to say to the guard.

"Maybe I'll ask him his name." I debated with myself. "No, maybe I'll just wait for him to start. Yes, I think that's a much better idea."

Finally, I saw him in front of my cell door.

"What's your name?" he asked.

My heart started pumping faster.

"Jafar," I responded.

"So, you're from Tizi-Ouzou?"

"Yes. But how do you know that?" I replied in a hurry, forgetting that I was the one who had told him.

"You told me earlier. Plus your accent is easy to recognize. Why are you here?"

"I'm just as puzzled as you. I have no idea."

"You don't?"

"Well, I haven't done anything. Where are we, anyway?" I asked.

Djaffar Chetouane

"You don't even know where you are?" he asked, furrowing his brow in disbelief.

"Can you please tell me?"

"Well, this is strange. Are you making fun of me?"

"Do I look like I'm in a position to make fun of you?"

"I'm sorry," he replied. "We are in Tindouf. Do you know where that is?"

"Yes, I do know." As soon as he said that, I felt fear shoot through my body. I was two thousand kilometers from home. Why had they brought me all the way here?

"You honestly didn't know that?"

"No. I didn't."

"What did you do? You must have done something against the government for them to jail you in a military camp."

"Back home, as a student, I wrote about *Tamazight*. I haven't done anything more than that. I just wanted *Tamazight* to be used in schools like French and Arabic. Is there anything wrong with that?"

"That's all you've done?"

"I've never done anything to deserve this. Are there more Berbers here?"

"No, you're the only one. Most people are just here temporarily."

"Where do they take them afterwards?"

"I have no idea. I'm just a *joondi*. I'm just waiting for my time to be up so I can go home."

"*Joondi*" is Arabic for a person who serves his two years of service with no rank. The entire conversation took only a couple of minutes, but to me, it felt like eternity. It was enough to establish a connection with someone from home, even someone who could probably be no help to me. I was simply happy to talk to him. And during the entire time I didn't even ask his name. He went back to his duties in a hurry, but not before saying that if I needed anything I should ask him. A warm light filled my heart upon hearing his words. I sat alone imagining the possibilities. Maybe I would find a way out of here after all? I knew there wasn't much I could do, but just having hope and something to think about made me more comfortable. I knew the border with Morocco was not far from Tindouf. Perhaps my new friend could help me get there? Deep down, I knew there was no way for him to help me escape, but still, I could imagine it.

As days passed by, my bond with the *joondi* grew stronger. We talked almost every day, in brief snippets, about all kinds of things. But in the hours between his short visits, there was nothing to do but think. It was essential to control the direction of my thoughts, to keep from going crazy from fear and isolation. I had to avoid thinking about my cell and how long I might be in it. To occupy my mind, I started to go back through chess games I had played. Sometimes I would remember an entire game I had played with someone, especially a game in which I had lost; I would think about what pieces I would have played differently. Other times I would think about my family, my childhood, or my friends. I knew my mother would be suffering terribly from my absence. She had just lost her husband, and now she had no idea where her son might be or if I was ever coming back. I kept thinking of Europe, thinking of the places I had been and how beautiful and green they were; the people I stole from, their faces, what they were wearing, where they were from, how and what exactly I stole from them. I silently asked for their forgiveness and understanding. My imagination went far and beyond the prison cell. However, it only strayed toward the past. I couldn't afford to allow a single thought about the future.

Finally, one morning, two new *joondis* came by and ordered me out of my cell for the first time. I followed them to a chamber. There I was told to sit in a chair, and they bound my hands and feet.

They said, "Today you'll get a clean cut. All this curly hair is no good for you here."

"If you're only giving me a haircut, then why are you tying me up?"

"A haircut? Is that what you think you're going to have?" one of them responded.

"Then what?" I said.

"Just stay put, someone will be right with you. We just do what we're told."

The two *joondis* left the room. In a few minutes, two officers walked in. Both of them had two V-shaped signs on each shoulder.

"Nice hair you have. Isn't it heavy?" one of them asked, with a sardonic smile on his face. I noticed he was holding a stove lighter in his right hand.

"How did you get those highlights? Do you paint your hair to look like a European?" the other one asked.

"No, I don't. My hair gets lighter from the sun."

"Well, today we'll take all that off, because we don't want any creatures living in that wooly mess. We can burn it or we can cut it. It all depends on you."

"What do you mean, 'burn it'?"

"If you don't answer our questions the way we want them to be answered, we'll burn your hair. So, you'd better cooperate and tell us everything you know."

My heart pounded wildly. I now knew I was in for my first interrogation here, and that it would not be the question-and-answer type. I had heard a lot about military style interrogations. In a word, they were physical. I had heard that they would beat the hell out of you and much more than that. But since I was never involved in any plot, had never harmed anyone, and had never interrupted any government work, what answers could I give them? There was nothing to confess. I knew I was in for a good beating at least, because I would have no information with which to satisfy them.

"Tell me everything you know about your people."

"What do you mean my people? We're Berbers." A fist crashed into my face as soon as I finished my last word.

"We're all Algerian and we're all Arabs. What is this Berber crap?" one guard screamed at me, putting his face an inch from mine. I could smell his breath and feel his spit on my face. He was a tall, dark Arab with a long face. Beneath his moustache, I could see he had a silver front tooth. His thick brows merged together in the middle, hovering over a pair of eyes so dark I could see my reflection in them. His expression told me clearly that I was nothing to him, not even human, and he would do anything to me that he pleased.

"You're here to torture me. You don't want to know about my people. So, you may as well do what you want and get it over with." A tear fell down my cheek as I stared back at him. I was committed and ready for pain, because I knew there wasn't anything I could do to avoid it. I was ready to just give up physically and emotionally, but I had to keep my inner self strong and remember that everything has an end, including what I was about to experience.

Djaffar Chetouane

He asked his friend to pass him the lighter.

"You see, I'm going to burn your hair, and after I'm done with it, you'll wish you were never born. I'm going to show you how we treat those who don't appreciate what the government has done for them, those who don't know the meaning of freedom and obedience. You will be here with us until you understand what it is to be Algerian, what it is to be a patriot, and how to appreciate your country."

He put the lighter to my hair. At first I wasn't aware of anything but the foul stench of hair beginning to smolder. It wouldn't catch fire easily, and it burned slowly. I was already bargaining with myself, telling myself that if I could just stand the smell, then there might not be so much pain. But as soon as I felt the first scorching of my scalp, all bargaining ceased. I started shaking my head desperately and screaming from the pain.

"You didn't think about that, did you?" he said with an evil grin. All I could bring into focus was the silver tooth. Then he told his friend to hold my head so he could continue his work on the rest of my hair.

The man put his hands around my face to stop me from moving my head, but I still resisted by shaking my head back and forth. So he used both arms to pin my face against the weight of his body. I was burning slowly and surely. I lost my voice entirely from screaming louder and longer than I ever had before.

When the silver-toothed man walked me back to my cell and locked me in, he said with satisfaction, "You'll never have curls again." I had never felt so much pain in my life. Tears were flowing like rivers down my cheeks. I sat on my wooden bed for a long time, conscious only of pain and the burning sensation on my head. After a long while, slowly, my head began to cool down. Exhausted and disoriented, I tried to lie down on the blanket. As soon as my head touched it, I realized my mistake. There was no way to rest, because I couldn't let my head touch anything. I sat upright the entire night, waking up when my head would bob forward on my weary neck.

The next morning, I began to try to touch my head gently, but it was far too raw. I wished desperately for a mirror so I could see for sure what they had done to me. Eventually, the *joondi* came by to serve me food. As soon as he looked at me, he dropped the metal plate he was trying to pass through the window, and his eyes widened in disbelief.

"What have they done to you?" he asked, completely horrified. From the look on his face, I realized I didn't need a mirror. I saw myself through his eyes—a feeling I will never forget as long as I live; an emotion that will follow me into my next life. Tears welled up in my eyes and dripped to the ground, where they would settle and keep me company for the rest of my time there. (To this day I still see the *joondi* seeing me. I still remember his look and his apologies for something he himself had never done.)

I slept sitting upright for days. Part of me wished I could just sleep forever. I couldn't feel my exhausted neck anymore, and my scalp continued to sear and prickle. But a glimmer of hope inside of me never let go, never once gave up on its promise: it never let death even come close. Exactly how many nights I slept upright, I cannot remember. All I remember is the pain that ingrained itself in me from maintaining that position for so many nights and days. Every day, the *joondi* would come by and talk to me, at least for a moment. We would talk about anything. He was so gentle. He wanted to ease my pain solely through words; I called them words of eternal peace. Sometimes one's suffering can be easily forgotten in the face of another person's recognition and compassion. I will never forget his gentleness, his wisdom, his sympathy, and especially his face. This one person gave me the capacity to resist my pain. Not that he even once opened the door for me, but his words and the look on his face enabled me to have hope about the unknown future. And I never did learn his name.

Then, finally, one day, I started to touch my head and it didn't hurt. I pressed harder and harder, but I felt no pain, just the hardness of the thick, dead scab that had formed over my whole scalp. I lay down for the first time in days, and I felt like I had entered heaven. The first thing I asked myself when I lay down was, "Will I ever have hair again?" If I ever left this place, would I spend the rest of my life feeling not only humiliated but also visibly scarred by what they had done to me? I lay down for a long time without turning over or moving once. My thoughts were far from my body and from my present situation. Eyes focused on the ceiling, images and shapes started to fill my mind, and I wondered.

I can't remember how many nights and days passed before the silver-toothed man returned.

"Get up, Berber!" he barked.

As he was opening the door, I sensed pain was on its way again.

"What are you going to do to me this time?" I asked. "I thought I was Algerian," I continued.

Right away he slapped me on the back of my head and said, "We're going to have a little fun with you. How's your head today?" He smiled and showed his silver tooth. I didn't respond to his questions. He pushed me ahead of him, then grabbed my arm and directed me into the same room where I had lost my hair.

"Sit down on the chair."

I sat on the same chair as before, and he circled around

behind me. Boom! A massive blow fell on the back of my head, and the ground rushed up towards my eyes. I huddled on the floor, hands on my head, squeezing all my muscles in pain. I have no idea what he struck me with, but I felt liquid pouring over my hands. As I brought my hands to my eyes, I saw that it was blood.

"Get up, Berber!" He was yelling and kicking me in my back. "If you don't get up, I will do it again and this time to your face, I swear!"

My head was spinning; still I found the strength to get up and sit on the chair. As I got up, he hit me again, and this time it knocked me unconscious.

The next thing I knew, I was waking up in my cell. I felt blood all over my face, and I was weak and nauseated, whether from blood loss or the blows, I didn't know. I pulled myself up to the bars in the door and screamed for the *joondi*. He came quickly, and as soon as he saw the blood all over my face, he hurried to bring me water and a bandage. He actually opened the door to the cell and came partway inside, helping me wash my head and telling me to lean over so he could apply the bandage.

As he left the cell, I heard screaming in the hallway. It was the silver-toothed man and the *joondi*. My friend was accused of helping me, but he was arguing that I could have died if I had been left to bleed. Of course, the silver-toothed man outranked the *joondi*, and he was enraged. I don't know whether that argument was all that passed between them, but after that incident the *joondi* barely said another word to me. My only friend was no more.

After many days and nights, I was called one morning by a voice far from the door to sit up. When the source of the voice appeared, it was the silver-toothed man, yet again.

"How is your head, you curly Berber?" he asked quietly,

with obvious enjoyment of what he had done to me. I stared at him silently, and he opened the door.

"Come on out. Today we'll show you how to just be alive and not worry about a thing."

This man telling me not to worry about a thing was an obvious reason to worry. Perhaps this man had once been brainwashed with the same kind of brutality I was about to suffer. Certainly, he was stuck in a dismal military post in the middle of nowhere, most likely for the rest of his life. For whatever reason, this man seemed to have been left without a trace of compassion in his heart.

I was directed to the same, awful room, and two new soldiers followed us in. But this time there was a new chair there. It was made of wood, with armrests, leg rests, and a headrest that was leaned back. There were leather straps at intervals on every portion of this contraption. I resisted when I first saw the chair, but my efforts would have been futile even if pain, malnutrition, and long imprisonment had not significantly sapped my strength by now. All three men forced me into the chair. They strapped down my arms, including my hands, my legs, my torso, and even my head. When they were done, the only movement I could manage was of my facial muscles. Last, they rolled in a metal stand with an intravenous fluid bag hanging from it. The tube extending from the bag was positioned about six inches above the skin between my eyebrows.

My old acquaintance (who usually accompanied the silver-tooth man) said, "This won't be like the first time. It won't hurt you at all—except it will." He stopped short of saying what they were about to do to me. He finished simply, saying, "You'll see."

Drops of liquid started to fall just between my eyes, and all

Donkey Heart Monkey Mind

three men left the room. At first I didn't feel anything. I could tell the liquid was just water, and that was fine. But because I couldn't move my head, not even an inch, the water drops soon started to irritate me. Then they began to infuriate me. They hit the same spot, over and over again, every two to three seconds, as my limbs and head remained bound to the chair. Suddenly the simple act of being able to raise a hand and wipe my eyes became simultaneously the most desirable and unattainable thing in the universe. The seemingly negligible physical sensation of the water was maddening in its inevitability, soon escalating into a new type of intolerable pain. The mind could not help but focus on each new drop, and yet the repetition was too much for the mind to bear. Eventually, as the droplets smacked at my forehead and the water coursed in steady rivulets into my eyes and down my cheeks, I began to go numb. I was aware of what was happening to me for a short while, but I eventually lapsed into a new kind of unconsciousness. It was not the same physical unconsciousness that had been induced by the vicious blows to my head, but it was mercifully just as complete.

I woke later feeling as though I were waking up from a long nightmare. It took me a long while to fully come to myself. My thoughts drifted, I was half asleep and half awake, and my brain seemed sluggish, as if it were emerging from paralysis. The first thing I did, I remember, was touch my head. To my surprise, I felt tiny hairs there. The last time I had touched my scalp, I had felt only bloody scabs and hardened scar tissue. It made no sense. My heart sped up. I tried to stand, but my mind wouldn't function. Maybe I was dreaming, maybe I was still in my nightmare, I thought. I was so confused that I couldn't differentiate between my awareness and my actual existence.

I remained lying on my back, my eyes wide open, as my

brain scrambled from one thought to another. I slowly became aware of an ache and dampness somewhere on my body. Again, confusion coursed through me, and I still couldn't sort out what exactly was happening. I remember a single tear coming to my eye, convincing me that I was alive and conscious of myself. Still, I didn't feel fully human. I was sure only that I was awake.

A long while passed with me lying on the wooden bed, struggling for understanding. Before they turned off the light in my cell that night, an unfamiliar man passed a metal bowl of food into the cell. Unable to get up, I stared at it for a while. I knew very well that it was food, but I couldn't find the strength to get up and eat it. I must have fallen asleep again, because I remember waking up once more, wondering whether it was night or day. The light in my cell wasn't lit, and I could see a little bit of light from the hallway passing through the barred window in my door. This made me understand that it was still night, and orienting myself just that tiny bit made me fully gain consciousness.

I became self-aware. I was alive.

The next day, I found the strength to get up as soon as my eyes were open. I stood up and sat on the edge of the bed. I shook my head, like a dog emerging from water. Next, I got up and walked a bit around the cell, and then I could identify the ache I had felt when I first woke up: the skin of my anus burned with a piercing sensation. I knocked on the door for someone to come, but no one responded. Looking around the cell, I saw the toilet in the dark corner. I tried using it, in the hope that clearing something out would relieve the burning, but it only worked temporarily. I went back to sitting on the edge of the bed, trying to imagine what had happened to me and coming up with nothing. I was very agitated, not knowing what was going on. It was clear that time had passed without my knowledge, but I didn't know how. I started to watch tears falling on the ground. Later I came to understand that they, my tears, were washing my head clear and getting me ready for an unbearable truth. They were cleansing my thoughts.

I sat like that on the edge of the bed for hours, until light crept into my cell. I knew the presence of daylight meant the presence of others. Knocking on the door once again, I found myself looking at a new guard.

"What a surprise! What is it that you need this early in the morning?" the man asked. "I've never heard you knock on this door before."

I stood there trying to get words out of my mouth, but I couldn't assemble a phrase to actually speak.

"Well, are you going to tell me something, or are you just wasting my time?" he asked calmly, leaning his face against the window bars.

I gestured to him to wait, and he said, "I've never heard you talk before. Are you deaf?"

The first word that came out of my mouth was a loud and clear, "NO." I cleared my throat, "I'm not deaf."

"You're the only one that never said anything before. I thought they'd cut out your tongue, but clearly they didn't. I'm busy at the moment. I'll come back later."

As soon as the man passed out of my view from my little window into the hallway, many thoughts stormed my brain all at once. The thought that dominated was that the man had said he had never heard me talk. Automatically, I started to talk to myself aloud. I stated my name, who I was, and where I was. My words were coming out all by themselves. My voice was coming back.

Djaffar Chetouane

Then I noticed that my memory had just resurfaced. It was like a river that had been dry for decades suddenly flooding and washing away everything that had settled during its absence.

I sat back down on the edge of the bed and started to think. As I leaned forward, I brushed my head with both palms and noticed once again that my hair was growing. I couldn't make any sense of this, though, because I had only recently remembered the experience of it being burnt. To me, it felt like it had happened only yesterday. Or perhaps it was a dream? I jumped off the bed and started to bang hard on the door. I now knew what I wanted to ask the man. My heart pounded along with my hands. As soon as I could see the man through a corner of the window, I asked the million-dollar question:

"What date is it?" I gasped, breathing hard.

"Why?" he answered with a question, smiling mockingly. "Do you have an appointment with someone today?"

"Please, I just want to know the date. That's all I want. Please tell me."

"April 30th," he responded.

"What year?" I asked, my fears confirmed.

"1989. What else do you want to know?"

I had been detained in November of the previous year. I grasped at my resurfacing memories: my interrogation in Blida, my transfer here, losing my hair, being strapped down under the i.v. bag. At the most, these accounted for two months. It should have been January. Where had the remaining months gone? Once again, the man smiled, obviously enjoying my reaction. From the look on his face, I could see that he knew more about me than I knew at that moment. I was so bewildered by his answers that I couldn't stand, and I went back to the edge of the bed without asking him anything else.

I sat on the edge of the bed that day, and many days thereafter, leaning over, elbows on my knees, holding my face with my hands. I felt tears streaming down my cheeks and watched as they splashed on the ground. I watched every drop disappear, trying to reclaim my entire life, trying to accept my present situation, and trying to remember the time I had lost. But I could only remember up to the water hitting me between my eyes. The edge of the bed and the ground represented exactly where I was in my thoughts. The distance to the ground I was staring at felt so far I could have been sitting on the edge of a cliff. The distance represented how much of my life I had lost. I was still alive, which was the most important thing, but losing four months' worth of memories paralyzed me. So I sat on the edge of that bed, in that same position, for days, stubbornly trying to recall what might have happened to me. The ground absorbed my tears thirstily, but my brain remained parched and unsatisfied.

Two thoughts came to me during those days that gave me the courage and will to persist. The first one was that I was still alive, still sitting on that edge, not yet fallen over the cliff. The second was making the decision to get out of that place alive or dead. Dying while attempting to escape would be preferable to remaining there. If my destiny is to remain here, I thought, I will cheat my destiny by choosing to die. I will make my own destiny.

I started keeping track of days by using my fingernails to scratch small lines on the wall. Then a few days after I regained consciousness, the guard who had been bringing me food appeared, unexpectedly, in the middle of the day. This time, instead of passing food through the window, he opened the door. As soon as he did, I knew something was wrong. I asked him where he was taking me, because that was the only reason anyone had ever opened that door before.

"You're not going anywhere," he answered, smiling. "I'm just going to have fun with you, as usual."

"What do you mean 'you're going to have fun with me?'"

"What's going on with you? You never used to talk at all."

As soon as he said that, I realized what I had done wrong. The torture I had undergone had been meant to be a brainwash: I was meant to have been cleansed of myself, cleansed of my past, and relieved of the ability to think for myself. For a time, their methods had worked. By talking to the guard, however, I might have given my captors a clue that I was coming to myself again. Who knew what they would do to me if they found out? I might be in for more of the same, or worse. I decided I had to play along with the guard and see what his intentions were.

"I need to clear my throat, it's been awhile since I spoke," I said to him.

"Pull down your pants and turn around," he answered, unzipping his own pants.

I was paralyzed by his words, and I didn't know whether to obey him or fight. I immediately understood the reason for the secret, searing pain I had become aware of when I first woke up. They had been raping me, probably for months. My mind raced, bewildered and horrified. But I didn't have time to process this new realization. I wasn't in a position to run away from the guard, and I could imagine that things would only get worse if he called his friends. In a split second, I realized I had to go along with him. I could survive this once and hope to find another solution later, I thought feebly. I started pulling my pants down.

"Hurry up," he said. His pants were already down and his penis way up. I turned around, and he did what he had obviously done many times before and then left. I was numbed by the experience, and I went back to the edge of the bed, my pants still lowered.

I sat there for hours, thinking of what had just happened. I was violated, humiliated, and I felt I was dead. I didn't think there was anything left in me. I was desperately ashamed, and I even blamed myself momentarily. I was just a shell lost on a vast beach. And that's when I knew that I would rather die than live this life that did not belong to me. I would rather die than live being used. Killing myself was not an option, so there was only one thing I could do: Escape. My chances of succeeding were slim, but I knew I could still try and hope for the best. I held on to what my grandmother used to say: "When you face one of the most difficult situations possible in life, there is still always a way out. There is always a solution out there waiting to be discovered. Innocence has its rewards at times of uncertainty."

And I was innocent.

ALI AND OMAR

It was in the middle of the night a few days later that I woke up and couldn't go back to sleep. I started walking around my cell to occupy myself until I could fall asleep again. At one point, I paused at the window, holding the bars with my hands. I leaned forward, putting my head on my arms and imagining that the door might just open for me and let me walk out. I leaned against it for a little while and thought about what it would be like to attain my liberty. I kept thinking of the things I would do if I ever had the chance to get out. And then, without even being aware of what I had done, I leaned backwards—and the door followed. It opened. There is no way to explain this, no magic trick or voodoo involved. The door just swung open. I was astounded. I stood there wondering if I was dreaming, but it was quite real. I pushed the door shut again and thought frantically about what to do.

I tried hard to remember the last time a guard had walked into my cell. It could only have been when the guard raped me, and that was three days or so ago. The only possible explanation was that he had been surprised enough to find me self-aware and talking that he had simply, incredibly, forgotten to lock the door behind him. He was either in a hurry, or he had simply enjoyed what he was doing too much. And then one thought rose up and shut all others out: What would happen if I just walked out?

My heart beat so hard I could feel my chest pounding. My pulse sounded like a drum beating in my ears. Taking deep breaths, I encouraged myself to take the chance. What was the worst that could happen? I asked myself. I could get shot, but what would I lose by that? It would simply be the end of my suffering. I told myself aloud that I had no life in this place; I would not accept that guard coming back to do again what he had done to me before. Without thinking about it anymore, I pulled the door open and moved forward.

I emerged from the cell and looked in all directions. To my right was more hallway, lined with cells. But to my left was a big opening leading outside. It looked like it must be the main entrance to the building, and there was an armed guard sitting asleep on either side of it. I shut my cell door slowly behind me and stood motionless in the hallway for a few seconds. Then I began to walk carefully towards the opening. I was barefoot, so my steps were silent on the stone floor, but my heart was pounding so hard I wondered if it might wake the guards up. I have no idea where I got the courage to keep walking. I just knew I didn't deserve to be where I was, and I wanted wholeheartedly, desperately to be free. I drew closer to the guards, and still they didn't stir. Then I found myself walking between them. I felt like a ghost. Finally, I was past them, and they had not so much as twitched.

It was night and I stood in the open air for the first time

in months and took my first look at the rest of the military camp. There were no artificial lights, but the dawn was approaching. By its light I could make out many single-level, flat-roofed quarters with clay walls, some of them slightly bigger than the others. It was like a small desert city with an enormous courtyard. I stepped forward and began to walk across the camp. I had no idea where the main entrance might be or how I would get out, and I couldn't really see very well. In a moment, I realized that it was not a good idea to be brazenly walking upright across the compound. I lay down on the ground on my stomach and looked around for an exit. In the desert at night you can see much better and much farther if you put your eyes as close to the ground as possible, and this proved helpful. Eventually, I made out the main gate, still a good distance away. I also noted that the entire camp was fenced in, with guard towers at each corner. By this time my heart had slowed down considerably.

I lay without moving an inch and tried to observe everything around me with calm. I was about a hundred meters from the sleeping guards, and I could barely see them by now. It was time for me to get out of there before I was seen. I was dressed in dark green pants and shirt, and they blended in with the reddish brown ground reasonably well. I decided that I had the best chance of not being seen if I crawled, so I set out on my belly. The ground was rocky and hardened, grinding and scraping at my elbows and knees, but I knew I must keep moving no matter what. On each previous morning, I had heard people singing the national anthem very early, and I imagined that the whole camp would soon be waking up. In a short while, one of the fences came into clearer view. I kept crawling towards it and away from the nearest guard tower. I kept my eyes on the tower, but I didn't see anyone in it. I assumed they were asleep, like the guards I had just walked between. I tried to move in the direction opposite the dawn light, and I just kept crawling until I reached the fence.

The bottom of the fence lay on top of the hard ground, supported by poles about every 10 feet. I was almost sure that it wasn't electrified, but I was still wary. It looked like it was made of very heavy-duty chicken wire. I moved one finger very close to it, without touching it, but I was still afraid and drew it back. Then I picked up a small rock and touched it to the wires. I didn't hear the sound of electricity, so I took the chance of touching it gingerly with my finger. To my relief, nothing happened. I immediately tried lifting the bottom of the fence, but it squeaked alarmingly, so I stopped. The dawn light seemed to be dimming, I noticed now. A small part of my racing brain stopped to wonder why it might be getting darker instead of lighter, but the bulk of my focus remained on the fence. Here I was, on the verge of being free! My excitement mounted, and I knew I had to hurry.

I sat for a minute or two, took a few deep breaths, looked around, and decided to lift the fence again. I lay down on my back, head next to the fence, and started lifting the bottom wire with both arms. Very slowly, I got the fence just high enough that I could scoot my forehead under. Next, I wriggled my neck and shoulders through. When the fence was just a few inches below my chest, I needed to reposition my fingers and arms, so I let the wire come to rest on top of my body. I tried to adjust myself as best I could, but when I moved my torso, the wire sliced into the skin below my right pectoral muscles. The pain seared through to the bone. I resisted the urge to cry out, slowly lifted the fence from my flesh, and kept moving. I repeated the same maneuver when the fence reached my stomach, and again I cut myself with the wire. Eventually, my whole body was through, and I found myself on the other side of the fence. I turned around, flat on the ground, and looked back into the camp to see if I could spot anyone moving. There were no signs of life, not even a sound. There was only the sound of my heart.

Thrilled but terrified, I turned and began to crawl again. Eventually, it became impossible to ignore the fact that it was almost completely dark now. I stopped for a minute to gather my thoughts and reorient myself. Flat on my back, staring at the stars, I finally figured it out: it wasn't the dawn at all. I had escaped by the light of the moon, and that moon was now setting behind some rocky mountains. Then, by luck, I spotted the morning star: I was heading east. I remembered the *joondi*, seemingly a lifetime ago, telling me that we were in Tindouf, on the far western border of Algeria. Therefore, the only safe direction for me to travel was west, toward the Moroccan border.

Before starting out in earnest, I stripped off my clothes and buried them under some rocks, just in case they sent people out looking for a prisoner. Now I was completely naked and it was cold, so it was time to get moving. I got up and started to jog slowly northward. I would have to pass the camp on my left before I could turn west and strike out for the border. After a little while, I noticed the mountains in the distance again, and I knew Morocco was not far from where I was. Now it was getting lighter quickly, with the leading edge of the light just appearing over the horizon. I turned, put the light of the dawn at my back, and ran toward the mountains in the west.

As I ran, I kept my mouth closed and tried to breathe only through my nose. This is one way to limit the amount of moisture your body loses in the desert, but it also limits how fast you can breathe and run. When I became too winded to run, I switched to walking, still maintaining as fast a pace as I could manage in my weakened state. At that time I didn't have any plan in my mind beyond just walking and walking as long as I could. I started to see daylight and accelerated my pace; I had to get as far possible from the camp before they realized I was gone.

They had almost never come to my cell in the morning, but who knew what terrible urges the guard might have that morning. If he came looking for me, they would see I was gone. By this time I could see the sun rising in earnest, so I kept watch behind me as well as ahead. I did not stop, even for a minute. The mountains, my singular goal, filled the entire horizon. If I were to have any chance of surviving the heat of the sun and not being discovered, I simply had to reach them. I could hide myself in a cave or crevice there, out of view of any pursuers and out of reach of the sun's rays until late afternoon. By then I would have regained my strength, and the sun would not be as hot. I knew I only had two hours or so before the sun would unleash its best, and at that point the ground could easily burn my bare feet. For the moment, though, I could swear my feet themselves were happy to finally walk without limits, as if they had a mind of their own. They carried me forward over the rough, dry ground, one in front of the other.

Thoughts flickered through my mind about what I might do if I actually succeeded in surviving beyond these first few hours of freedom. I knew that once I reached the mountains, I would still have to cross them. I was headed towards Morocco, but how would I know when I had crossed the border? I would feel safe, I thought, when I saw a town, a flag, or people. Then I would know I was on Moroccan soil. But how would I face people naked? I chose not to dwell on these thoughts. I had not even made it to the foothills yet.

Donkey Heart Monkey Mind

Two of the most dangerous things in the Sahara are dehydration and sand storms. The sooner I got out of the open, the better. But by this point I had to stop and rest from time to time. There was no shade anywhere. All around was a vast rocky landscape, dreary and desolate. After walking awhile longer, I started to feel the heat of the sun on my skin. It was still morning, but I was out in full view, with no protection. I covered my mouth with my hand to conserve as much moisture as I could and decided I would not stop until I reached the protection of the mountains. For a moment I thought of the shirt I could have kept and used to protect my head, but it was too late for regrets.

I arrived at the foothills of the mountains at midday. Exhausted, I was tempted by the sight of a rock to sit and rest. But as soon as the stone touched my naked buttocks, it burned. I leaped. The ground was hot, the rocks were hot. Where would I sit down? I looked back in the direction from which I had come and couldn't see anything except the haze of the heat on the horizon. I was truly in the middle of nowhere. Despite my isolation, despite the heat, despite the gravity of my situation, I was elated. Just hours ago I was in a military prison, my whole world a stone cell and a wooden bed, my own body the plaything of bored, sadistic men.

Now I was all by myself, beyond the walls, beyond the guards. I didn't know what to do with the happiness I felt. There was no one to share it with except the desert and the rocks. So I started screaming as loud as I could. I jumped up and down, and even though it was very hot, I rolled around on the ground. I wanted to share my joy with the ground, if no one else. I didn't stop to think about all the energy I was wasting and the fact that I had no water or food to keep my strength. I felt I had all the energy I needed just from being free.

Djaffar Chetouane

After I exhausted all my happiness and calmed down, I looked around. The mountains were not terribly high, but there were no trees or water sources to be seen. The entire range was rocky, red, and brown. Finally I found a large, overhanging rock where I could sit down and rest. I eventually began to doze, and then to dream. I was riding on a brown horse through a cool forest. There was no one around me. I saw a pond. Dismounting to take a drink, I lowered my head to the surface of the water—but as soon as I tasted it, I woke up. My mouth and lips were parched. I yearned for the scene in the dream to be real.

Looking out from my shelter under the rock, I found myself looking at one of the most beautiful sunsets I had ever seen. It reminded me of the time I had spent in Egypt. The sky was purple above me, the rocks of the mountains were thrown into sharp, burning relief, and I sat in a sea of red. As the sun set behind the mountain, it reassured me of my westward direction and my goal. So I sat there enjoying the sunset for a while, feeling a little saliva forming in my mouth and my strength beginning to return. There was not a single living thing around me, and no one was looking for me. I was alone in a vast region of rocks.

My next realization was that I was very hungry. I looked down at my gurgling stomach and saw for the first time how red it was from being cut on the fence and how dirty from my rolling around on the ground. The cut just below my chest was still bleeding a little. I could see my ribs sticking out of my skin, and I touched my face and felt how bony it was. It made me shiver with fear and trepidation. How would I make it over a mountain range in this state? But I had to remain calm, remind myself that I was still alive, and that all this would be solved in a matter of time. Maybe I could even catch and eat some creature while I walked,

Donkey Heart Monkey Mind

though I had not yet seen a single living thing.

The next step was to start looking for the easiest route through the mountains. I started out northwest up the foothills, scouting around. This stretch of the mountains ran from north to south and lay entirely in Algerian territory, I remembered from a geography class long ago. I kept walking and walking until I found myself in the heart of the mountains. It started to get dark and I couldn't see more than a few meters ahead. So I sat down for a little while until I happened to look around behind me, and I saw the biggest moon I had ever seen. It wasn't full, but it was huge, hanging right above the mountains on the horizon. It seemed close enough to touch. I sat there for a little while enjoying the view, planning to use the moon to light my way when it got high enough. If I kept walking through the night, I reassured myself, I should be in Morocco by morning. Most people who have never lived in a desert do not realize how cold it can get at night, but I knew a chill was coming—another reason to keep moving. Soon the moon was high enough to provide adequate light, so I set out again. The reality of being in the mountains alone was not comforting, despite the fact that I was still relishing my newfound freedom.

I walked long into the night before I realized how much my feet were hurting from treading over the rocks. I did not know that my feet were bleeding until I stopped to rest. I looked down and saw that they were covered in cuts. The blood was flowing freely enough that I was sure I was leaving bloody footprints. Despite the pain in my feet and through my exhaustion, the view of the mountains excited me. I hadn't seen such beauty in such a long time.

I finally decided to try to fall asleep for a little while, so I simply dropped in my tracks, out in the open. I don't know how long I slept before an unfamiliar noise woke me up. I could tell it was an animal but not one I recognized right away. No animal had yet shown itself to me, but I knew there must be some. I had no idea whether it was a large animal or small, aggressive or harmless. Was it something I could catch, or might it have a much better chance of catching me, especially considering how weak I was? I didn't hear the sound again. Still, I decided to get up and start walking again. I had never before been attacked by an animal, whether wild or domestic, though I had been near wild ones many times in my life.

My grandmother taught her grandchildren respect for animals, saying that all of them, even humans, are connected, and that how you treat one animal will determine how other animals treat you. If you treat them well, you will not be in any danger, but if you fail to respect an animal, you will eventually be attacked by it or another one. As far as I knew, I had yet to offend any creature in these mountains, but the precariousness of my situation was becoming ever clearer. I had no weapon, not even the thin defense of clothes or shoes, and my strength would continue to wane if I didn't find food or water. There were also other human animals to worry about. Who knew who might patrol the mountain range somewhere? If I were lucky, they would be Moroccan, but they might still be military, and there was no way to know how they might deal with me. I had to get to the other side of the mountains and find a village—before anyone found me.

I continued moving and searched continually with my eyes to see if I could spot the animal I had heard. My feet still ached and burned, but not with the intensity of the previous evening. By then it was getting a little light, and I confirmed that it was the dawn behind me this time. I also saw the moon still lit in front of me. Finally, as it became completely light, I began to be able to see that the mountains were coming to an end, though I couldn't tell what might be beyond them. My feet were hurting more and more. Then a vast area of sand came into view in the distance. I sat down and rested my feet while I thought about what to do next. From the look of the sand, it wasn't a good idea to walk over it under the full sun. I could see the heat reflecting off the sand and knew I would be cooked in no time. But staying in the mountains would not get me anywhere. I decided to continue walking until I reached the very edge of the mountains and decide from there. When I arrived and could see the steep, jagged foothills I would eventually have to descend and then the dunes stretching into the distance, I decided to stay exactly where I was.

Again I stopped for a moment to enjoy the view of the desert, and again the sight of natural beauty—unbounded by cruel walls—lifted my spirits. The very next moment, however, I started to wonder how in the world I would cross all that sand in all that heat with no water. I found a place to hide from the sun and thought about what to do next. Suddenly, it seemed perfectly clear that there was only one thing I could do: I started crying like a baby. I don't know where my body found the moisture to produce all those tears, but I was too scared, weak, and lonely to control it. All I could see behind me was rocks, and all I could see ahead was sand. What was I doing? What was going to become of me?

Still, I had no energy or water to waste, so I finally wiped my face and just stared out at the view in front of me. And in just a few minutes, I discovered what I believed was the source of the noise that had awakened me before dawn. A fox appeared, standing and staring at me. I hadn't suspected that foxes actually lived in that harsh environment, but there it was, eyes steadily on me, creeping curiously forward. What joy I felt looking at that animal! I was sure it wouldn't harm me, and it was the first living creature I had seen since setting off on my desolate journey. I started laughing and calling it to come closer. As I spoke, the fox stopped. It was about 25 meters away, and it sat down calmly and did not move. I relished looking at it—this beautiful animal, company to talk to—and the fox in turn did not take its eyes off of me. I was sure I was safe with this creature; in fact, it seemed to me that the fox was assuring me that I would be all right. Immediately, I began to feel more confident.

I sat there with my friend until I could feel the heat subsiding. The sun was in front of me now, so it was time to get up and start walking again. To my amazement, as I got up, so did the fox. I stared at it for a moment and then spoke again.

"Are you waiting for me to die so you can have a feast all to yourself?" I asked. The fox didn't respond. It just stood there staring at me.

I asked the fox if it was male or female. It didn't answer, of course, but it turned sideways, almost as if to let me have a better look. I think I wanted it to be a female. According to my grandmother, females of any species do not harm you unless you provoke them or threaten their young. I couldn't see any evidence to the contrary, so I decided my friend was female.

"Hello girl," I said. "Would you like to accompany me?"

Still, no answer.

"Well, I will have to give you a name, but I'm not sure what it should be. Would you like that?"

Silence.

I turned away and began my descent down the mountainside and, amazingly, the fox followed. She kept her distance, but she accompanied me the whole time as I walked and watched the sunset. Even when there was too little light left to see her anymore,

Donkey Heart Monkey Mind

I still felt her behind me, and her companionship gave me courage to begin the next stage of my trek. I finally reached the foothills of the mountains, and I began to feel more sand with every step. Silently thanking the fox for keeping me company, I pointed myself north-northwest and entered the desert again.

The sand felt much better on my ragged feet than the rocks. Still, I was loath to leave the mountains entirely, because they had at least offered some kind of shelter. So I trudged along, following the contour of the foothills for as long as I could. But by the time night had fallen completely and the moon was high in the sky, I noticed that the mountain range began veering off to the northeast. On my right, eastward, was another enormous moon and the mountains, perhaps even my fox friend, while on my left, to the west, lay only sand dunes. I could not risk heading east, however, because that would take me back into the territory of my captors. So I walked northward. I must be in Morocco now, I reasoned, searching my memory for details of the mountains' relationship to the border. Still, even if I had managed to recall any details, there was nothing around me to tell me whether or not I was on the right track. There was just sand, sand, and more sand ahead, and the mountains fading ever farther into the distance on my right. The dawn was approaching and there was no shelter to seek, even if I had the energy or will to look for it. Finally I was so exhausted I sat down right where I was and fell asleep.

As soon as the sun hit my face I woke up, famished and dehydrated. I imagined the fox appearing and just giving herself to me so I could eat her. But I saw no fox, nor any other living creature. What I did see, to my excitement, was a fence. It was a very low fence, consisting of only a few wires, off in the distance to the west. In just a few minutes it was before me. Here must be the

Djaffar Chetouane

Moroccan border, at last. I climbed over the fence and immediately spotted a sign that made my heart pound. It said that this was a minefield, that crossing here was illegal, and that the Moroccan government hereby warned all trespassers away. Why would they have minefields here? I asked myself. Who crossed here in the middle of nowhere often enough to necessitate such a sign? I just stood there for a time, considering this new information.

I eventually concluded that this must be a place where smugglers cross and that, most importantly, there were probably no mines. It would be a typical North African military move, to concoct such a lie in order to scare people. There might, however, be real Moroccan military personnel not too far from here, on the lookout for traffickers. Still, I was naked, half-starved, and wretched with scabs and scars. If the military spotted me they were unlikely to accuse me of criminal activity. I could only hope they would understand my situation.

Back at the fence, I realized I had no idea what a mine might look like, nor what I should do if I saw one. (Thanks to the soldiers who popped out of the ground in Egypt the year before, I was still blissfully ignorant about landmines.) Even though I thought it unlikely that there really were any there, I still remained watchful as I inched forward. I did know enough to understand that if I stepped on a mine it would be the end of me. To think of having managed to escape, coming all this way into the desert, and dying by stepping on a mine! It wasn't much consolation, but at least it would be quick. If it were my destiny to die that way, so be it, I kept telling myself, even as my eyes scanned the ground for mines and the horizon for the Moroccan military. I continued walking north-northwest, until the fence was out of sight and the mountains began to disappear into the horizon. Of course, by the time midday arrived, it was so hot that I wished I might see someone, even a Moroccan military officer, if it meant I would have some water. I tried to stop to rest but realized that the sand was too hot for that to be an option. So I once again closed my mouth, concentrated on breathing through my nose, and continued walking at a slow pace.

Much to my relief, the landscape was beginning to change. I came upon an area that was not very sandy, with some small rocks and even a cactus tree in the distance. The presence of the cactus meant water, so I headed straight for it. The tree was a good size, even casting a bit of shade. I pried off some thorns, sat down, and rested my back against the shady side. My feet burned, and I was desperately thirsty and weary beyond anything I had ever known. I dug a small hole and realized the sand was much cooler just below the surface, so I stuck my feet in the hole. My plan was to stay there until the sun went down and then continue my walk during the night. Before I knew it, I had fallen asleep.

I woke up in the early evening, again immediately aware of my hunger and thirst. I scraped at the cactus with one of the thorns I had taken off earlier. A white, milky liquid oozed out. I didn't know if it was safe to drink, so I rubbed a small amount of it on my lips, just to get them a little wet. It tasted very bitter, but it was satisfying to feel even a tiny bit of moisture on my mouth. I decided to begin moving again. The landscape started to change again. There were more and more cacti, as well as some other trees in the distance. Since it was once again nighttime, I was a bit cold, and that kept me walking. Each time I passed a cactus I would scrape out some of the milky liquid and wet my lips. My entire third night since my escape passed in this manner. I trudged forward, garnering the tiniest bit of relief from each plant, hoping that I wasn't mistakenly passing by a town in the darkness.

Djaffar Chetouane

As morning drew near, I started scouting for a sheltered place where I could sleep. Again, there was nothing in my vicinity. I used the first light of dawn to look as far as I could into the distance in the hope of spotting a town, but I saw nothing. No town, no people, and no water. The landscape changed once more, becoming hilly. Now I couldn't see anything at all around me, my view blocked as it was by hills and boulders. For the first time, I felt completely lost. I knew I was done with sandy dunes, and where there are hills there are usually people, but how many more days might pass before I found them? How many more days would I last without food or proper water? Loneliness and despair eventually overcame me again, and I sat down and started to cry. Only the fear of dehydrating myself further forced me to control my tears. Who knew how much farther each of those precious drops of tears might have taken me?

I slept under a tall tree with very few lower branches. I woke up at the end of the day in great pain; for the first time my stomach was twisting and cramping from hunger. The landscape, once again, renewed my hope. I could see mountains very close by, and I was sure that I would bump into people in a short while. I decided to start walking right away, rather than wait for the sun to set further. The only advantage of walking in the dark, aside from protection from the heat, was that I would be able to see the lights of a village from a distance, but the dark also meant I couldn't navigate as well. So I continued walking until night fell completely, and then I stopped and spent the night next to a big rock.

It was the next day—my fifth day after escaping from my cell—that rescue finally appeared. I had set out towards the mountains again, and at midday, I spotted a camel caravan on the horizon. I was so overjoyed that I was suddenly filled with enough energy to run. The caravan was heading in the opposite direction, so I knew I had to get to them before they disappeared out of sight. My life depended on my reaching them, so I ran as fast as I could.

Though camels can run quite fast, caravans normally travel at a walk, so even in my pitiful condition I was able to gain on them. By the time I drew close, I could tell that one of the men had seen me and alerted the others. They halted their camels, and I stopped as well. For a moment, I had forgotten that I was naked; when I remembered I was immediately embarrassed. I picked up a rock to cover my genitals, out of respect, and I headed towards them slowly, keeping my distance and waving at them.

One of the men was looking in his bags, and he pulled out something brown. He walked towards me, holding the object in his hand, and as he got close to me he unfolded the *djellaba* and handed it to me. I put it on immediately.

The man looked at me amazed and asked, "What are you doing here, young man?" He spoke in Moroccan Arabic. He was dark skinned, short, and wearing a *djellaba* that looked exactly like the one he had handed me. Having run all that way to catch up with them, it was quite awhile before I could catch my breath enough to answer him.

"I'm an Algerian. I just escaped from a military prison, and I've been alone for five days. Could I please have some water? I'm dying of thirst." My speech was labored and my voice was creaky as I tried to clear my throat. Naturally, I was severely dehydrated, my throat was parched, and I felt the skin of my face cracking as I spoke.

"Bring some water, quickly," he called to his friends, gesturing to me to come with him and join them. Another man produced water in a small leather bag that felt cold to the touch. I drank a small amount and took a break to breathe.

Djaffar Chetouane

"Have some more. Drink more. You need it," the man insisted.

He continued to urge me to drink until I had emptied the small bag. Just as I finished the last drop, it came right back out of my eye as a tear of joy; I felt a relief that transcended mere words. I couldn't believe it. I was so happy to finally drink water.

"What's your name?" he asked.

"I'm Jafar," I answered. By then my breathing had slowed down, and I even had a smile on my face. Of course the smile only confirmed how dehydrated I was; it hurt my cheeks. I continued, "Thank you so much for your help. I needed the water so badly, and I apologize for running at you like I did. I didn't have a choice."

"Did you say you escaped from a prison?" asked the man that gave me the *djellaba*.

"Yes, I did, but please don't think that I've done anything wrong. In fact I didn't at all."

"Then why were you in prison?"

Before I could answer, one of them said, "You must be hungry. Aren't you?"

"Yes, I am very hungry," I responded.

By this time all the men had dismounted from their camels, and the camels had settled down on the ground to rest. One of the men went to his mount, dug through his things, and came back with a bag full of food. He opened it and laid the food out on a small cloth on the ground.

He said, "Please eat all you want. I'm so sorry for what happened to you. We hope you don't mind us asking you questions."

"Thank you so much. I don't mind you asking at all. I promise I'll answer all your questions," I said, sitting down and starting to eat eagerly. There was dried meat, homemade bread, camel milk, and couscous mixed with many vegetables. They watched me without saying a word.

"Where are you heading?" one of them finally asked me.

"I have no idea where I am or where I'm going," I responded, still eating. "I was just running away and hoping to get to a town."

"Naked," one of them interjected. They all began to laugh, and I laughed with them.

"You were not lucky enough. You could have been greeted by a woman instead of us," another man said.

They started to laugh even louder, and I continued to only smile along with them, since I couldn't really laugh yet. We all thought it was very funny though.

I asked, "How far is the nearest town?"

"Not that far at all," one of them answered. "It would take you about a day to get to Ait Ben Haddou. People there are very nice. You'll be treated like family."

"Are you from Ait Ben Haddou?" I asked them.

"No, we're from Tislit. We are traveling merchants," said the man who had first greeted me.

"Would you please point me in the right direction?" I asked eagerly.

"Well, it would take you about a day to get there on foot, but I wouldn't recommend it in your state. Besides, you will not make it there before dark. We can loan you our horse if you promise to give it back to a friend of ours. That friend will gladly help you, and you could even stay with him for a few days while recuperating."

"I don't really need a horse if it would only take a day to get there. Besides, how would you get your horse back?"

"It would take you less than half the time on the horse. Besides, the horse knows the way. It can get pretty hot around here;

Djaffar Chetouane

I think you should use the horse. We're not worried about getting him back. You made it this far all by yourself, and we don't think you would steal the horse."

"Don't you need the horse with you?"

"We have the horse in case we need to catch something. Sometimes we hunt, and we use the horse to bring in our catch faster."

Having no further arguments to offer, I said with a smile, "I need pants to ride the horse. I can't do it in a *djellaba.*" They all smiled in response and agreed with me. One of them went digging through his bags and came back with billowing white pants. There was no need to worry about them fitting, because they were the kind of traditional Arabic pants that have an enormous waist that you tie with a drawstring. The man also handed me a shirt to replace the *djellaba* and a pair of sandals that looked like they had been locally made. When I had dressed myself again (this time hiding behind a camel to be more modest) and given back the *djellaba,* I turned around to thank them, but I couldn't find words that could possibly express my profound appreciation for their kindness. As I tried to think of something, tears started coming down my cheeks.

"I don't know how to thank you," I said, wiping my eyes.

"You don't have to thank us. It is our duty to help those in need," one of them said, patting me on the shoulder.

"I will never forget your help and generosity."

"Where are you from, anyway?" another man asked.

"I'm from Tizi-Ouzou. I'm a Berber."

To my amazement, they started talking to me in their Berber dialect, *Tashelhiyt.* They were *Chleuh,* a Berber ethnic group that lives mainly in Morocco's Atlas Mountains and Souss Valley (I came to know later that part of this area is a UNESCO Biosphere Reserve).

Donkey Heart Monkey Mind

The Moroccan Berber dialect is a bit different from mine, but I could still understand what they were saying. Of all the people I could have bumped into, I thought to myself, I bumped into my own.

"Were you in prison for political reasons?" one asked.

"Yes, I was." At that moment, I felt sorry that I had ever been involved in politics. If I hadn't been, I would never have been in the situation in which I now found myself, however monumentally improved it had become.

"We understand what you've been through," said another.

"When you get to Ait Ben Haddou, make sure you ask to see Omar. Everybody knows him. He makes pottery. Anyone you ask will tell you how to find him," said the man who first greeted me.

"Just tell him I sent you. Tell him Ali sent you," he went on. It was the first time I had heard his name.

"I want to kiss you all goodbye," I said.

"Come here. Start with me," Ali said.

I kissed each one of them on the cheeks four times. Then I mounted the horse and they all mounted their camels, covering their noses and mouths with light scarves to keep the sand out. I started out in the direction they told me to follow, looking back over and over again to watch them leave. I counted the 11 men who had saved me. Then I counted 11 camels, plus the horse they had loaned me. As I was leaving, I thought to myself, "Eleven is now my lucky number. I will think of the number 11 for as long as I live."

The horse knew the way to Ait Ben Haddou without any input from me. The entire trip was through rocky hills and over a sandy landscape that looked very much like the sea that had dried there millions of years ago. I thought almost constantly about the dream of the horse and the cool pool that I had on my first day as a free man in the mountains—my dream had come true. Was it a dream or was it a vision? I wondered. The sun was getting ready to set when I spotted the town in the distance. My first thought as I drew closer was how beautiful it was. In the evening light, the entire town looked like a single, ornate, reddish-hued castle. It was built of clay, as are most desert towns, a warren of walls, square buildings, and rectangular turrets piled up a hillside. All the houses are connected, with small alleyways in between them. I asked the first person I came across where I would find Omar, the man who makes pottery. The young man directed me straight to Omar's house.

As I dismounted from the horse when I arrived at the house, I felt pain all through my hips from riding for hours on top of so many days of walking. I had to stretch my legs and my lower back before I could actually walk, and I could still feel the pain as I walked towards the door. I knocked on it, and a very young girl opened the door for me.

Smiling, she asked, "What do you need, mister?"
The girl had a darkish complexion and long, braided hair. She wore a beautiful multi-colored dress and a very large necklace (too large for her I thought) that may have belonged to her mother. Her feet were bare.

"I came to see Omar. Ali sent me."

Right away, she invited me to come in, without consulting her parents. Life must be so peaceful, I thought, in a place where a girl of nine or ten can invite a strange man into the house without fear.

"What's your name?" I asked.

"My name is Houria," she responded. (Houria means "liberty" in Arabic.)

"I have a sister named Houria as well," I told her. We entered the courtyard, and I asked, "Are your parents home?"

"Baba, Baba, there is a man here to see you!" she called

loudly in *Tashelhiyt*. I immediately knew they were also Berbers.

A man emerged from one of the living quarters and greeted me, smiling.

"*Mss lkir*," the man said.

"*Mss lkir fllawen*," I responded. "Are you Omar?"

"Yes, that's me," he answered.

"Ali told me to come and see you to return his horse. It is outside." I spoke in my dialect.

"Ali asked you to return the horse to me? Why? And where are you from? You don't sound like you are from here." Omar directed me outside to see the horse. "We need to put him in the barn," he continued.

"It's a long story. Ali and his friends saved my life."

"Are you not from here? You don't sound Moroccan."

"I'm Algerian. My name is Jafar, and I'm a Kabyle from Tizi-Ouzou."

"What brought you here, and how have you come to have Ali's horse?"

"As I said, it's a long story."

"Well, I would love to hear your story, but first, let me take care of the horse," Omar said. "Please follow me."

Omar was in his forties. He had a moustache and black hair salted liberally with gray. I could tell he was a little confused and curious to hear what I had to tell him. Still, he didn't stop smiling at me. After we put the horse in the barn, Omar suggested that I wash my hands and join his family for dinner, after which I was invited to spend the night there. We went back into the house, where he introduced me to his wife, Malika, and his two younger daughters, Sabiha and Noura.

He directed me to the bathroom, gave me some handmade

soap and a towel, and said, "You have good timing. My wife is preparing a lamb dinner tonight. We don't eat lamb every day, and I'm very excited. Hurry and wash up so you can come and join us."

"Ali said that you would take care of me like family, just as you are doing," I said gratefully.

"Anyone who enters this house becomes a family member, no exception," he answered, with complete sincerity.

He truly displayed what I call North African hospitality. North Africans can be generous enough to give you their eyes if you need them. I washed my hands and forearms, my face, and my feet. It had been months since I had seen that much water. I used as little as possible, because water in that region is not abundant, and every drop gave me back my sense of life. It was like a dream to escape from prison and find myself suddenly in a house with a beautiful Moroccan Berber family, about to eat one of my favorite meals, with a bed waiting for me at the end of the night.

As I was drying my face I saw a small mirror hanging on the wall next to the door. I looked at it for a few moments, debating whether or not to pick it up. It was a small hand mirror, about six inches long by four inches wide, with a green plastic frame. At first, I hesitated, but I finally picked it up slowly and turned it towards my face. I only caught a glimpse of maybe a quarter of my image before I put my hand down again suddenly. I had seen what looked like a skeleton with skin stretched across it. I touched my face with my other hand to confirm that it was still my own. Then I brought the mirror up to my face with my eyes closed. As I opened them slowly, I couldn't believe what I saw: I looked like a dead person walking. My face looked so different that I had the sensation it wasn't mine. But it did look like me. I couldn't deny it was me. I put the mirror down again and began crying in sorrow and disbelief. One of Omar's girls peeked in at me and went right back to where the family was waiting.

I was washing my face once again when Omar came in and asked, "Are you okay, Jafar?"

"I just cannot believe what I just saw," I responded.

"What did you see?"

"My face," I answered, still full of sorrow and disbelief.

Omar looked at my watery eyes and said, "You are here now. There is no need to cry. Everything will pass." He patted me on my shoulder and continued, "Come on now, dinner is waiting. Don't worry about a thing."

When we walked in the whole family was seated around a fire, waiting for me. The lamb smelled delicious. Malika stood next to the gas stove, checking the couscous steaming on top of the lamb sauce with her fingers to see if it was ready. The three daughters were sitting quietly in a row, and Omar sat cross legged on a Berber carpet, poking the fire.

"*Mss lkir fllawen,*" I greeted the family.

"Welcome, welcome. Sit down, Jafar," Malika said.

"Thank you," I said.

I sat down between Omar and his daughters. I put my hands on Houria's head and smiled.

"What brought you here, and how did you meet Ali?" Omar said, eager to hear my story, "If you don't mind me asking."

"Well, I didn't tell Ali much about myself when I bumped into him in the middle of nowhere, but I think I now have time to tell you how I came to know him," I said. The entire family had their eyes fixed on me. Malika stopped checking the couscous, the three girls were attentive, as if ready for a bedtime story, and Omar got comfortable in his seat. I, on the other hand, had my eyes fixed on the couscous. I was feeling thrilled to have my first real dinner in such a long time.

Before we touched any of the food, I had told them the entire story. I related the circumstances of my arrest, my imprisonment, the way I was treated and tortured, and my escape. I told them everything that had led me to their doorstep. While I was telling them of my adventure, they completely forgot to eat. My words were their nourishment. Malika did not even check the couscous. The only move she made after I started talking was to turn the stove off.

"*Subhan Allah* (By the grace of God)," said Omar, when I had finished.

We sat silently for quite some time, until Omar remembered dinner and said to his wife, "I think it's time to eat now. Make sure you serve Jafar the biggest piece in that pot. I want him to eat until he can't stand up, even if you have to give him my portion."

"Thank you so much Omar, but I'm already imposing and I'm certainly not eating your serving," I said.

"No, you will not get up until I tell you to. You will not stop eating until I tell you to. And you will not say 'no' to me at all. My house is yours for as long as you want; my family is your family. And speaking of family, does yours know where you are?"

"No, my family does not know a thing about me. They don't even know whether I'm still alive or not," I responded.

"Tomorrow I will accompany you to the post office so you can call your family."

"I don't think I want to call them just yet. I will wait until the time is right."

"Your mother must be worried to death! I think you

should call her," Malika said, as she spooned the couscous and lamb into pottery bowls. "I'm a mother, and I know how it feels. You should call your mother."

"I must wait at least a few days until I get to Spain, then I'll call her," I responded, but I thanked her for her kind words.

"You're headed to Spain?" Omar asked.

"Yes, I have to get away, as far as I can from Algeria," I answered, and he could see my anger towards my country on my face.

Dinner was served: couscous with red sauce, full of garbanzo beans, carrots and green beans, with chunks of perfectly cooked, tender lamb. The first spoonful seemed to pause in midair, en route to my mouth. I was so happy just looking at it.

"Eat, eat." Omar insisted.

We all ate quietly, just like my family at home, back when my father was still alive. Most Arabic peoples, and also Berbers, do not speak while eating; it is considered disrespectful to the food that God gives us. So we ate the whole dinner in silence, looking at each other and smiling. After a few spoonfuls I couldn't continue. My stomach had clearly shrunk from being fed so little for so long.

"You have to eat more," Omar pressed.

"I really can't," I replied. "I'm very full."

"When was the last time you ate?" Malika asked.

"The last time I ate a full meal? I really couldn't tell you."

"I should have made you a soup. It would've helped loosen up your stomach."

"That would have been a good idea," said Omar.

"Don't worry about it. I'm so happy. I ate all I could, so please don't worry."

"Wait awhile, and then you must have some more."

Djaffar Chetouane

We sat there for a while talking, and I ate a few more spoonfuls. As much as I appreciated the food, I really relished drinking all the water I could. Soon my shriveled stomach could hold no more. I was so stuffed I couldn't stand up, just as Omar had wanted. By then it was about nine o'clock, and Omar asked his wife to make up a bed for me.

"I haven't seen a real bed in months," I said.

"Tonight you will sleep in my house. You are my guest, and I want you to feel comfortable," Omar said with a smile.

As soon as I lay down on the bed, I felt tremendous relief. I felt safe for the first time in recent memory, and I knew I would sleep very comfortably. Not surprisingly I couldn't fall asleep for quite a while. Everything that had happened over the last months came rushing back into my mind. I saw images of my imprisonment, and I saw the image that had faced me earlier in the mirror in the bathroom. Then finally I dozed off and slept like a baby.

The next day when I woke, early in the morning, I felt an urgent pain in my abdomen. At first, I couldn't understand why, but I quickly realized that my bladder needed to be emptied. This feeling of having drunk enough liquid to have a bladder full to bursting was another sensation that was new again. I hurried to the bathroom. My urethra burned terribly as I urinated, and I tried to remember the last time I had actually done this. I realized that I had not urinated for the last five days, since there had simply been nothing in my body. My first few bowel movements would also be extraordinarily painful because of the injuries I had suffered in prison. These were only two of many ways in which I began to understand that escaping from that cell was not simply a matter of physically removing myself; its cruelties and humiliations were indelibly marked on my body and in my mind.

Donkey Heart Monkey Mind

Exhausted by the effort of emptying my bladder, I went back to bed. When I heard noises in the kitchen, I got up, intending to go in, but I first stopped to reexamine my face and head in the mirror in the bathroom. I had two scars on my head, a scar between my eyes, and very short hair growing from my scalp. Fortunately this time my appearance was less shocking. The sumptuous meal and comfortable bed had done me an enormous amount of good. I walked into the kitchen looking well rested.

Omar greeted me and said, "I heard you speaking while you were sleeping last night, but I couldn't make out what you were saying."

"Was I?" I asked.

No one had ever told me that I talked in my sleep before; Omar would become the first to hear the sleep-talking that would last for more than two years. I would talk, walk, toss, and yell in my sleep. However, I was never more upset by these nocturnal activities than when I was told of this night that they apparently began.

"Well, today is a brand new day and a brand new life," Malika said, serving me tea and fresh fried bread. Like any good host, she had baked for her guest, and I thanked her for her kindness. Omar very much wished for me to stay with them awhile longer before trying to make my way to Spain, but I was reluctant to impose on this wonderful family any longer. He asked me whether I had any money to take a bus to a border city, but of course I didn't even own the clothes in which I had arrived, much less any money with which to travel. A general plan to hitchhike to Spain had been forming in my mind since the time I had met the camel caravan.

"It would take you forever to get to Spain hitchhiking," Omar said. "I will buy you a bus ticket to Tangier."

Djaffar Chetouane

"You absolutely don't have to do that."

"Well, stay and rest with us for a couple days, and if you want, we can go to the station today and ask when the next bus to Fes will be. You can get a bus to Tangier from Fes. But I will pay for the bus ticket."

I had no idea how to thank Omar. I assured him that I would do my best to pay him back someday, and that if I did not manage to personally, someone or something would return the kindness he had shown me.

"That's not what you should worry about right now," Omar responded, shaking his head. "There is something else you need to consider." He explained to me that every major road in Morocco had military checkpoints, and he asked what I would do if I were stopped and asked for my papers. I was aghast. We didn't have such things in Algeria, and it hadn't even occurred to me. Still, I promised Omar I would think of something when the time came, and I was sure I would. After all, I had made it this far.

I spent two more days with Omar's family. Then he bought me a bus ticket through Fes to Mallatcha, near Melilla, a smaller, less crowded city than Tangier, from which I thought I was less likely to get caught trying to cross into Spanish territory. The ticket cost Omar more than a whole day's earnings, for which I felt terrible, but he insisted. It was wonderful to spend time with such a generous, kind, and caring family. They shared everything with me. Omar showed me around, introduced me to his friends, and even took me to his shop and showed me how he made his pottery. He also took me to the Kasbah, a fortified old town on the other side of the river, and told me that many American movies were filmed at the site. (Later I learned that the Kasbah of Ait Ben Haddou has been a UNESCO World Heritage Site since 1987.)

Donkey Heart Monkey Mind

Before I departed, I asked Omar for a final three items: a white *djellaba*, a *shashiya* (a traditional Islamic prayer cap), and a Koran. Naturally, he was curious as to why I would ask for these things, so I explained my plan. I would wear this traditional religious garb and read the Koran aloud on the bus the whole way to Melilla. Omar acknowledged that it was a very clever idea. In the Muslim world, it is considered so impolite to interrupt someone who is praying that even the military might not bother me.

"I have no doubt in my mind that you will succeed in your life, and that no one will stop you. After going through what you have and coming up with an idea like this one, I'm sure you will be fine. I have all that you asked for at home."

On the day of my departure I embraced Omar's family before I got to the bus. It took a day and a half to get to the outskirts of Melilla. Over the course of the trip, we were stopped at about five military roadblocks. At each stop, soldiers boarded the bus and asked a few passengers for their papers. But not me. My plan seemed to be working. I looked devoutly Muslim in my *djellaba* and *shashiya*, and the book of God in my hands. I read the Koran aloud—not too loud—but loud enough for others to hear me and make no mistake that I was reading the Koran. Even the other passengers did not speak a word to me. (Nowadays, I think a person who looked so utterly Muslim might be the first one the military would ask for identification.)

After I got off the bus in Mallatcha, I walked to Melilla. I crossed the border easily, as if I were simply walking into another town. As soon as I found myself in Spanish territory (which includes two cities on the North African coast), I walked into a residential neighborhood and found some clothes on a drying rack in an alley. Although I felt terrible for stealing again, I exchanged what I was wearing for some of the clothes on the rack and hurriedly put on the new ones. The day was coming to an end, and it was time for me to think of what to do next.

BRIAN

      After I put on the jeans and t-shirt from the rack, I looked totally different—no longer like a Muslim but like a European. As I walked through the city, my brain wouldn't stop working even for a second on what to do for food and shelter. I finally decided to go to the police department and tell them that I had lost all my belongings. From my previous travels in Spain, I knew about charities that provided help to homeless people. But before I could go to one of them, I had to come up with some sort of identification. To do that, I had to go to a police station, and I knew my prospects would be best if I looked as European as possible.

      I decided to go to the beach and see what I could come up with. My first look at the ocean was like nothing I could describe. There is perhaps nothing more diametrically opposed to a small concrete cell than the infinite stretch of the rolling ocean. I inhaled the smell of the water and felt it fill me with happiness. Then, as I strolled along the beach, I saw a few North African youths hanging around, laughing together. I approached the group and told them that I needed a drink and didn't have any money. They immediately recognized that I was Algerian and reached into their pockets to give me money. They gave as though they had a lot of money, but they can't have had much to spare. They clearly felt sorry for me and wanted to help. In all, they gave me enough for a meal—though that was definitely not what I had planned to do with the money.

I went back to town and bought a clip-on earring and a razor. Back at the beach I shaved most of my head, leaving only some hair in the shape of a crucifix, to look more like a European youth. I put on the earring, tore my jeans a bit, got myself wet, and headed to the police station.

I arrived at the police station and declared that I was a French citizen whose belongings had been stolen by a bunch of North Africans while I had been swimming at the beach. I felt terrible saying that, especially after just being helped by North Africans. Unfortunately I had very few options at this point so, inside my head, I asked for their forgiveness. With no trouble at all, the police typed up a report that showed the false name I gave them (François Gilbert, a very typical French name), a Paris address (that of my father's cousin's restaurant, as nearly as I could remember it), and a picture they took at the station. After I had the paper in my hands, the female officer who had taken my report admonished me, stressing that I would need that document to get back to France and therefore must not lose it. Since she seemed sympathetic, I decided to ask her for further help. She wrote down the address of a Catholic charity, and I was on my way.

On the way to the charity, I thought about how easy it had been to get a document that would eventually help me cross to mainland Spain by boat, and how fortunate I was. A moment ago

Donkey Heart Monkey Mind

I had only been able to think as far as finding a place to sleep and eat, but I left the police station with more ideas than I'd had going in. When I got to the address the police officer had given me, they welcomed me and spoke to me in broken French.

"We are sorry about what happened to you here," a nun with a soft voice said to me gently. She was wearing a dress that covered her whole body and a scarf that covered her head (just like a Muslim woman, I thought).

"Could you help me find a place to sleep for the night and maybe some food?" I asked.

"That will not be a problem," she answered.

"I would greatly appreciate anything you can do for me."

"Where are you from in France?" she asked.

"I'm from Paris, but my parents live in Lyon," I responded, making up the story on the spot.

"How will you get back to France?"

"I have no idea at the moment."

"Well, for tonight we will give you a voucher, and you can go to this small hotel. They will feed you and give you a bed for the night. It is where we send people when they need help. You will be among other people there. It's not a regular hotel with your own room. You understand, right?" she said with a smile.

"Of course I do, and I thank you very much."

"Tomorrow you must come back here and we'll try to figure out a way for you to get back to France."

"I just need to cross into Spain. I can hitchhike the rest of the way. How much do you think a ticket will cost?"

"We'll figure out something tomorrow. For now, go and have a good night's sleep."

"Thank you so much. You're very kind," I said, gratefully.

Djaffar Chetouane

The place where she sent me was a shelter for home-less people. I gave the voucher from the nun to the man at the reception desk, and he directed me to an eating area and assigned me a bed among a dozen or so others. During the night, I lay there recalling everything that I had gone through up to that very moment. I thought of how fortune seemed to have been embracing me throughout my journey and reasoned that I mustn't do anything that would jeopardize my luck. I also thought with some regret of the clothes I had stolen in that small alley. Ironically, I felt worst about stealing just at the time in my life when it might have been considered most excusable.

The next morning I woke up feeling ready to face the crossing to mainland Spain. The thought that my false identity might be exposed and I might be captured made me nervous, but my resolve was also bolstered by the idea of making it to my destination. After eating the breakfast I was offered, I went back to the Catholic charity. The nun welcomed me with great news.

"We can help you buy a ticket to Malaga. The boat is leaving at about seven this evening," she said with a smile on her face. "All you have to do is go to the ferry building, tell the cashier you were sent by us, give them your name, and they will provide you with a ticket. Everything is taken care of."

I was amazed at how quickly she had found such a perfect solution for me, to the point that I couldn't believe it when I first heard it. I wasn't going to be stuck in Melilla, waiting to be dis-covered, casting about for an escape plan. Even more wonderfully, before I left, the nun gave me vouchers to purchase food at a local grocery store for my trip back "home," to France. Those grocery store vouchers were like gold. I bought three ham sandwiches, a large bottle of Coke, and plenty of fruit. Fruit! I couldn't stop eating it, and each piece gave me tremendous joy. Bananas were my favorites, and I had six of them that day.

I spent the entire day walking around town, thinking about what to do once I got to Malaga. Each phase of my escape had been fraught with peril, and the danger was far from over. I was free from my prison, yes, but where was I going to go? I needed to get as far as I could from Algeria, but every border I crossed meant security checks and scrutiny of my identity. And how would I eat? How would I live from here on out? Doing something illegal increased my chances of getting caught and deported back home. But I couldn't just depend on charity. Still, the kindness I had encountered so far gave me hope. At that moment, my only choice was to get on the boat to Spain and hope for the best. So I continued walking around town, killing time, and all of the marvelous fruit was eaten long before I got to the docks.

I made sure I gave myself plenty of time to be on the boat that evening. There was a police checkpoint to pass through before boarding, though, and there I hesitated. A Moroccan officer might recognize that my accent was North African, not French. So I got in line in front of the officer who looked the most Spanish to me. When I got to him, I presented the police report with my picture on it, and to my surprise he didn't say a word about it. *"Buen viaje,"* he said simply, wishing me a good trip.

I boarded the boat feeling a bit shaky. There were sleeper cabins on the boat, but my ticket, of course, was one of the cheaper ones that only reserved a seat. I was completely happy with it, though, because all I wanted to do was spend the entire night outside on the deck smelling the ocean. I even slept in a corner on the deck for a short while, not caring how cold it was. The ocean air smelled like freedom rising right up from the bottom of the sea. Imagine, I thought, just a few days earlier I was in the desert, desperate for water, and now here I was on board a ship. Here was all the water I could need for the rest of my life, and all the water for the rest of everything that breathes on this planet. From one extreme to another extreme, I thought, from imprisonment to freedom, from sadness to happiness, from feeling practically dead to feeling utterly alive, from Africa to Europe. It gave me the feeling that nothing could stop me for the rest of my journey, no matter where I might be headed.

The next morning I disembarked onto the streets of Malaga. Right away, I started hitchhiking towards Barcelona. My first night in Spain was spent on the beach in Almeria, and my second in a youth hostel in Valencia, paid for by money from the very kind man who gave me a ride there. At the end of the following day, I found myself once again in one of the most beautiful cities in Europe: Barcelona. I had exactly enough money left to pay for a bed in a youth hostel and not a penny more.

It was here in Barcelona that I finally called my family. The last time my mother had seen me or heard from me was November 16, 1988, nearly seven months before. When she found out it was me on the phone, she fainted, and I had to wait several minutes while my sisters used perfume to wake her up. Tears came to my eyes as I heard the voices of my family members. To my dismay, by the time my mother was revived, I was almost out of change. I had to limit myself to telling her where I was, that I was okay, and not to worry about me. I could only promise to call again soon.

It was also in Barcelona, at that youth hostel, that my reluctance to tempt karma by stealing anything wavered. Sitting in the lobby, I saw the many tourists coming and going, friends laughing together, and people drinking beer at the bar and eating

Donkey Heart Monkey Mind

dinner. I, on the other hand, had no friends, no money, and no food in my belly. The thought of stealing wouldn't leave my head; I was jealous, sorry for myself, and sad that I was alone. I watched a young man around my age take his wallet out of his pants pocket and pay for a drink at the bar, and I decided it just wasn't fair. I had been burned, beaten, and subjected to innumerable humiliations, plus I had walked across a desert to get here. Had this young man done more than I, to deserve his fat wallet? Why shouldn't I have some of what he had? Besides, it was harder to find help in big cities, I told myself. I was going to have to steal in order to survive.

I watched that same young man, planning to let him get drunk and then do what I needed to do. When he finally went to the men's dorm, I found that his bed was only a few beds away from mine. I went to bed, too, and lay there for a while thinking about the sin I was about to commit. Praying for the gods to forgive me, I got up very slowly and went to the head of his bed, reaching for the small backpack in which I had seen him stow his belongings before he fell asleep. I picked up the bag very slowly, and before I knew it, it was in my hands. I immediately left the room and went to the bathroom. Fishing out his wallet, I helped myself to as much money as I thought I could take without him noticing, including a few larger bills in Spanish pesetas and some others I hadn't seen before: British pound notes.

Back in the room, I placed his bag carefully back where I had found it. Marveling at how easy it was and at the trusting nature of these "sons of Jesus," as we called Christians in Algeria, I went back to bed. For a moment I considered stealing money from the rest of the people in the room, but I knew it wasn't the right thing to do. I was acutely aware of the irony of going from being a vulnerable person helped by kind people, to stealing money from those that hadn't done me any harm.

I lay awake most of the rest of the night, pondering my choices from here. Settling down somewhere and finding a job was not an option, because I could only work in illegal jobs, increasing my chances of having a run-in with the police. I couldn't risk having any contact whatsoever with cops. In Europe, when they catch someone without legal documents, that person will be on the next flight back to his country of origin. For this same reason, I couldn't stay in Spain at all, especially Barcelona, because it is full of North Africans. Moroccans migrate to Spain as Algerians do to France and Tunisians do to Italy, and wherever there are illegal immigrants there are police officers on the lookout for them.

In fact, I couldn't stay anywhere in Europe for long. France, Spain, Belgium, the Netherlands, Scandinavia—all these places would have authorities on the lookout for illegal immigrants. In addition, I wouldn't always have money for a room, and I couldn't risk wandering the streets and sleeping outdoors. I needed to be inside at night to avoid being picked up. Finally, I had to appear well dressed and decent, in order to avoid catching anyone's eye. I had no choice but to keep stealing in order to be able to keep moving, stay inconspicuous, stay free, and stay sane. And I absolutely could not, under any circumstances, get caught. This would be easily accomplished in youth hostels. What else could I have done? I felt sorry for those who would come my way. Again, I asked the gods to forgive me and to understand my plight. I figured I had gotten this far, so they must have understood. How else could I have been this lucky if the angels were not near me? I must have had someone's forgiveness.

When I woke up the next morning from a fitful few hours of sleep, there didn't seem to be any problem in the hostel. No one had reported any theft, so I left there and went straight to a mall. I bought myself a small backpack, a new set of clothes, and a pair of sunglasses as a disguise. From there, I took a taxi to the outskirts of Barcelona and started hitchhiking along the coast towards France. After rides with several different drivers as far as Portbou, Spain, I walked overnight through woods across the border into Cerbere, France. Arriving at dawn, I bought a train ticket from there to Toulouse, where I settled myself into a youth hostel.

It was at this youth hostel that I met Brian, one of the most important people I would ever meet in my life. I first encountered him in the hostel's cafeteria, and I was sizing him up as my next mark. He was heavily built, bearded, and wearing a hat with a Canadian flag that he had sewed onto it himself. Recognizing the flag on the hat, I said hello to him in French. He greeted me in return in Canadian French. (At the time, my experience of the world was limited enough that I didn't even know there were also Canadians who spoke English.)

"How are you doing?" I asked.

"I'm a little tired from the train ride I just took from Madrid," he responded. "How are you?"

When he asked me how I was doing, I felt a knife of sadness stab into my stomach. Something about that commonplace phrase coming from this man made it sound like he actually cared how I might be doing. For some reason, without knowing him at all, I was inclined to answer honestly.

"To tell you the truth, I'm not well at all," I answered.

Brian offered to buy me a drink, and when I said that I didn't drink alcohol or coffee, he got up to get me a Coke at the bar. As he stood, he had to hitch his pants up over his ample buttocks. As he left, I wondered if I could still consider robbing him in the night. His kindness caught me off guard. As he sat down, he said, "I sense that you're going through a lot. I would love to hear your story."

Once again I was surprised by a person's sincerity, so I deflected it. "At this very moment I'm fine, sitting here having a conversation with you. I'm fine now," I said.

"But you weren't."

"How could you tell?" I asked.

"I could see it in your face," he responded.

"What else could you see?" I asked, hoping that he might be able to see my thoughts. If he could tell that he was going to be my next robbery victim, maybe he would run away, and then I wouldn't even be tempted. I knew he didn't deserve to have his money stolen.

"I see that you're a smart guy," he answered.

"Out of all the answers you could choose, you chose to say that. Why?" I asked, surprised again.

"Because that's how I feel. Since you sat down here, your eyes haven't stopped checking everything around you. You seem to be in alert mode."

"Well, to be honest—" I stopped for a minute, hesitating to explain, unsure whether or not I should. "To be honest, I am on alert. Very much so."

"Why?"

"It's a long story."

"Well, tell me about it."

So, inexplicably and wonderfully, I did. I told him everything that had happened to me from the day I was arrested in class in Algeria. I told him of my imprisonment, my torture, my escape, and the astonishing kindness I had encountered along the way. However, I did leave out one thing: I didn't confess to him that I had started stealing in Barcelona and that I had been thinking of doing the same to him.

Yet I wanted very much to tell Brian the complete story. He seemed so honest, and I felt terrible for even thinking about making him my next victim. The thought came to my mind to ask him for help directly. Before I could do that, though, I had to find out more about him.

"This really happened to you?" he asked.

"Well, you tell me. You trust your instincts, don't you?" I responded.

"I believe you, but it's just so unlikely to actually meet someone who has gone through what you have. I've never actually met anyone from a third world country."

I wanted to change the subject and hear about Canada, about the whole continent, in fact. I had only barely set foot in the Americas once, and I wanted to know what else I had missed by not managing to stay there.

"Tell me about your country," I invited, eagerly.

"My country is nothing like yours," he said. "We have a democratic government." He went on, telling me all about Canada. I got to hear about Canadians' social lives, their political system, their economy, and even their cold winter weather. Then he told me about the United States and Mexico, patiently answering all the questions I asked as best he could. A very talkative person, he didn't mind keeping me company and teaching me things. As we talked about the Americas, my mind started traveling there. I imagined how free I could feel there and how far I would be from the terror I had been through. But getting there was unimaginable. It was too far for me to aspire to.

"I know you probably need help, and I want to offer you

what I can," Brian said next, out of nowhere.

His words made me feel like my heart would bleed. I was deeply saddened, remembering again that I was about to steal from this person. Of course, I reminded myself, I hadn't actually done it, only thought about it, and it wasn't too late to change my mind. So I cleansed my thoughts and forgave myself for having had evil intentions, and I decided to truly share my thoughts with him.

"Can I be honest with you?" I asked.

"Please," he responded.

"You see, I don't deserve your help."

"Why?"

"Because I had an evil idea about you."

"Tell me about it," he urged.

"This may scare you, and it may end our friendship, but I must tell you. You deserve better and you need to know. But before I begin I would like you to try to understand my reasons."

"What is it?" he insisted.

"I had planned to steal money from you tonight while you slept." The words came out of my mouth then without hesitation.

Brian simply said, "I understand."

"Is that all you have to say?" I replied.

"Suppose I weren't a nice guy," he said. "Suppose I didn't have a kind heart, suppose I didn't offer my help. What would you do then?" he asked.

"I would try to steal from you," I answered.

"That is my point exactly. If I didn't offer, you would try to steal, and since I offered, you told me about it. That makes you an honest person," he replied.

"I'm sorry for it," I said. "It was just a thought. I would never do anything like that to someone like you."

Donkey Heart Monkey Mind

"Well, believe me, I do understand. In fact, I wouldn't mind being in your shoes for a minute."

"Oh no, you don't want to be me. Trust me," I said.

"Yes, I do. I want to experience your kind of adventure. Not many people can say they escaped from prison."

"Not many people would want to go to prison just so they could experience an adventure."

"Yes I understand that, but to be you is to be full of life."

"How is that?" I asked.

"Life is even better when you earn it yourself," he said.

"You can earn it, but you don't have to be in prison for life to be better."

"I do know that, but you didn't go to prison because you wanted to. You were sent there against your will, and you escaped on your own. That's what makes life more interesting. You took a big risk and won."

"I had to take the risk," I replied.

"Not everyone is strong enough to take a risk like you."

I started to understand that Brian was intentionally encouraging me. He was trying to lift my spirits. He was also sincere in saying he wanted to experience an adventure. I gathered from what he told me about his life in Canada that he was brought up in a safe and secure environment. Coming to Europe was his first time ever leaving his country. He was my age and he was anxious to experience some harshness in his life, because he believed that he would then be able to truly own his life and appreciate it more fully.

We continued talking until past midnight. I forgot all about the fact that I hadn't slept much the night before. I didn't feel tired at all. Meeting and talking to such a wonderful person went a long way towards easing the loneliness and desperation I had been feeling for so long. That same loneliness might be facing me again in the near future, but for now I savored our conversation.

The next morning, Brian insisted on buying me a train ticket to Paris. It was his last destination before going home to Montreal. We picked up our bags and headed to the train station, where Brian purchased two tickets directly there. On the train, he started asking me about my plans in Paris, but of course I really didn't have any. My plans consisted simply of keeping moving and not getting detained anywhere. Paris was not a safe city for me, I explained to him, because there are too many Algerians and the police are always on the lookout for those of us who don't have proper documents.

"So, I think you're a clever man," Brian began after a while. He paused for a few seconds before continuing. "I would like to help you, but you have to come up with a plan for how I can. I believe there is something you are going to need more than you will need money."

"What do you mean? What kind of something?" I asked, confused.

"Isn't there something else you need, besides money, to help you get to a place where you'll be safe and you can start your life all over again?"

"Getting out of Europe would be the best thing for me to do. But how can I do that without a passport?"

"That's what I'm talking about," he said firmly. "You have to come up with a plan, and I'll try to help you."

"Well, I really have to think about this very hard," I said.

The truth was I really didn't need to think very hard at all. I was simply surprised at Brian's offer. I had already done the same thing that he was suggesting once before, in Melilla. It was a matter of taking on a false identity: this time, Brian's. After thinking about the details for a while, imagining how I might leave Europe and where I might go, I explained to Brian how I thought it could work. He thought the plan was brilliant.

In Paris, we finalized our scheme and said our goodbyes, promising to see each other again. He then left on a shuttle to catch his flight to Montreal. Our promise to find each other again was more mine than his, and such promises between friends made on the road are easily broken. But I was no casual college traveler in Europe, nor was my promise a casual one. It could be a matter of life and death for me to get out of Europe. (Thankfully, I would be very much alive when I saw Brian again a year later.)

ACROSS THE ATLANTIC

I had found new hope. I had made a real friend, which meant I no longer had to feel alone in my new situation. I was in Paris, a city full of beauty and possibility, and I had in my pocket five thousand French francs that Brian had given me (as if he owed me any more kindness). What's more, I hardly needed that kind of money in Paris. Plenty of relatives and people from my village lived there. I could easily find a place to sleep and eat, because I had rendered numerous favors to various people here in the past, and they would welcome me with open arms. Before deciding where to go and who to see, however, I had to call my family.

My brother Brahim picked up. Apparently I had created a terrible mess when I called from Barcelona. My family's phone was bugged, and the government had been listening. Military police descended on my family's home to question everyone, including my mother and sisters. As if this kind of treatment at the hands of the police were not bad enough, the family was then subjected to the judgment of the entire village. In a small community, it takes all of a few hours for every relative and friend to know that the police have shown up at a family's house and grilled everyone about the whereabouts of their son. It brought shame upon my mother and only added to her fear for my life and the safety of the rest of her family.

Brahim told me firmly not to call again. After I hung up with him, I had to sit and think for a few minutes. Suddenly, all the doors had closed again. I knew I couldn't go see anyone and couldn't call in any favors. The Algerian government knew I was in Europe, they would be looking for me, and Paris was a good place for them to start. I didn't even have any identification to present to a hotel or a youth hostel, because the false French identity papers that had gotten me into Spain would be useless in France itself. I spent the next three nights sleeping huddled in a bush on the *Champs de Mars*, right next to the Eiffel Tower. Eventually, I had no choice but to get moving again.

Now I was even more grateful for the money Brian had given me. I bought a train ticket north to Lille, where I spent the night at a youth hostel. There, I gave quiet thanks for another favor Brian had done for me; I gave the youth hostel Brian's name and date of birth, which he had given me permission to use, and this got me a youth hostel identification card. The next day, I hitchhiked to Toufflers, a small town near Belgium, and crossed the border on foot, avoiding checkpoints. From there I continued walking to Nechin, another small Belgian town, and finally bought a train ticket to Brussels.

At a youth hostel in Brussels, I had another tremendous stroke of luck. It was there that I met a young woman from Kentucky named Sarah. She was with a group of other teenagers traveling through Europe on vacation. Anxious to practice her French,

Donkey Heart Monkey Mind

she approached me and said hello, explaining that she wanted to make new friends with whom to practice her language skills. We sat at a kitchen table in the hostel and talked for a while. My mind started to race when Sarah showed me her home state on a map. She was the first American girl I had ever met, and listening to her describe her home country filled my mind again with the possibility of actually living there. I had been there once already, only too briefly, and I had never forgotten it.

Sarah and I talked comfortably for a long time, even having dinner together. She didn't want to stop talking, and I didn't want to stop asking her questions about the United States. I wanted to dream. I also asked her questions about Canada, though she couldn't tell me much about it other than to say that going to Toronto was just like visiting another American state. Incidentally, she mentioned that crossing the border to Canada only required a driver's license, and that stuck in my head. It meant that crossing into the U.S. from Canada was the same. No passport required. When she said that, I started dreaming in earnest.

When I said goodbye to Sarah the next day, she wrote down her Kentucky address and phone number for me on a piece of paper. I then got on my first bus in Europe, to Amsterdam. The whole way there, I couldn't stop staring at the piece of paper. I kept imagining myself in America, and my enthusiasm continued to flourish. I already knew I couldn't stay anywhere in Europe for long. Might I actually be able to make it to the United States?

I had never been to Amsterdam, and it contained quite a surprise for me: Marijuana. I had never even heard of the drug before. In Algeria, people smoked hashish, but the effects seemed quite different; the hashish smokers I had seen yelled and screamed at each other. In contrast, at the youth hostel—which happened to be in the heart of the café district (as well as the red light district)—groups of youth sat around smoking outside, quiet and spacey. The café system struck me as one of the strangest things I had ever seen in my life, where people sat and smoked drugs out in the open. Of course one of the first things that occurred to me was that Amsterdam would be an excellent place for me to lay low for a while. I could subsist for quite some time on small amounts of money picked up from those too high to notice. And no matter where I went from here, whether the United States or another place in Europe, I needed to amass a fair amount of money.

I stayed in Amsterdam for a few days, stealing from everyone I could. As before, I followed the same principle of never totally cleaning anyone out, but I took money from a lot of people every night in the youth hostel. At the same time, I was exploring the possibilities of leaving Europe. I just needed enough money to sustain me for a few months, but I was using a lot of the money that I stole to eat. I was eating all kinds of food: meats, vegetables, fruits, cheese, and bread, making up for months of deprivation. I spent much time and money during the day just eating food, still trying to gain my strength back. When I decided I had been in this one place long enough, my next stop was Hamburg, Germany. Then came a small German town called Harrislee, and from there I crossed by foot to Padborg, Denmark. From there I purchased a train ticket to Copenhagen.

When I arrived in Copenhagen, I decided I finally had enough money to put the next phase of my plan into action. Basically, I was going to do the same thing I did in Melilla, only this time I would be impersonating someone who actually existed. Brian had given me all of his information, most of which I memorized, and some of which I had written down. I had his name, date of birth, passport number, father's name, mother's maiden name, his address, and his phone number. The plan was that if anyone asked any questions, as long as I gave Brian a heads up, he would pretend to be his father on the phone. I called Brian when I got there, letting him know I was going ahead with my idea, and the next day I went straight to a police station.

"Someone has stolen all my belongings, and I have lost my papers," I said to the woman officer they found to translate for me.

"How did you lose them?" she asked.

"I was in Tivoli taking pictures, and my bag disappeared. It had all my papers in it."

"It happens all the time over there. Many tourists like you come here and say the same thing," she assured me.

I had chosen to say that I lost my papers in Tivoli because I had seen so many North African pickpockets at work there. It is an excellent place for those who steal money, passports, and cameras.

"What do I do now?" I asked her.

"Well, since you lost your passport, we'll take down your information and submit it to the Canadian Embassy. They'll tell you what to do next," she answered.

True to her word, she copied down all of my (Brian's) information as I gave it to her, and then she told me to wait until she heard back from the Embassy. About an hour later, she summoned me back to her desk.

"Your Embassy has verified all the information. They even called your father and informed him of your situation," she said. Brian must have played his part well. She went on, "If you wish to stay in Europe, the Embassy wants you to go over there so they can issue you another passport. But if you wish to leave Europe and go back home, we can just attach your picture to this document that your Embassy faxed us. You can use it to go back home. It's written in French, Danish, and English."

"Can I see the document?" I asked.

"Of course."

I looked it over, not really reading it in my excitement. I simply scanned the French words, since they were the only ones I understood anyway.

"I don't have much money to stay in Europe," I said to her, trying to look sad instead of thrilled, "so I'd better go back home."

"Maybe you should call your father so he can buy you a ticket," she suggested.

"I will most definitely do that."

"Okay. Come with me and I will take your picture and staple it to this document. Then you'll be on your way," she said.

She led me to a side room with a camera and took my picture. In just a few minutes, two pictures emerged from the camera.

"Here, take this other one. I only need one," she said, handing me the second picture.

I walked out of the police station and called Brian right away. That day was my happiest since the day I wriggled out from under the fence around the Algerian prison compound. With a new identity, a Canadian one no less, all things were open to me. I went back to the youth hostel to start planning more seriously. Could I really get into Canada with just this piece of paper? I sat down on the edge of my bed and put my head in my hands. Immediately the memory of sitting at the edge of my wooden bed in prison came rushing back, but I pushed it from my mind and concentrated on the task at hand. I didn't speak French with a Canadian accent, nor did I look particularly Canadian. If I were stopped at immigration, it would be the end of my journey in more ways than one.

Donkey Heart Monkey Mind

Then Sarah from Kentucky came to my mind. I picked up the piece of paper with her address on it and stared at it for a while. I asked myself whether or not I could really get into the U.S. with only my new documentation. Yet it was all there: Brian's officially recorded information, my picture, the logo of the Canadian Embassy, and the stamp the police had placed over my picture. It was a legal document. Why wouldn't it work?

The next day I went to the Scandinavian Airlines office to find out how much a ticket to Montreal would cost, just to explore the possibilities. The ticket agent explained that I would have to connect either through Chicago or New York. I turned these options over in my mind. Having already been in New York City once, I decided to try my luck with Chicago. When the agent told me the cost of the ticket, however, I found that I didn't have enough. I asked him to hold the reservation for me anyway, and I left.

Back to the youth hostel I went. As soon as I saw my chance, I stole a camera, a nice Nikon with a zoom lens. At a camera shop the next day, I showed the owner my papers, explaining that I needed to sell the camera to get money to go home. He was happy to oblige by taking it off my hands in exchange for 1,000 Danish kroner. Now with more than enough money in my pocket, I headed straight back to the Scandinavian Airlines office and purchased my ticket to Montreal via Chicago. The departure date was set for the next day, July 8, 1989.

I arrived at the airport in Copenhagen very early, even though I didn't have any bags to check. Checking in and heading for immigration, I held my breath and presented the document with my picture on it. In no time at all I found myself at the gate, and a few hours later, I was in the air on my way to Chicago, absolutely astounded. I couldn't believe I had pulled it off. If all went well at U.S. immigration, I thought to myself, I would finally be in a land far from home, where I could start thinking about my life instead of thinking about who to steal from next. Naturally, I was very sorry about all the people I had stolen from, and I already planned to make it up somehow. I knew I couldn't repay them directly, but I could make it up in kindness to others. It is never too late to do good things for those who are in need, as so many people had done for me over the last several weeks.

To say I was very nervous when I landed in Chicago would be an extreme understatement indeed. Proceeding to the immigration officer, I presented my document and told him I was Canadian. He asked me something I didn't understand. Taking a guess, I said, "French," and he understood.

He picked up a receiver, and soon the inevitable female translator appeared.

"Are you Canadian?" she asked.

"Yes, I am. I'm from Montreal," I answered, doing my best to imitate Brian's accent.

"Did you lose your passport in Copenhagen?"

"Someone stole all my belongings, and I'm headed back home."

"Do you have your ticket to Montreal?" she asked.

I showed her my airline ticket to Montreal and she handed it to the Immigration and Naturalization Service officer (also known as the INS). They spoke briefly, and then she turned around and said, "Your flight will leave in about four hours. Do you need help finding your plane? You have to go to a different terminal."

"If you can just point the way for me, I'll find it myself. Besides, I have four hours."

Donkey Heart Monkey Mind

The officer stamped my paper, and the lady walked me out to direct me towards the terminal for the flight to Montreal.

As soon as I was out of her sight, I started looking for the fastest way out of the airport and into Chicago. I stopped momentarily at a trash can to dispose of every shred of paperwork I had on me, including my plane ticket and the false identity documents. I immediately regretted my actions, wondering what I would do if someone asked me for ID, but my mind was overwhelmed with fear that someone might apprehend me and realize that I was not Canadian. I had concluded the papers were evidence of the fraud I had just perpetrated. Utterly elated and, at the same time, nervous to the point of paranoia, I set off into the United States for the second time in my life.

I saw arrows pointing to the train to Chicago. Stopping at a currency exchange window, I got $23 and some change for my leftover Danish kroner. I didn't speak a single word of English, but I was determined to get out of the airport and into the crowded city before I could get caught. When the train arrived in downtown Chicago, I was dismayed to find it full of buildings but utterly devoid of people. (I didn't understand this until many months later, when I learned that the financial district of an American city was no place to find crowds to blend into on a weekend.)

By now I only had a few dollars left on me. When a homeless person asked me for money, I gave him two dollars and tried to ask him to help me make a phone call. Unfortunately, we couldn't communicate at all. I continued walking, and I finally spotted a police officer. I summoned up all the courage I had and tried to look as calm as possible, then showed him my youth hostel card and asked him to direct me to such a place. Somehow he understood me, and after radioing in a question to headquarters, he wrote down an address and a telephone number and did his best to tell me how to get there.

Much to my relief, there was a young man at the hostel who spoke French. He was tremendously helpful, including calling the home of my one American friend, Sarah, for me. Sarah's mother picked up, and the young man translated. She didn't know who I was at first, but when she realized that I was a friend of her daughter, she invited me to visit her. With nowhere else to go, it didn't faze me a bit that I was in Chicago and she was in a tiny town in Kentucky. The fellow at the youth hostel explained that the Amtrak train could carry me to Kentucky—and being Algerian means knowing how to ride a train without paying for a ticket.

The following Monday evening, I got onto a train that would stop in Fulton, Kentucky, planning to hitchhike the remaining 120 miles or so to Hanson. A few minutes after the train departed, I sought out the ticket collector and told him that my ticket had been taken from my seat while I was in the bathroom. I didn't really speak any more English than I had when I had arrived in Chicago two days earlier, but the man at the youth hostel had given me a book with a few basic phrases in French and English for tourists. I picked and chose from them and made myself under-stood. The ticket collector put a temporary pass on top of my seat and told me the train would arrive in Fulton at 4:30 a.m. It was that simple.

Although Fulton is several times the size of Hanson, it is still very small. You can imagine how unusual a lost Algerian youth must have looked disembarking in a small Kentucky town at dawn. I was still quite thin, and my tight black curls were still just growing in over my scarred scalp. With no idea how to get to Hanson, I simply started walking through Fulton. To my dismay, a police officer soon stopped me and asked where I was going. I quickly pulled out the youth hostel card that proclaimed my Canadian identity and showed it to him, trying to tell him I only spoke French. Not understanding anything he said to me, I then pulled out the piece of paper with Sarah's address on it and said something like, "Me go here."

The officer examined the address and started talking into his radio, and fear shot through me. I froze when he gestured for me to get into his car. I needn't have worried, but I had no way of knowing that. The officer had actually called Sarah's mother, who must have confirmed that she knew who I was, and then he explained to me with simple words and gestures that he was going to drop me off on the road to Hanson. He pulled over on the side of the rural highway a few minutes later and then took the time to show me my route on a map, write down the names of the towns I would have to pass through, and point me in the right direction.

I had hitchhiked all the way to Hanson by the end of the day. There, a car salesman at a local dealership was kind enough to call Sarah for me. In a show of hospitality much like that of Omar's family in Ait Ben Haddou, Morocco, Sarah's mom picked me up from the car dealership and took me straight to her home. Already my English was improving, and I understood when Sarah's mom explained that her daughter was at summer school in a different town, and that we would go visit her in a day or two. In the meantime, I was invited to stay for as long as I liked.

Over the next eight days, I recuperated from my long journey in the heart of rural Kentucky. Their house was nestled in the countryside like nothing I had ever seen before, covered in clean grass and dotted with horses. I was introduced to Sarah's brother, who had long blonde hair and loved rock and roll music. A typical American teenager, he listened to music all day long. I helped Sarah's mom mow the back lawn, and she drove me to Sarah's summer school to visit her. She fed me, helped me practice my English, and even allowed me to call my mother several times (and never once asked me to pay the bill that must have been several hundred dollars by the time I left).

I had explained that I wanted to try to settle in a big city, but I knew my limited English would in turn limit my options. When her daughter told her I spoke Spanish, Sarah's mom suggested Los Angeles. The following week, she bought me a Greyhound ticket in Fulton, and off I went toward the "City of Angels." Through St. Louis, across to Tulsa, Albuquerque, Flagstaff and Riverside, then finally to Los Angeles, I marveled at my new country through bus windows for the next two days and nights.

When I arrived, Los Angeles struck me as very different from the city I had seen in movies and heard so much about. The downtown streets were very bumpy and dirty. I remember gesturing to the driver of the bus when we got to the terminal and asking him if this were indeed L.A. My English was still only 12 days old, and I couldn't really ask a full question, but I remember pronouncing only the words "Los Angeles" and asking the rest of the question with my hands. The driver was frustrated at my persistence when he didn't understand me, and he was irritated that I was blocking the aisle for the passengers behind me trying to get off the bus. He shouted at me, and though I didn't understand enough English to know exactly what he said, I know it was something like, "Get off my bus! Of course this is L.A!" His tone of voice still rings in my ears. I was definitely not in Kentucky anymore, so to speak.

I started walking the streets of the city. There was no beach to be seen and no Hollywood, not even the famous Hollywood sign. The moment I left the bus terminal, people started asking me for money, and others followed me and talked at me continuously. I did not understand a word they were saying, of course, so I just kept walking and walking. Here I was in a big city with skyscrapers and only $20 left in my pocket from the money Sarah's mom gave me before I left. I decided to simply keep my eye on the tall buildings I could see and keep walking towards them.

I eventually came upon a small park where people in suits and nice dresses were having lunch. The dirty streets seemed far behind me now. I sat down on a bench and had been there for a little while when a woman sat down next to me. She said hello, then opened a small plastic box and started eating her lunch. "*Bonne appétit,*" I said to her. She immediately replied, "Thank you." She was about my age, dressed in a dark blue skirt with high heels and a black jacket (that did not match her skirt, I thought to myself). I sat quietly and decided I would strike up a conversation with her after she finished her lunch. While she ate, we exchanged a few looks and smiles, and I figured she must be a bit curious about me.

When she finished her lunch, I asked her if she spoke French. To my surprise, she answered, "a little." I introduced myself and told her that I had just gotten into L.A. Then I explained that I did not know anything or anyone there and asked if she could direct me to the closest university. There, I might find someone who spoke French and could help me find a place to spend the night, since I did not have enough money to stay in a hotel. The woman's French was good enough for me to understand, and she was very helpful. Her name was Terry, and she asked me all the questions one might expect, such as where I was from, how I got to L.A., and so forth. We sat there chatting pleasantly, though I did most of the talking. After a while, she pulled out a piece of paper, wrote her phone number on it, and asked me to call her after 6 p.m.

Djaffar Chetouane

Terry went back to work, and I started walking down Figueroa Street towards the University of Southern California (or USC, for short). When I found the campus, I just wandered around and enjoyed the beauty of it until it was time to call Terry. She then came and met me and invited me to spend the night at her place in the campus dormitory. She had a studio, a very small one, she told me, but I could sleep there, and she would make a few phone calls to try to help me find a place where I could stay for a few more nights. The next morning, in response to Terry's inquiries, an older man came to pick me up and take me to his house, where he said a few other young men were staying. It turned out he was a Catholic priest, and as soon as we entered his house he asked me to make the sign of the cross over myself. This made me too uncomfortable, and I decided to leave right away. Heading back to USC, I called Terry, but she had already left for work.

I went to her building anyway and when I got in the elevator, another man came in just as the doors were closing. He was very outgoing and full of frenetic energy. I started up a conversation right away by asking him the usual question of whether he spoke French. He responded just as Terry had: "a little." His name was Jeff, and he was very curious about me. Finally, he asked me to follow him to the apartment he shared with two other men. We had a rather amusing conversation, with him asking me so many questions so fast I couldn't keep up, and then I, in turn, having to repeat my answers multiple times so that he could understand me. After a few minutes of this, he asked me to follow him again.

We went outside and then into a building where professors had their offices. There, Jeff introduced me to his French professor, a Belgian in his mid-forties named Alain. Alain helped translate and all three of us sat talking for a while. I told them my whole story, and both were fascinated and saddened. Ultimately, Jeff invited me to stay with him as long as I needed. This would give him a chance to practice his French, he said, and I could help him with his homework. Alain laughed and assured me that he would know if I were doing Jeff's homework for him. Jeff also told me that he would help me financially, and that I had nothing to worry about. He became one of my first real friends in America.

I stayed with Jeff for more than two months. He introduced me to many people, including his family, took me to many, many places, and paid for everything. The man was my angel. The most important person I met through Jeff, though, was an older Pilipina woman who worked for a Catholic charity. Unfortunately I cannot remember her name, but it was she who introduced me to the immigration lawyer who then guided me through the paperwork necessary to apply for United States residency. I also met a man by the name of Peter (my first male translator!), who acted as my interpreter during my Immigration and Naturalization Service interview on October 11, 1989. That very same day, I was granted my first work permit.

For a 15 year stretch, from 1989-2004, I didn't see a single member of my family. I did talk to them often, of course, racking up phone bills that became my biggest expense every month. Throughout that period, I never stopped thinking about my childhood, my adolescence, my adulthood, my pain, and my happiness. I kept these aspects of my past at the forefront of my mind and never let go, for fear of forgetting them. There was one thing I could not stop thinking about, however, which I did very much want to forget: my imprisonment. I relived it in terrible nightmares every single night.

During my first two years in America, by far the worst period in terms of nightmares, I was terrified of falling asleep. I dreamt the same dream over and over, again and again—about being raped. According to those around me, while I slept I screamed, I kicked, I sweated, I talked, and I would even sleepwalk. More than once I left the building and walked outside in my underwear. I have never remembered sleepwalking, but the thought of wandering around outside wearing hardly anything at all and frightening the neighbors embarrassed me deeply. Once I was spotted by a neighbor who had to run and wake up my girlfriend, and then the two of them grabbed me just as I was about to cross a busy street. That last episode convinced me that I had to do something about the nightmares and so, on the advice of my girlfriend, I reluctantly started seeing a psychiatrist.

Where I came from there was no such thing as "psychological help." In fact, I had never heard of anyone in Algeria that practiced psychology or psychiatry. The idea of telling a stranger everything about myself, especially being raped, frightened me terribly. How could I bring myself to talk to another human being about that horrific period of my life, the experiences that had not allowed me to sleep soundly for years?

Some part of me must have known what I needed, because after a few sessions with the therapist, my macho resistance broke down. Some therapists have a way of bringing out the best and the worst of a person, and this one certainly succeeded with me. He became the only person who knew the full extent of my suffering for more than seven years. After I had been thoroughly examined both mentally and physically, he suggested that I pursue a non-traditional method of getting rid of my nightmares. Because he felt I had an addictive personality, he didn't want to put me on a prescription drug. Instead, he suggested I try smoking marijuana. Because marijuana drastically impairs short-term memory and, according

Donkey Heart Monkey Mind

to him, dreams are the shortest-term memories, smoking marijuana should enable me to sleep with no problems and no dreams.

On the first night I tried marijuana, it was not a pleasant experience. It burned my eyes, dried out my throat and mouth, and muddled my thoughts. But the next morning, I realized that I really had slept like a baby, with no dreams whatsoever. I did it again the next day, and the same thing happened. So I continued smoking every day. My girlfriend then introduced me to one of the quintessential experiences of the American marijuana smoker: she took me to a Grateful Dead concert. There I saw all the people smoking the herb, dancing, singing, and selling all kinds of things outside. Every one of those people, who I later came to know as "hippies," seemed kind and happy. I was exceedingly attracted to their lifestyle, including the friendly atmosphere, the mellow high from the marijuana, and especially the music. Still, the most important aspect of smoking was that it relieved me of my nightmares, enabling me to finally sleep peacefully. I would smoke marijuana every day for the next ten years, and despite my therapist's best intentions, I had become addicted to it.

During those years I held a wide variety of jobs, and I stayed high while working at every single one of them. After having been employed as a busboy, a French teacher, and a salesperson at a pager company, I became a hair model. One day a hair stylist spotted the curls that had mercifully grown back, and in a gracious twist of fate, the hair I once feared might never return became a lucrative source of income. I made good money having people wash and style my hair, and I got a good (silent) laugh listening to salespeople tell potential customers that this product would make their hair look like mine. I became a limousine driver for a while and later I became successful at landscape design.

Djaffar Chetouane

In the summer of 1996, during President Bill Clinton's re-election campaign, I actually got to meet him in San Francisco. It was one of the happiest days of my life. I managed to get to pose for a picture with President Clinton, and I sent a copy home to my family. Not surprisingly, the picture was the major talk of our village. My brother even made money by selling copies of the print. It was also in that same year that I came to own my very first bicycle, a very rare object in Algeria when I was a kid. I began by biking all over the San Francisco Bay Area high on marijuana. Later, I would explore California, the West Coast, South America, Europe and Asia—still on a bicycle but not always high on the herb.

Every four months I would go to the INS office to renew my work permit, until finally I received my "Green Card" in the mail, on October 1, 1991. Because I had no proof whatsoever of my background, I had to write down my whole story for the INS on my first appointment on October 11th, 1989. Evidently that account—the precursor to this one—was sufficiently persuasive. Exactly five years after the date I received my Green Card, I applied for U.S. Citizenship. I was granted American citizenship on June 10, 1997. The very same day, citizenship certificate in hand, I applied for a passport and paid an extra fee to have it issued the following day, which was a Wednesday.

Wednesdays have always been significant for me, and I am a sentimental man. I was born on a Wednesday, according to my mother (although my birth was not registered until that Friday, because my father was nowhere to be found). I got my first Algerian passport on a Wednesday. I first left Algeria on a Wednesday. I was arrested on a Wednesday. I escaped from prison on a Wednesday. I received my first American work permit on a Wednesday and started my first American job, as a busboy at USC,

Donkey Heart Monkey Mind

on a Wednesday. Finally, the twentieth anniversary of my arrival in the United States was Wednesday, July 8, 2009. Wednesdays have been turning points in my life, so I always think of Wednesday as my special day of the week.

SECOND CHANCES

Meanwhile, as I was living week after week of a life in America that poor Algerians could only dream of, my country was being turned upside down politically, physically, socially and morally. Because I had been forced to flee, I narrowly missed being present for a period of civil war, martial law and terrorism that would turn Algeria into a killing field for more than a decade.

After President Chadli Bendjedid was re-elected in 1989, he announced reforms including privatizing government-owned enterprises, liberalizing the economy, and allowing the formation of political parties other than the ruling National Liberation Front (Front de Libération Nationale, or FLN). The president also allowed exiles—who had been erased from history books after independence was won from France—to return to Algeria. Sixty political parties were formed in a short time, and all wanted seats in the parliament. The Islamic Salvation Front (Front Islamique du Salut, or FIS) stood out as most likely to win a majority of parliamentary seats.

Two men played a major role in creating the FIS. Abassi Madani had studied Islam in Egypt and returned to become a university professor in Algiers. Second in command was Ali Belhadj, who had studied Islam in Tunisia and returned to become a junior high school teacher and a mosque preacher. Both held the title of "Islamic Science Professor," used for those who research and interpret the Koran. They founded the FIS to institute governance according to strict Islamic values and laws. Both FIS leaders drew many students, members of government, and mosque worshippers into their plan. Historically the Berbers have always been a more secularist people, however, and they reinterpreted the acronym, FIS, as standing for *"Fatima Interdit de Sortir,"* or "Fatima is not allowed to leave the house." If the FIS were in power, women would not be allowed to walk outside as before and would have had to cover themselves from head to toe.

Madani and Belhadj never seemed to have the interests of the country at heart. Instead they sought to exploit Algeria's resources and people as others had in the past. Nor did they deserve the title of Islamic science professors, because true scholars know that Islam does not preach violence. The Koran is a book of peace and discoveries, a book of harmony. And science should always include an invitation to other possibilities, other convincing evidence, and other findings; it should never call for dogmatic adherence to a set of absolute rules.

However, Madani and Belhadj had the support of hardcore Muslims. These supporters were men who thought they were well-versed in Islam; they enthusiastically fomented public discontent and recruited many followers, especially soldiers who had recently returned from helping the Taliban oust the Soviet Union from Afghanistan. In the early 1980s, a few thousand Algerians were trained in Pakistan; some went because they had nothing to lose by leaving Algeria and others were conservatives helping their brothers repel invasion by a communist country. After the Soviet-Afghan War ended in 1988, many of the Algerian fighters came home more fervently Muslim than ever—and found that the FLN governed over a fairly liberal Algerian Muslim society.

These soldiers who had been part of an international network of Islamic fundamentalists fighting a brutal guerilla war, suddenly found themselves in a peaceful (though impoverished) country. These soldiers weren't taken care of, weren't taught how to live as noncombatants, and they weren't given psychological help to ease their pains and memories of war. They were ignored, and the moral absolutism they had adopted in order to make sense of their bloody crusade was not even considered. Of course the militant, power-hungry Madani welcomed these men into his ranks.

Lack of education and personal despair helped the fundamentalists win young people over to living by strict Islamic rules in Algeria. Like the soldiers from Afghanistan, the youth had nothing to lose. An Algerian kid had to be in the top 10% of his or her class to get into a university; a full 90% would never make it. Most lived with their parents in small apartments, with no jobs and no money. Depression lurked in the minds of many and women suffered a great deal more than men, because women had far less freedom. Men who got fed up were free to try migrating elsewhere, legally or illegally. Women, on the other hand, could only wait to get married, nothing else.

From 1989 to 1992, the FIS would use the country's 12,000 mosques to gather more and more desperate people to their cause. The FIS held 1,000 meetings a day, and Madani and Belhadj gave 4 to 5 speeches daily. Throughout 1989, the FIS was winning local legislative votes and putting itself everywhere. Madani met with President Bendjedid in early 1990 and was assured of the president's support. The president wasn't worried about Madani because the president assumed the FLN would dominate parliamentary seats during upcoming national elections, since these would include the many new parties that had formed. He sorely underestimated the FIS.

By 1990, the FIS had won important local legislative votes throughout the country. The ruling FLN finally realized it had reason to worry, and the Algerian military—which controlled the FLN and smaller parties throughout the country, including the few new Berber parties—also worried about the allegiance of the Algerian people. Many European countries with interests in Algeria, such as France, also grew nervous about the potential of strict Islamic governance in Algeria if the FIS won national legislative power.

In 1991, armed conflict broke out between the military and the FIS, whose leaders had signed a declaration of Jihad against the government. Madani and Belhadj were arrested, increasing the fervor of their followers at the same time public trust in the government was in decline. On December 24th, the president held a televised press conference to assure the people that the government would rule through a democratically-elected majority. Of course the FLN actually planned to manipulate the votes, but this was not to be the case.

In the national election of December 1991, the FIS won a majority of parliamentary seats, but the FLN was not ready to concede power. A second round of voting was to take place shortly thereafter, but in January of 1992, President Bendjedid resigned unexpectedly. Some say General Khaled Nazzar forced the president to resign at gunpoint—because if the president resigned, the military could take power and cancel the upcoming election. The details of the resignation remain unclear, but the military did indeed take control of the government and did cancel the election, and then brought in a provisional president. The new head of state, Mohamed Boudiaf, was a veteran of the war for independence who had been in exile in Morocco since 1963.

In response, Madani and Belhadj ordered their forces to attack the government, killing police officers and military personnel, and the FIS started stockpiling weapons for war. As they grew more aggressive, President Boudiaf ordered the arrest of over 10,000 FIS members. His plan backfired, however, and he was assassinated by one of his own bodyguards. Algeria was in a state of shock, and the military appointed a man named Ali Kafi to be the next president.

After the FIS was prevented from taking control of parliament, its supporters joined the numerous new armed Islamist groups. The Armed Islamic Group (Groupe Islamique Armé, or GIA) was the largest and most influential, the result of the merger of many disparate cells in the Islamist movement. Some contend the GIA was at least partly controlled by the Algerian military, or that the military created it to discredit the FIS, since armed attacks linked to the FIS would justify martial law. Throughout the 1990s, the GIA conducted terror campaigns throughout Algeria (and also in France) as part of a campaign to destroy the government and establish absolute Islamic rule.

The Prophet would never have approved of what Madani, Belhadj, and their followers did to so many innocent people in the name of Islam. True Muslims would have educated and organized the people—not used violence and intimidation—to claim the parliamentary seats that they had been denied. Despite their lack of moral authority, they did have power; during most of the 1990s, while Madani and Belhadj were imprisoned at Blida, many government officials visited them to try to convince them to order a ceasefire. Both refused to do anything unless they were first set free, but the ruling FLN did not want to take that chance.

As is often the case in such conflicts, the Algerian government itself also bears responsibility for many of the atrocities that took place during the Algerian Civil War. Many sources even allege that the Algerian army generals were the true terrorists. After all, Minister of Defense, General Nazzar, was the one who had ordered the army to open fire on protesters only a few years before during Black October, which resulted in over 500 killed, overwhelmingly civilians, more than 2,000 injured, and 3,500 arrested.

According to many sources, including journalists, historians and French security forces, Nazzar and his colleague, General Kamel Abderahmane, had a hand in the creation of the GIA itself. The generals allegedly plucked a political prisoner by the name of Djamel Zitouni—a former chicken seller with little education and a passionate commitment to the FIS—from a prison in the Sahara and helped him attain leadership of the GIA in 1994. One source cites a former Algerian security officer who said "army intelligence controlled overall GIA leader Djamel Zitouni and used his men to massacre civilians to turn Algerian and French public opinion against the jihadis." An article in the British newspaper, *The Observer*, called the grooming of Zitouni as a military collaborator and GIA leader "the creation of a monster," because the violence perpetrated by the GIA increased so dramatically under his leadership.

The FLN-led government eventually quelled the extremist uprising, but not before the entire country had suffered almost a decade of brutal civil war and over 200,000 people lost their lives. A new president came to power in 1999, Abel Aziz Bouteflika, and made a bargain with the terrorists, offering amnesty and immunity if they would lay down their arms. Subsequently, over 2,000 were released from prison and given monthly compensation in exchange for resigning as terrorists. Madani got a passport and cash and was allowed to leave Algeria, but Belhadj is still there, and no one knows how he was appeased. Of course some terrorists rejected the government's offer, and some regrouped and are committing acts of terrorism in Algeria and Europe to this day.

Matoub Lounes, the Berber singer and songwriter who had been shot by police during Black October, continued his activism as the conflict between the Islamists and the Algerian government raged on. He continued to tour, performing his songs and advocating for Berber cultural rights all over the world. In February of 1992, he was in New York City, and I had the honor of sharing a bottle of 1864 Madeira with him (and I still cherish the empty bottle that bears his signature). In September of 1994, Matoub was kidnapped by members of the GIA and held hostage for two weeks. The terrorists hoped to use Matoub to gain the support of Berbers to help fight against the government. The Berbers didn't want anything to do with either the government or the terrorists, however, and a tremendous public outcry arose, demanding Matoub's release. When he was freed and told the people where he had been held, Berbers chased the terrorists out of their hiding place in the mountains.

Matoub's final album featured a parody of the Algerian national anthem that insulted both the government and Muslim extremists. That song made him even more popular among Berber people because it spoke to exactly what they were experiencing. He

Djaffar Chetouane

warned in that album that death would be coming for him, but he also told the people that he didn't mind dying for truth. On June 25, 1998, Matoub was assassinated in a hail of 78 bullets, when he, his wife, and two of her sisters were stopped at a fake checkpoint. I, like most Algerians, remember his death the way Americans alive in 1963 remember the assassination of John F. Kennedy. When Matoub was murdered, I was on a bike ride through Nice. Two days later, over 5,000 Berbers took to the streets of Paris in protest and in mourning. Who actually killed Matoub? No one knows if it was the government, Islamic terrorists or Berbers who disapproved of his activities. Regardless of who pulled the trigger, Matoub is immortalized by his music and lives on in the hearts and minds of the Berber people.

The 1999 amnesty that the Algerian government offered to the country's terrorists also applied to anyone who had ever fled Algeria for political reasons. Therefore, of course, the amnesty also applied to me. I was not ready to trust the act until five years later, in 2004, when I set out to visit the country of my birth once more. I flew from San Francisco to London, and from there I boarded a plane bound for Algiers. It was the longest and most difficult plane ride of my life, not because of the plane, but because of how nervous I was about seeing my home after 15 years of absence. During the entire flight my hands were soaked with sweat, my body could not remain still, and my mind raced from thought to thought.

The Algerian Embassy in the United States had issued me a visa (necessary because I only have a U.S. passport), and I had contacted the U.S. Embassy in Algiers to inform them of my impending arrival—but I was still worried that I might be detained. My brother Mustapha came to pick me up from the airport with two high-ranking government officials, just in case. I had to pay them quite a bit of money to secure my entry into my home country, but I suppose the extra "insurance" was worthwhile. When I arrived the immigration officer at the airport punched my name into his computer and asked me to go ahead. I passed through without a word.

The ride from the airport to Tizi-Ouzou took about two hours, and it proved all that I had heard about the Civil War to be true. My brother told me all about the ravaged landscape, pointing out various places where tragedies had occurred as we passed. The land also bore the scars of the earthquake of 2003, which kept the region on high alert for more than three months; people slept outside for fear of dangerous aftershocks and structural collapse. The country was different from how I remembered it in every aspect and domain. I was shocked.

When I got home, my mother and two sisters greeted me with tears. I immediately noticed how old my mother looked; although she was only 63, she looked no less than 93. She had lost height and weight, and her face bore the wrinkles of a much older woman. My sister Souad, who had been 12 when I last saw her, stood in front of me as a grown woman. Houria, on the other hand, did not look much different to me. Although she is only a year and half younger than me, I didn't notice her age. All four of us hugged each other for a long time, tears flowing freely down our cheeks. My other two brothers, Brahim and Sid-Ali, and I kissed each other formally, with no hugging or any other contact. Sid-Ali, the youngest in the family, started in right away, asking me to bring him to the U.S. Brahim-the-merchant had changed the most. He had lost most of his teeth, had a big belly, was wearing eyeglasses, and limped as he walked, like an old man. Worst of all, I learned, he had become a drunk.

Shortly after my arrival, neighbors started knocking on the door. Everyone wanted to see me and tell my mother how happy they were for her son's return. Mom had already prepared my favorite meal: couscous with steamed fava beans and a full jar of buttermilk. As I ate, everyone stared at me, and I stared back. I could not believe this moment had come. The only person missing was my father (though I wasn't missing him). We sat there chatting until night came, and I went to bed with my sisters and mother. I slept between my mother and Souad on one bed, and Houria slept on a single bed next to us.

I woke early the next day, and so did my mother and sisters. There was only one person in my mind to see right away: my grandmother. When I was a child, I always got excited going to see her, and this time the feeling was even more extreme. I wanted to go see her the old fashioned way, the way I always had in the past: walking the entire distance to her house in the valley. And so I did. As I made my way through the valley that I remembered as green and full of crops, I saw that it was now completely different. All was brown. No vegetation, no green, and none of the sprinklers that I used to love to watch and listen to as they watered the crops. The smell of freshly watered crops always brought my childhood to mind, but now none of those memories came. I was deeply disappointed and surprised. Still, I walked the same path I had walked so many times. As I got closer and closer to my grandmother's house, my heart started beating as if I were going into battle.

Tears of joy came to my grandmother's eyes when she saw me. She hugged me close to her and said, "I knew I wouldn't die before I saw you again." She looked tiny, but still strong and healthy at 87. I was amazed just looking at her. I spent the night there, and we talked through most of it.

I would stay in Algeria for three weeks before leaving, although I had planned to stay two months. Environmentally, economically, and psychologically, Algeria was not the same as I had left it in 1989. It was all shocking to me and, to be perfectly honest, I was scared. After hearing all kinds of stories about all that happened in the 1990s, I couldn't bring myself to stay any longer than I did. I needed to return to my new life in the United States, at least for a time.

A week before my return to America, I traveled to the highest village in the Kabylia Mountains with my brother, Brahim. We went to visit our second cousin, whom I hadn't seen since 1984, and to buy traditional Berber Rugs, known for their intricate designs and beautiful colors (much like Navajo Rugs). I looked forward to seeing my family and also to getting the rugs as mementos of my heritage, since I had lived in the U.S. for 15 years without any.

Our journey began with an hour and a half bus ride to Michelet, a very well-known town in the mountains, surrounded by Berber villages. Our second bus suddenly came to a halt, where the paved road ended and the dirt road began. My brother explained that we must continue on foot because the terrain was very hilly and no cars could make it through. He laughed and noted that Algerians would use SUVs if they had them—unlike Americans, who have plenty of SUVs but never drive them on real dirt roads.

It was June and past midday when we started our hike. The sun was high in the sky and very hot. We had plenty of water and also a selection of fruit, as it is customary among Berbers to bring something when you visit family members. We were walking and enjoying the view of the mountains and the prickly-pear cacti on the side of the road. Soon we came upon a steep hill that climbed upward for over 2 miles. We figured we would get a good cardiovascular workout since we both smoked cigarettes.

Halfway up the hill, we caught up with an old man and his

donkey. The donkey was so overloaded with household goods, the poor thing looked like a huge mound of packages with legs. From a few meters away I could hear the donkey breathing heavily, flies swarming around his rump, while the old man yelled, jabbed and called the donkey all kinds of names—as if any of this could make the donkey move faster.

When we got close, I spoke to the old man calmly and respectfully. I began, *"Baraka"* (which means "your highness" and is customary when speaking to an elder you don't know), "it would be very nice if you took it easy on the donkey since he's loaded so heavily. It's very hot and he's walking uphill."

The old man turned around surprised, since his own yelling prevented him from hearing anything but himself. He seemed tired and disgruntled. He wore traditional Berber clothes and carried a baton that he used as both a donkey whip and a walking stick.

"If you feel sorry for the donkey, then you should buy him!" he said in a cranky tone.

"How are you?" I asked.

"Pretty damn tired and this stupid animal is not moving fast enough. I'm hungry and want to get out of the sun," he replied angrily.

"Well, maybe if the donkey's load was lighter, you would've been home by now," I replied.

"I'm an old man, and I can't keep going up and down this hill just to take it easy on this stupid animal," he said firmly.

"You're still very strong if you're able to load this much onto a donkey," I pointed out with a smile.

By now we had all come to a complete stop. My brother and I caught our breath, took a sip of water, and offered some to the old man. He drank and handed the bottle back to me (with no thanks offered), then turned around, smacked the donkey on his rump and continued on.

"Please, take it easy on him. It's very hot, he's walking uphill, and he's loaded with all that stuff—and you're still hitting him. There is no need to hit him," I said.

"Like I said, if you feel sorry for him then you should buy him," the old man repeated.

"How much will you sell him for?" I asked.

My brother interrupted, "What are you doing?"

Again, I asked the old man how much for the donkey, ignoring Brahim.

"10,000 dinars," said the old man.

"They cost no more than 6,000 dinars," my brother said to him.

"I'll give you 20,000 dinars—if I can buy him right now," I said in all seriousness.

"20,000 dinars? Are you crazy?" my brother asked.
Again, I ignored him and told him to let me handle it. I turned towards the old man, "So what do you say?"

"Are you serious?" he asked.

"Very serious," I said, pulling a wad of cash out of my pocket and starting to count 20,000 dinars (about $220 U.S.D.).

"A handshake will be sufficient to make the deal. And this gentleman," referring to my brother, "will be our witness. Just like the old days," the old man said.

"That's fine by me," I said as I handed over the cash and shook his hand.

The old man started counting the money, and I went straight to find the main knot holding the load together, to untie it and get that heavy burden off my donkey. By the time he finished counting, the load had slipped to the ground before I could catch it. My brother froze in his tracks and didn't say another word. When the old man heard the noise, he lifted his head and started yelling at me.

"Wait a minute young man. I still need to get my stuff to my house!"

"I apologize, but this donkey is mine now. We had a deal, you took the money, and my brother here is our witness. The donkey is mine, and I don't want anything on him," I replied.

"How am I supposed to get all this stuff to my house?"

"Well, like you said, we did it the old fashioned way, we shook hands—and I paid you double what you asked. So how you'll manage is not my problem," I answered him proudly.

The old man couldn't move, couldn't speak. He knew all I said was true, and it was he who hadn't thought far enough ahead. I stripped off the donkey's saddle and bridle and asked the old man for a measure of rope, so I could take my property with me. He cut a small piece and handed it over without a word. I tied the rope around my new donkey's neck and off we went, without even looking back to say goodbye.

After turning the matter over in his head awhile, Brahim stopped and said, "Aren't you even a little bit sorry for the old man? Leaving him there with all his things and no way to carry them home?"

"Brother," I said, "look at the donkey's rump, how much it's bleeding. Did he feel a bit sorry for this guy?"

"But that's a donkey. He's made for that kind of stuff," he responded.

"What do you mean 'He's made for this kind of stuff?' And who made him?" I asked with a furrowed brow, anxious to hear my brother's explanation.

Donkey Heart Monkey Mind

"Come on man, he's a donkey," he said with a grin.

"Yes, he's a donkey. I can see that," I spoke seriously. "And he's also a living being who works hard for us and therefore deserves to be taken care of and respected."

"So you come from America and buy a donkey in the middle of nowhere. What do you intend to do with him now?" he asked.

"I'll set him free somewhere," I replied.

My brother just shook his head and we continued uphill. After a while my brother asked if he could at least hop on the donkey to take a break. I told him that nothing and no one shall ever climb on my donkey again. He laughed and continued limping along, bewildered by my actions.

As we entered the village, donkey in tow, people could tell we weren't from there. They kept staring at me and the donkey. I knocked and my cousin, Houria, opened the door and asked who I was. (My brother was somewhat embarrassed by the donkey, so he stayed on the side where she couldn't see him.)

"What can I do for you, sir?" she asked.

"Don't you recognize me?" I asked her.

Then my brother came into full view. They kissed each other, and again she asked who I was. After a few moments of studying my face, she recognized me and couldn't believe her eyes. As she was kissing me on the cheeks, she noticed the donkey behind me.

"What's with the donkey? Is he my present?" She asked, laughing.

"You don't want to know," my brother answered. "Where is Djamel?"

"Somewhere in a café in the village," she told him.

"I'll go and get him," he said.

My brother left, and I tied up the donkey and went inside.

Djaffar Chetouane

My cousin and I started chatting about America, and she forgot all about the donkey. She was far more interested in my new life. A little later my brother and Houria's husband, Djamel, came in. We kissed on the cheeks and he was smiling, having heard the donkey story.

"After 15 years in America, you came back just so you can buy a donkey from an old man on the way here?"

"You bought the donkey?" asked Houria.

"What are you going to do with him?" Djamel interrupted.

"Wait a minute. Can anyone tell me what's going on?" asked Houria, with a puzzled expression.

Djamel started telling her the story as he'd heard it from Brahim. Djamel exaggerated a bit for dramatic effect, but the real thing was every bit as funny as his version. We all laughed as he acted out the scenes, playing the different characters. Djamel's retelling made me feel very proud of myself and not a bit sorry for the old man. Djamel is a high school teacher, well-versed in various subjects, and he acknowledged my compassionate act, having never heard of such a thing. Houria was very proud of my kindness but also pointed out that a question remained: What to do with donkey?

"I'll take him to the forest and set him free," I said, as if it were the obvious thing to do.

"Pardon me, Jafar, and I apologize for what I'm about to say, and I mean no disrespect—but if you do that, the donkey will find his way straight back to the old man's house. You'll lose your money for nothing, and that alone will make you about as smart as the donkey." He chose his words carefully and displayed an apologetic expression for comparing me to the donkey.

"I have to find a place to keep the donkey safe and sound, where he won't ever be used or poked, cursed or abused again," I said firmly.

Donkey Heart Monkey Mind

My cousin and her husband understood. They looked at each other briefly, then Djamel said, "Well, we have about four hectares of land that is just outside the village, all fenced in, with a barn that's all torn out. You can keep him there if you want, but you have to buy his hay."

"I'll buy enough hay to last him two years if you'll keep him for me, and I'll be more than happy to pay you if you want for the use of your land," I answered quickly, before he could change his mind.

"The land is not being used at all. It's just an empty lot and you can keep him there without paying us," Houria said.

"Well, that is so nice of you to offer and I accept. Where can I buy the hay?"

"There is a man who sells it here in our village, and he's pretty reasonable," Djamel responded.

"Can we go now and see the man?"

"You want to go see him now?"

"Yes, I want to buy the hay today," I answered, "if it's at all possible."

"Why don't we sit and enjoy each others' company awhile. You guys have to spend the night anyway, and you can do your business tomorrow," said Houria, and Djamel concurred. We stayed up late into the night talking and then went to bed.

The next morning, Djamel, my brother, and I took the donkey to his new home. The lot was perfect, with more than enough space for the donkey to roam and graze without getting into anyone else's land. Next, we found the man who sold hay and bought a truckload. The hay was placed neatly near the barn and covered with a tarp to protect it from the rain.

The next task was making sure the donkey would be

looked after. He would not require much work, but someone had to feed him and make sure he was okay. When I asked my cousin's eldest son and offered to pay him, of course all three boys jumped at the offer, each trying to convince me that he would do a better job than the others. I said I'd let their parents decide, since they would be the ones holding the money.

Both parents promised me that the donkey would be fine and never used again, under any circumstances. Overnight, those who had laughed at my actions at first, changed their minds and ended up fully agreeing with what I had done. Though Djamel kept saying he had never heard of such a random kindness in his life, he fully agreed that we need to take care of our animals. He said he'd tell everyone the story (and I'm sure he has).

By the time my brother and I reached home in Tizi-Ouzou, my family had already heard the story. My mother was proud and affirmed my actions without words. Within a day, everyone in my village knew about the donkey, and some even came and thanked me. As people spread the story in their own words, some added a joke: People come from France, they bring a Peugeot. From America, maybe a Mercedes. But what does Jafar do? Comes all the way from the United States, and what does he have? A Donkey!

Although there was no donkey in my plan for this trip to the mountains, I was given the opportunity to honor my namesake and do what any "Best Friend of the Donkey" would have done. (The donkey is old now, living out his retirement in the tranquility that all hardworking donkeys deserve.)

It wasn't until the summer of 2006 that I went back to visit Algeria again. I found it the same as it had been in 2004. Bombs aimed at government forces would still periodically explode in different cities, at police stations and on military bases. By this time, the Islamic extremists were targeting only the police and the military, though, and the general public was not affected as directly. The perpetrators would even make sure to inform the public not to be anywhere near a government building or police station that they were planning to attack.

I only stayed for three weeks and spent most of my time getting reacquainted with my family, especially my grandmother. Throughout the trip, I couldn't wait to leave and tried my very best to avoid hearing about the ongoing terrorist attacks. Rather, I focused on enjoying my time in the Kabylia mountains visiting my extended family and eating Berber foods, almost always including couscous. It wasn't that I wanted to leave so quickly, it just didn't feel right, didn't feel like the place for me to be.

The following January, in 2007, I decided to go to Algeria again, but this time with different intentions. I wanted to go all the way to Tindouf, the town near which I was imprisoned. I wanted to see the place where I had been held and relive the days that remained ingrained in my memories. I was no longer smoking marijuana, and I wanted to face my fear and experience my past in the present time. Every person I knew in Algeria warned me, begged me, not to go back to the place where I had been held and tortured. But to me, it was the only way to see where I had been, the place where I had decided that I would rather die than live in a cell as a worthless human being. I wanted to rediscover the courage I had found to escape. I'd seen myself in this place countless times in my nightmares. The smell of a rocky desert anywhere in the world still makes me shiver. But I had to go there. I had to see it for myself, feel it, and live the moments again through the vibration of my own blood. I wouldn't risk going back to the military prison itself, but I wanted to draw as close as I could.

Djaffar Chetouane

It took two and a half days to get to Tindouf by bus, roughly 2,000 kilometers from Tizi-Ouzou. Tindouf lies a few dozen kilometers east of the Moroccan border, as I had found out 18 years before by marking every meter of it with my feet, and there is nothing there but military bases and rocky mountains. To the north, east, and south of Tindouf, there is also nothing but rocks and sandy desert. It is in the heart of the Sahara. I returned bearing little more than I had with me when I escaped; I carried a little duffle bag (with a small laptop inside), the clothes on my back, and a brown *djellaba* worn over them. I didn't want to be recognized as a stranger, so I hadn't shaved in days and my papers, including my American passport, were hidden inside my underwear from the moment I left Tizi-Ouzou. I'd sent all my other belongings on to Paris, where I planned to be in a few weeks. I had wanted very much to bring my camera, but I couldn't take the chance of being caught with it.

The risk I took in visiting the area was not limited to the fact that I was a former political prisoner. The mountains near Tindouf are full of uranium, phosphate, and gold, and the presence of these natural resources, combined with historical border disputes with Morocco, are two reasons there are so many military bases in the area. All the area's inhabitants are connected to the military in one way or another and any stranger is immediately a suspect. I had learned through people who had the unfortunate luck to serve their obligatory two years of military service in this area that if anyone sees you with any sort of camera you'll be arrested immediately by the military, with no exceptions.

Yet I simply had to come back. This place, these people, my experiences, were so powerful to me, filling me with just a little fear, but also anxiety, sorrow, and even happiness. When I found myself there again, I desperately wanted to talk to someone back home in the U.S., to assure myself that I hadn't become totally unmoored and traveled back in time. But I couldn't remember any of my friends' phone numbers. They were all stored on the phone that I sent with my other belongings to Paris. For the moment, once again, I was completely alone.

For a while, the old heightened consciousness of my imprisoned body returned. My feet seemed to recognize where they were. Although I stood thirty kilometers from the military base, my feet felt as though they were poised exactly over the spot where they had walked back and forth in a small cell, with no conscious brain to guide them. My legs trembled, as if to ask why my head had brought them back to this place. My hands asked the same question and shook.

But I stood there and I could think, "What happened to me happened where I am right now. It happened under the same sky, on top of the same constantly shifting Saharan sand. Although the exact grains of sand where my feet stepped as I ran may have traveled on the wind all the way to the Middle East by now, I have also traveled on the wind all the way to America. It seems just as probable that those same grains have returned here just as I have. I never once thought I'd ever see this place in person again, but I'm here, am I not?" And now I had brought the past in front of my own eyes, in the present. Not just as memories, but as part of me. My skin shivered and the hair on my arms stood on end, and then both settled with confidence.

I stayed in the city of Tindouf for two days before heading to Morocco. As an American with legal documents, money, and credit cards, I didn't anticipate any problems crossing the border. But I wanted to walk at least one full day and night in the desert by myself on the Moroccan side, just as I had in 1989. So I began this second stage of my journey by bus, to Bechar, Algeria, across the border to Rassani, Morocco, and from there almost two days through the Atlas Mountains and desert towards the town of Agdz. When I got there and asked around I found out that it would take more than a day of walking to get to Ait Ben Haddou, where there was someone I very much wanted to see. So I purchased another bus ticket to Ait Ben Haddou. About 25 Kilometers before we got there, I asked the bus driver to drop me off. He was amazed and perplexed when I told him that I wanted to walk the rest of the way, but this time I had plenty of water and food and a road to follow. I had made a walk like this once before with no water or food and very little idea of where I was going, and I had survived. So I knew I would be fine now.

It was the middle of the day when I began my trek towards Ait Ben Haddou. It wasn't hot at all; in fact the weather was perfect for a stroll in the desert. I took my time getting there and even spent the night outside. While walking, I thought in amazement about the luck I had had when I first escaped. How in the world did I ever survive for five days in the desert without a drop of water in the middle of summer? To this day I still have a hard time believing it myself, even though it happened to me. Or maybe I can't believe it because it happened so long ago and I've been softened over the years. I can only conclude that I had angels watching over me. Now I walked towards the homes of two of my angels, simultaneously amazed at my past and joyful at my freedom.

I had to ask around a little when I got to the town, just as I had the last time I was here, but I soon found myself on Omar the potter's doorstep. His wife Malika opened the door. She was wearing her same traditional Moroccan dress with a scarf covering her head. Her eyes were large and dark, her lashes accentuated by mascara, and her wrists wrapped in silver bracelets. She had aged over the years, but time was very kind to her; she looked beautiful. After I greeted her, we stared at each other for a few seconds, and she recognized me without a single hint. I was amazed that she knew who I was after so long. The first time I appeared in her house, I had barely any hair on my head and was starved, scraped, and bruised. Now I had long curly hair and was healthy and well-fed. But she saw the same face as she had many years ago.

"How did you recognize me?" I asked, smiling.

"Whoever enters this house always stays in my eyes," she answered with confidence and a wide smile. She continued, "Besides, I've had a few dreams about you over the years, and I never forgot your story and how you came to our house."

I opened my arms to embrace her. She came right into my heart. We stood there hugging each other, like mother and son.

"Thank you so much for your kind help and words. I, too, never once forgot about you and your family, and I'm here as I promised." I spoke to her with a soft voice that came from the bottom of my heart as I hugged her.

"I've always known you would come and visit us someday," she replied.

"Where is Omar?" I asked.

"Oh, let me send my neighbor's child to go and fetch him."

"Is he still at his shop?"

"Yes, he is," she answered.

"Actually, I'd rather go myself. I want to see if he will recognize me as you did. But I could use some direction from the child, if you don't mind."

We went outside and she knocked on the neighbor's door.

Djaffar Chetouane

In a moment my guide and I were off to the shop.

When I arrived, I pretended to just look around. I saw Omar washing his hands in his muddy apron. He must have just finished making something.

"*Assalam aalaykum,*" I said in Arabic.

"*Wa aalaykum assalam,*" he replied, still washing his hands. The man did not recognize me. I was in for some fun.

I pretended to look for some traditional Moroccan clay vases. I asked the cost of a few of the items in the shop and kept looking at Omar. He still didn't have a clue of who I was, though he had dried his hands by now and was giving me his full attention. I picked up the most beautiful vase he had, with gorgeous, colorful, traditional Moroccan designs on it.

"How much is this one?" I asked in Arabic.

"1,000 dirhams," he replied. Costing the equivalent of about $120, the vase was well worth the money, but it was a large amount of money in a place where most people earn an average of $500 per month of hard work. I could see from his face that he was willing to bring the price down a bit so he could make the sale. But before he spoke again I said, "I don't have that much in dirhams. Can I pay you in U.S. dollars?"

"U.S. dollars will work as well, but you can go to a bank and change money," he said, smiling at having made the sale.

I pulled out my wallet and counted out $1,000 in $100 bills.

"Here, this should be enough," I said, handing him the money.

"That's way too much. Why are you giving me this much?" he said with a bewildered look on his face, hesitating to take the cash.

"Well, you didn't let me finish what I was going to say.

Donkey Heart Monkey Mind

This also should cover the money you gave me about 18 years ago," I said, lifting my eyebrows.

Omar furrowed his brow and couldn't seem to get any words out of his mouth. He was amazed, and he couldn't understand what I was talking about.

"I gave you money 18 years ago? Who are you? I don't think I know you."

"You know me. Not only did you give me money, but I stayed in your house. And you bought me a bus ticket, too," I said, but this time I spoke in *Tamazight*.

As soon as I said that, the man looked like he had just been hit by a ton of bricks.

"Jafar, is that you?" he cried.

"Yes, it is," I answered, glad he finally recognized me.

He rushed out to me from behind his desk, tumbling to hug me with his whole body. He came at me so forcefully that as he reached me, I dropped the vase and broke it. He didn't seem to worry about it at all.

"*Subhan Allah* (by God's grace)," he said, and continued, "Is that really you Jafar?"

"100%. It's me."

I was upset that I had broken the vase, but Omar wasn't bothered at all. He continued kissing me on the cheeks, keeping his arms around me and looking at me over and over with deep, wide-open eyes.

"How did you get here?" he asked.

"I went to your house and your wife asked your neighbor's kid to guide me here."

"My wife will be very surprised to see you," he said, forgetting that I had just mentioned her.

"I already saw her."

"Oh yes, I forgot. I'm sorry. I just don't know what to say."

"I'm still paying for the vase," I said.

"No way and don't worry about it. Put your money away," he said firmly, dismissing the long hours he had put into making it.

He wanted to go home right away and close the shop without even cleaning up the mess I had just made by breaking the vase. To him, my presence was all that mattered. He was happy beyond words.

"We'll clean it later. Let's go," he insisted.

Over the five minutes or so it took to walk back to his house, he didn't take his arm off my shoulder, and he just kept looking at me and smiling. We seemed like old buddies, even though we had only known each other once before in our lives and for only a few days. Although Omar was in his sixties, he seemed rejuvenated from the joy of seeing me again. As for me, I felt as though I was walking down the street with the father figure I never had. I was reunited with my savior, my angel, my friend.

I stayed with Omar's family for three days, just as I had in 1989. The same day I arrived, I went out without consulting Omar and bought a whole sheep. I brought it home with me and asked that we slaughter it in celebration of seeing each other again. Omar and Malika were honored and amazed by this extravagance. Omar then called all three of his daughters, now married, to join us at the house with their husbands and children, and they all arrived the next day. Omar, his sons-in-law, and I attended the slaughtering of the sheep. After it was done, Omar built a fire and started grilling the inner parts of the lamb. In every Arabic country, the inner organs of an animal are everyone's favorites. When the meat was fully cooked, Omar served me first, with a good chunk of the liver and the heart. Malika and her daughters had taken the rest of the animal and made us a delicious Moroccan lamb stew for dinner. We all sat around talking and laughing. Omar told his sons-in-law the story of how we met. Then, of course, as he was recalling how we met, he mentioned Ali, the nomadic merchant. I interrupted him.

"I would very much love to see Ali again. Where can I find him?" I asked. As I asked about Ali, everyone's faces changed, and silence fell briefly over the table.

"He's passed away, *Allah yarhmou* (May God forgive him)," said Omar.

Then one of Omar's sons-in-law spoke, "Ali was my father, and I do remember him talking about your story. He recounted the story several times. I remember very well." He spoke softly.

I felt a knife go straight through my heart upon hearing his words. Then I turned and asked Omar why he hadn't told me that the man was Ali's son. He responded that he had simply forgotten to mention it.

"I wanted so much to see him again," I said to Ali's son. "Your father saved my life. He lent me a horse without even knowing me. I can never forget him. *Allah yarhmou.*"

"Amen," everyone said.

"Where is he buried?" I asked.

"He is buried in our home town of Tislit," his son, Mabrouk, said. "I'll take you to him if you like. We live there."

"I would most definitely like that," I replied.

As we went to bed that night, my thoughts remained on Ali. His image would not leave my eyes for the entire night. I hardly slept. I had wanted so much to see him again. Could this second journey be complete if I did not get to thank Ali, the man who had found me naked in the desert in the nick of time? It was as if I had needed to make this pilgrimage again to prove to myself that I had truly survived. And yet there I was, lying in bed at Omar's house, in the exact same room where I spent my first nights in 1989. I had at least had the satisfaction of thanking Omar and his family for all they had done for me, and Ali's son would know how indebted I was to his father for his generosity.

After my third night at Omar's house, I left with Mabrouk, his wife (Houria, who had first opened the door to me so trustingly at the age of 10), and their son, whom he had named Ali. But before I left the house, I embraced the whole family and insisted that Omar accept the original amount of money that I had tried to hand him before I broke the vase. Naturally he tried to refuse, but I wouldn't take no for an answer. It was my obligation to at least attempt to repay him, though of course his kindness was priceless.

As we were approaching Tislit, we stopped so I could get a bouquet of flowers (artificial ones, of course). Then I asked Mabrouk to take me straight to Ali's grave, where I placed the flowers inside a vase Omar had given me for the purpose. The family paid their respects, and then I asked Mabrouk to leave me there alone.

I sat on the edge of Ali's grave just as I had sat on the edge of the wooden bed in the prison cell 18 years before. I sat with a mind crowded with competing memories, the unwelcome ones from long ago shoved aside for the moment by new, joyful ones. My thoughts sprang from branch to branch of my memory, just as they had once sprung from option to option as I struggled over how to survive. The agility of my thoughts once saved me, but I wondered now if I might not be ready to let them settle. I had made my pilgrimage. Could my mind now be content to rest for the next portion of my life and whatever lay ahead?

I stayed at the grave until sunset. Then it was time to take up my journey again. I would spend the night at Mabrouk's house, and then I would be off to Paris, free now to move across continents and oceans without fear or deception. Ali had lived his life as a nomadic merchant traveling with camels, then one day he helped a stranger, and his help meant the difference between that stranger's brutal, solitary death by dehydration and a chance at a new life. I had been born with no greater influence or opportunity than Ali's son, and I had come close to an early death, but now I had succeeded far beyond anything anyone in Ali's family could expect for themselves.

Have I been lucky? I was imprisoned and tortured by my own country, yet it was that very cruelty that led me to escape when I did and miss the worst of the violence that the rest of Algeria's citizens have suffered. Has it been destiny? I was born a member of a powerless minority, and I now hold a passport from the most powerful country in the world. I have been forever marked by the poverty and corruption of the country I was born into, by the want and desperation that drives small children to learn to survive, but I have also been marked by the perseverance of the people that doggedly cultivate that country's fields—and the beasts of burden that help them. I have been abused by people who learned cruelty at the hands of their parents, commanders, and government leaders, but I have also been embraced and cared for by strangers who had almost nothing to give themselves. It is my hope that such generosity, optimism, and perseverance will touch many more people, and that other desperate, driven youth like the one I was when I first set out to see the world can find at least a temporarily peaceful place like that which I have found.